THE
FLESH
SEASON 3: TRANSFORMATION
CARTEL

RACHEL HAIMOWITZ
HEIDI BELLEAU

RIPTIDE
PUBLISHING

Riptide Publishing
PO Box 6652
Hillsborough, NJ 08844
www.riptidepublishing.com

The Flesh Cartel, Season 3: Transformation
Copyright © 2013 by Heidi Belleau and Rachel Haimowitz

Cover Art by Imaliea, http://imaliea.deviantart.com
Editor: Sarah Frantz
Layout: L.C. Chase, http://lcchase.com/design.htm

ISBN: 978-1-62649-080-2

First edition
December, 2013

Also available in ebook across four episodes:
ISBN: 978-1-937551-96-4 (Episode 7)
ISBN: 978-1-937551-97-1 (Episode 8)
ISBN: 978-1-937551-98-8 (Episode 9)
ISBN: 978-1-937551-99-5 (Episode 10)

THE FLESH

SEASON 3: TRANSFORMATION

CARTEL

RACHEL HAIMOWITZ

HEIDI BELLEAU

RIPTIDE PUBLISHING

TABLE OF CONTENTS

THE FLESH

SEASON 3: TRANSFORMATION

CARTEL

EPISODE 7: HOMECOMING

MAT

M at had few regrets in life, but the ones he held on to, those were *big*. Being too afraid to leave home at eighteen when Coach Darryl had first offered to take him on. Begging his parents to make the long drive to Bristol to watch some stupid fight, then pushing them away from the after-party (*I'm* nineteen *now, Mom, I don't need a babysitter!*), and waking up at 3 a.m. to news of the accident that'd killed them on the way home. Losing Dougie to foster parents for five long years after that.

But none of that—*none* of that—compared to the regret he felt now at what he'd let happen in that room with Nikolai's sick-fuck pedo client. At what he'd let Dougie think. The heartbreak, the betrayal on Dougie's face, was the single most painful thing Mat had ever laid eyes on. How had he let Nikolai convince him that was *right*? How could he have abandoned—no, *shoved away* the most important person in the world to him? The one person in the world to whom he, in turn, was also most important?

God, he was a *monster*.

He rolled onto his back, then curled up on his other side, away from the family photo and younger-Dougie's innocent, beaming grin, hugging his blanket tight around his shoulders. Moving hurt. *Existing* hurt. But whatever. That was fine. No less than he deserved.

He lay there awhile. He didn't know how long. No sense of time in the endless merry-go-round of recrimination and self-loathing he was riding. Every so often, he'd escape it long enough to think about the safety razor in the bathroom. Maybe he could break the blade free somehow. All eighth of an inch of it. Yeah, fat lot of good that'd do him.

He must've slept at some point; he woke to the door opening, soft footsteps on the hardwood floor. Not Nikolai—no click of dress-shoe heels. He kept his eyes closed. Couldn't be bothered to look.

The bed dipped under someone's weight. A gentle hand brushed across his shoulder above the blanket. "I brought food. You should try to eat."

Roger. Mat didn't deserve the sympathy in the man's voice, in his touch. He lurched away, didn't bother to stifle the moan of pain at the motion.

"At least take these?" A hand appeared near his face, three little white pills cupped in an open palm. "Tylenol with codeine. You'll feel better."

Mat snaked one arm out from under the blanket and knocked Roger's hand away.

"Hmm." A thoughtful noise: half sympathetic, half disapproving. "The master said you might feel that way. I'll just leave them right here in case you change your mind." A soft tap—the sound of the pills being placed on the nightstand. Roger stood, disappeared into the en suite. Ran some water. Came back a moment later. Another soft tap—probably a cup of water. The man was *babying* him, for fuck's sake. He didn't deserve to be babied.

Roger sighed. "All right then. I'll come check on you again in a little while."

Mat ignored him some more.

"Try to eat," Roger said again, then left, shutting the door softly behind him.

CHAPTER ONE

For the first time in a long time, Dougie drifted lazily into wakefulness, like sleeping in until past noon on a Sunday. He shifted inside his cocoon of warm covers and cool sheets, sighed, stretched . . . and *remembered*.

That horrible man.

Mat, standing by and doing absolutely nothing.

For the first time in his life, Dougie woke up in a world where he was alone.

No. He had Nikolai now.

Nikolai. Last night . . . yesterday . . . when had it . . . No, it didn't matter. Before he'd gone to sleep, he and Nikolai had . . . They'd kissed. Dougie had been a good boy for him. Pleasured him. *Pleased* him. Nikolai had been good to Dougie in return. Not just good. Had *loved* him.

Love seemed to come so easy to Nikolai; why was it so hard for Dougie? He'd felt it for a moment last night, he was sure of it—an instant of clarity, transcendence, his heart light and full. And yet now it was just . . . gone. Slipped away.

He'd found it once in Nikolai's arms. Maybe he could find it there again.

The last time he'd been a good boy for Nikolai, he'd woken in those arms. And this time? He reached out, searching by feel, not ready yet to pull back the covers and actually face the light of the outside world.

The bed was empty.

Alone, then.

But why? Hadn't he been good enough? Had Nikolai sensed he was a fraud? Nikolai had promised to help Dougie be who Nikolai wanted him to be. He'd *promised*. Dougie couldn't do this without him, he knew that now, just as surely as he knew he couldn't *not* do this and stay alive in this place. Strange how he felt no more fear about that, no more fear about changing, becoming something else—though the lack of fear itself did frighten him a little. But what frightened him most was the possibility that Nikolai had lied. That he *wouldn't* help. That Dougie would be thrust back to the dark days of endless pain and need and terror and uncertainty and never, ever get to be at peace again.

Had it all been another mindfuck, one he didn't yet comprehend? God, what was about to happen here?

Regardless, he couldn't stay under the covers much longer, because this wasn't a lazy Sunday. Lazy Sundays were for free men. Not their pets. Not their *slaves*. He should get up. Do something. Show Nikolai he deserved to be a cherished pet, not a kicked and broken one. Trust that this wasn't a mindfuck—that Nikolai had meant all the things he'd said—or that if it *was* a mindfuck, it was all for the best.

Trust Nikolai. Be the person Nikolai wanted him to be. Which started with waking up.

Except the room spun when he threw the covers back, and his limbs felt strange, heavy, not quite under his control.

"Easy, easy, it's all right, Douglas. Don't get up."

Nikolai. Soft voice, then softer hands at Dougie's shoulders, urging him back down. Fingers stroking his cheek. Petting his hair. Relief so profound he could've wept—*he's not mad at me he hasn't abandoned me he won't hurt me*. Objectively, he knew he shouldn't feel that way. But in his heart, he couldn't change it. Didn't *want* to change it. Not when the alternative was going back to how things were before. Or going to a monster like the man who'd hurt him yesterday. No. He'd take this, grab what Nikolai was offering with both hands and never let go. Nikolai would show him how.

"I just went to fetch you some breakfast. I was hoping you wouldn't wake while I was gone; I didn't want you to think you were alone."

Nikolai's smile could've soothed a wailing baby back to sleep. Dougie focused on it, tried to match it with one of his own. Tried to feel something more than . . . than what? Gratitude, perhaps. A lessening of fear. Tried to recapture the affection he'd felt last night, when he'd taken Nikolai into his mouth and sucked him and it hadn't been a chore at all.

For a moment, Nikolai became two Nikolais, then coalesced back together. Dougie rubbed his eyes, and when he opened them again, Nikolai was sitting beside him, leaning in close, still smiling that soothing smile. He brushed the hair off Dougie's forehead and followed his fingers with a brush of his lips. "You were quite restless this morning. I gave you something for the pain. Perhaps that's why you look so confused now."

No judgment in those words. Mild amusement instead. "Th-thank you, sir," Dougie managed. He sounded like he'd swallowed a frog.

No, just Nikolai's cock, spat some quiet little voice in a far corner of his mind. Dougie shoved at it, pushed it farther into the darkness and slammed a door on it. He couldn't afford to listen to that voice anymore.

Nikolai handed him a glass of orange juice.

"Thank you, sir," he said again, and made a show of taking a sip. *Thank you* was easy. Gratitude was easy. And maybe gratitude wasn't a far step from affection. Maybe that was how all love began. Mothers took care of their babies, and their babies loved them for it. Maybe he just needed to be patient.

Nikolai was watching him closely, but that soothing smile was still on his lips, in his eyes. Crinkling the bridge of his nose, even. He was so handsome when he smiled like that, like he meant it. "Do you think you can sit up?"

Dougie nodded. Nikolai took the juice from him and propped pillows behind Dougie's back so he could lean against them. Brought over a tray with short legs from the table and placed it over Dougie's lap. Breakfast in bed? When was the last time *anyone* had brought him breakfast in bed? Pattie, maybe, back when he was . . . fourteen? When he'd caught bronchitis and missed two solid weeks of school. When he'd wept inconsolably for his dead mother and Pattie had tried so, so hard to fill her shoes.

And now Nikolai was here, filling Mat's shoes.

And just as with Pattie, Dougie would do his best to let him.

Nikolai didn't have to tell Dougie to eat, not anymore. Even though he wasn't hungry at all, he dug into the omelet on the tray, trying to look appreciative as he did so. He told himself that his willingness to choke down food was out of gratitude for Nikolai's kindness and not out of fear of his wrath. But Dougie remembered all too well what had happened the last time he'd refused to eat.

I can't let myself be afraid of him anymore. Maybe love and fear could coexist—because what were abusive relationships, if not that exact combination?—but he had a feeling that for that to happen in nature, the love had to come first. And it hadn't for Dougie and Nikolai, which meant . . . Dougie was sure the fear had to go, even if that meant it had to be surgically excised. Subtract fear. Add love. Nikolai would know the math, have the right prescription.

"You know," Nikolai said, and though his voice held the same gentle amusement as his smile, Dougie still jumped. "When I was first brought here, I didn't eat for almost a week."

Brought here? Nikolai? "I . . . You . . .?" *Intelligent, Dougie. Really intelligent.* He put his plastic fork down, looked into Nikolai's eyes. "*Brought* here, sir?"

Nikolai picked up the fork, cut off a bite of omelet, and held it to Dougie's lips. Dougie's mouth knew what to do all on its own: open, accept, chew, swallow. God knew he'd done it enough, with whatever was pressed to his lips. Nikolai smiled; Dougie felt a warm little shiver travel down the back of his neck. That was good, right? He'd pleased him, and Nikolai's pleasure had pleasured Dougie in return. A step in the right direction, surely. Maybe Dougie could do this after all.

"Yes, brought to this very house, actually." He speared a cube of cantaloupe and fed it to Dougie. "I was five. I came with my mother. Didn't speak a word of English."

"Your mother?" It was hard to imagine Nikolai having parents like a normal person, even though it had to be true. This was the real world, even if it didn't feel like it anymore; Nikolai hadn't been decanted. He hadn't risen fully formed from the shadows. He was . . . just a man. And all men had once been boys.

"A miserable woman," Nikolai said with a nod. "Until . . . Well. My mentor was her mentor as well. He took care of us both. Made us into our best possible selves."

Dougie nearly gagged on the bite of toast Nikolai was feeding him. A *five-year-old*? Here? Being . . . *Ugh.* He shuddered, swallowed hard. No wonder Nikolai was—

"You misunderstand, Douglas. I was like you, but not. I suppose I could have wound up a slave, had the dice rolled differently for me, but as it was, my mentor was a specialist, like I am now. He had no interest in training a child into service. He did, however, have great interest in raising an heir. I think sometimes perhaps that's the only reason he acquired my mother at all."

Swallowing his toast became easier, but not by much. God, to be five years old and ripped from your world, from everything and everyone you knew. Well, not everyone—Nikolai had had his mother after all—but after how things had gone down with Dougie and Mat, Dougie wondered if maybe it was better to be alone. Nikolai had always been so sure of the fact that Dougie and Mat's relationship couldn't survive their training. Had he spoken from experience?

"So, um, your . . ."

"Mentor?" Another gentle smile, an arched eyebrow. Had Nikolai always looked so warm and inviting when he was happy? Had Dougie just failed to notice before? Or had he just not managed to make Nikolai happy before today? Nikolai didn't say anything after that, merely sat there smiling, waiting for Dougie to finish.

"Was he . . . I mean, was he very patient with you, sir?" Dougie didn't know how else to phrase it. Being any more blunt when talking about a child—even a child who'd grown up to be Nikolai—made him want to be sick.

Nikolai nodded. "Always. Though he wasn't a man accustomed to repeating himself. Or dealing with children, I don't think. When I refused to eat for a time, he grew very cross because he *worried* for me, you see. He didn't want me to fall ill. I understand that now, training boys of my own. I know now, in my heart—" he flattened his hand to his chest, patted twice "—how wretched the worry can be. How deep one's love can go. How very much you *ache* for the best in life for your boys. He no sooner wanted me to suffer than I want you to suffer. But, like any good guardian, he was unafraid to punish me to protect me from myself. And for a long time I couldn't understand that. So I feared him. I even hated him. I tried to run away. I picked fights. I said terrible things."

Just like me with you. Dougie picked up his second slice of toast and ate it on his own. *See? I can learn. I won't make you worry about me.*

"I was a particularly terrible teenager," Nikolai said, and Dougie surprised himself by laughing.

"You don't say. Me too."

Nikolai's grin grew expansive, mischievous. "I ran away. Packed a bag, stole a credit card from his wallet, and hitched a ride into the city."

No way. "Me too! Well, except I stole forty-two dollars and eighteen cents and took a bus downtown." Dougie chuckled, shook his head at the memory. God, what a hopeless idiot he'd been. "Mat found me four hours later, nursing a soda at the diner and working through my third plate of waffle fries." His smile faded; he finished off his toast and took a long pull on his orange juice. He didn't want to finish the story, didn't want to think about how it ended, and yet now that he was talking, he just wanted to get it out. Like an exorcism. "He knew exactly where I'd go. I didn't talk to him for like a month."

Strange, but reminiscing about Mat almost felt like reminiscing about his parents, now.

Maybe that was why Nikolai didn't scold him. Just put an arm around his shoulder and tucked him close, let him pick at the remnants of his breakfast on his own. "Eventually I came to understand my mentor better, and the running away and the fighting and the back-talking all stopped. I realized that if all he'd wanted was a son, he could have purchased me on my own. He could have been selfish. But he took my mother as well. He not only gave me the gift of her continued presence in my life, but he also gave me the gift of seeing her *happy*. She'd never been happy in Russia. I don't think I *ever* saw her smile there."

"And she was happy here? Even though she . . ."

Was a slave? Like me?

"Not at first. Not for a while. But eventually. Eventually she saw the light, as they say. Saw how much more fulfilling her life could be when put to purpose. I think it helped, too, to see that her son was cared for. She never could have given me that, otherwise. We were always too poor, too afraid. Too many dangerous men in and out of her life. Animals, all of them. *We* were animals. And do you know what I saw when I ran away, Douglas? I had enough money in my pocket to stay at the finest hotels, eat at the finest restaurants, buy the finest things. And yet all I saw, all around me, were more animals. Unhappy, unthinking beasts beholden to their urges, crushed beneath the weight of the emptiness in their lives, the sheer *purposelessness.* And then I came back, and I saw my mother at my mentor's feet, and I understood."

Dougie didn't understand. He wasn't an animal. Mat wasn't an animal. Pattie and Mike and Mom and Dad . . . none of them had been animals. None of them had seemed empty to him. They'd led good lives, hadn't they? Happy lives. And so what if Mom and Dad had worried about money, or if Pattie and Mike had argued sometimes, or if Mat got beaten up for a living or Dougie stressed about making good grades. That didn't mean they were stuck on a hamster wheel.

Nikolai cupped Dougie's chin in his hand, lifted Dougie's gaze from the contemplation of his tray to meet Nikolai's eyes. "It's all right not to understand now, Douglas. You will in time. Can you trust that I'll get you there?"

Dougie licked his lips, stared into Nikolai's eyes, and let himself search for answers—no, for *faith*—within. "Yes, sir," he finally said. "I just . . . I don't . . . I don't know *how.*"

The thumb on Dougie's chin swiped gently across his lips; Dougie parted them, let the tip graze his teeth. This seemed to please Nikolai, which raised that warm shiver down the back of Dougie's neck again. He reached after the feeling, clung to it. Touched his tongue to Nikolai's thumb. "That's all right too, Douglas. Nobody springs fully formed from their father's head, you know." *Except Athena. She did.* "We have mentors for a reason. Trust me to be yours."

"Yes, sir," Dougie murmured against the pad of Nikolai's thumb.

Nikolai's smile turned mischievous again, and he pulled his thumb free. "So, waffle fries, eh?"

The tension popped, just like that, and Dougie laughed. Blushed. "Contraband, sir. I don't ever remember a time when Mat wasn't watching his diet. We never had any junk food in the house. We never went out to eat at greasy spoons. Wasn't fair to him, Mom used to say—made it hard to stick to a strict regimen if we were waving it under his nose. So there I was, little bro, following in his footsteps, even though I wasn't athletic in the slightest. Honestly, I'm still like that. Sneaking junk food: Red Bulls and sour cream and onion potato chips and Snickers bars. And Burger King hash browns. I know they sound disgusting, but . . ." His mouth watered just thinking about them, even though he'd just eaten more than his fill. "Actually, the night I—"

He stopped. His heart pounded. No, he would talk about this too. His former life. He would talk about it like it didn't matter, like it wasn't taboo, and then it wouldn't hurt so bad. "The night I was taken, that was what I was most worried about. I'd bought some junk food I had to eat before Mat got home." How clearly he remembered weighing the change in his pocket, contemplating the shuttle schedule: Could he afford to splurge? Would he miss the bus? It all seemed so ridiculous now, somehow. "I guess it wasn't the worst of my worries in the end, was it?"

"Was it ever?"

No, he supposed not. There were the bills, and not getting calls from Mike recently, and keeping his grades up, and getting permission to do research, and Mat's mysterious bruises. "I guess not," he admitted.

"Soon you will know, Douglas, what it's like to have no worries at all. You'll never worry again. You'll give of yourself, and be taken care of in return."

He'd been so eager these last few years to "grow up," to *do* the taking care of instead of *being* taken care of like he had his whole life. But really, what was so great about that? About worrying about everything all the time? And who was even left to care for? Mike had his own family, didn't need Dougie anymore. Pattie and Mom and Dad were dead. And Mat . . . well, Mat was gone, wasn't he. Gone and never coming back, and Dougie deserved that, deserved all of it.

But maybe, just maybe, he deserved love too. Nikolai had been right about so many things already; maybe he was right about this as well. Maybe being cared for *was* his destiny. And to be honest, right about now, it didn't sound so bad. Not scary or sad or depressing or anything. Just . . . safe, maybe. The natural order. What he'd been born for, made for.

Now if only he could figure out how to love his caretaker in return. Then, he thought, he might finally be happy.

Nikolai hadn't thought of his mother in a long time. He'd failed her, in the end—failed to anticipate her loss of purpose when his mentor had died, failed to staunch her despair, and worst of all, failed to predict the bloody mess she'd make of herself and his mentor's en suite in time to save her life—and his memories of her were always tinged with sadness now, with a sense of preventable loss, with the chastisement of irresponsibility. He'd vowed never to make such mistakes again. Never to so disastrously misread another in his care. He owed them more than that.

And it was precisely *because* of what he owed them that he'd been willing to face those memories once more to help Douglas find peace.

Strange how this time the recrimination didn't feel quite so powerful. As if Douglas had brought him some measure of peace in return.

Perhaps they were more alike than he'd realized.

He stroked the boy's dozing head, combing fingers through downy-soft hair grown out past his ears, then reluctantly stood.

After their breakfast, he'd given Douglas more painkillers and talked about nothing with him as he'd slowly and peacefully nodded off.

If the cruelty he'd carried out yesterday was his least favorite part of the job, then this was his most favorite: gently guiding a newly willing and pliant boy to accept and understand the role he'd always been destined for. It was complicated, careful work, with harder tests ahead. And then, when Nikolai's work was through and Douglas's transformation was complete, would come the hardest part of all . . .

But for now, Nikolai would enjoy these sweet first days and, as always, worry about the future when it came.

Speaking of worrisome futures . . . Nikolai tiptoed out of Douglas's room and then headed up the stairs to his office, where Roger had left a tea tray just how he liked it. He poured himself a cup and settled in to watch this morning's "conversation" between Roger and Mathias. All exactly as he'd expected: Mathias in the throes of unbearable guilt, convinced he'd made a catastrophic mistake he was powerless to undo. Given how deeply his sense of self was wrapped up in the role of his brother's protector, Nikolai knew there'd be no reaching him now—no fear of consequences, no motivation to behave. The animal would probably welcome any punishment he'd force Nikolai to inflict; he no doubt thought he deserved it. So rather than tempt the beast, Nikolai was having Roger care for him instead, doing what Roger did so well and worming his way beneath Mathias's skin. The man seemed to have a certain sympathy for Roger anyway. Best to use it to his advantage.

Was it selfish and irresponsible to hand off Mathias to Roger while Nikolai tended to Douglas, the brother without a buyer? Perhaps. Some would argue most certainly. But any attempt to work with Mathias would only end in violence now, and Nikolai suspected not even the serum would make him pliant. But Roger could slip through cracks Mathias didn't even realize he had. And Roger was Nikolai's right hand. Nikolai could use him to accomplish what he himself could not. There was no shame in that.

If that rationale allowed him to indulge his growing affection for Douglas? Well. He was the master, after all.

CHAPTER
TWO

Days passed. Nikolai slowly nursed Douglas back to health until he was able to get out of bed unassisted, until the bruises faded. He visited the boy daily, keeping training to a minimum. They ate together. Talked. Well, Douglas talked, mostly, and Nikolai listened. The boy always spoke softly, rarely making eye contact, but it seemed almost a compulsion for him, a purging of his prior life, as if by speaking of it he might hope to put it to rest.

And so Nikolai let him speak of what he would, rarely steering the conversation. Mostly inane things, things he couldn't even use in future training. But that was all right. They had all the time in the world, and not everything had to serve a purpose. He *liked* Douglas. He liked hearing about his family vacations, and the year he'd almost been held back for failing geometry, and how his father had sneakily taught him and Mathias basic math as children by playing penny poker with them every Saturday afternoon. How he looked forward to those games all week, even when they'd long outgrown their purpose. How they seemed like the only time Mathias ever sat still for longer than the span of a meal, how much that time had meant to Douglas.

Other times, Nikolai had the boy read aloud to him, or give him massages—nothing sexual, nothing below the belt—or other assorted tasks associated with personal service. All useful skills, but all selected to be the least emotionally trying of exercises. Pleasant, small things they could both enjoy and that solidified the growing bond between them. He could see the boy trying so hard to *feel* during those tasks, to find the root of his own fondness and plant it firmly in this new soil. The boy offered his friendship like a flower he wasn't sure how to keep alive. He knew it needed care he couldn't manage on his own. Nikolai did his best to nurture it, to help it grow, counseling patience over and over, and promising a future filled with warmth and sunlight, and in exchange the boy was ever eager to please. It wasn't love, not yet, not by a long shot. But the bud was there.

And now that the boy was well enough again to smile and walk and feed himself, it was time to stretch the boundaries a little more. Combine a slightly more intensive training exercise with a memorable, worthwhile reward.

He gathered up the shopping bag Roger had prepared and took it down to Douglas's room. When he unlocked and opened the door, Douglas was stretched out on his belly on the bed, nose stuck in the book of poetry Nikolai had given him to memorize. Nikolai's eyes lingered for a moment on the delicate curve of his ass, on one strong thigh. A runner's legs, like his brother. He'd finally begun to fill out a little these past few days, soften a bit as he recovered from his earlier deprivation. The sight pleased Nikolai; very few, himself included, liked their boys quite so . . . stringy.

"How go your lessons?" Nikolai asked, placing the shopping bag on the table by the door.

Douglas startled, turned around, and slid to his knees on the floor. He must've been quite engrossed. And trustful. Only a boy who'd learned to shed his needless fear would miss the sound of his door opening. He opened his mouth, presumably to apologize, but then his eyes landed on Nikolai's smile, and he said instead, in an uncertain, breathy rush:

Being your slave, what should I do but tend,
Upon the hours, and times of your desire?
I have no precious time at all to spend;
Nor services to do, till you require.

He paused, blushing fiercely, eyes sliding from Nikolai's mouth (curved now into a very firm smile, oh, his clever, clever boy!) to somewhere around Nikolai's chest. Douglas's fingers twitched on his thighs, and he cleared his throat, an oddly delicate sound, almost a nervous cough.

"Please," Nikolai prompted, as encouraging as he knew how to be. Douglas had chosen this sonnet for a reason. Nothing so apropos could possibly have been for Nikolai's benefit alone; no, Douglas's unconscious mind was seeking to make poetry of his own life—find beauty and meaning in his servitude—as surely as he was seeking to please Nikolai. "Continue."

Douglas nodded, pulled his gaze back up to Nikolai's face, and held it there, their eyes locked. And this time when he began again, it was firmer, surer, the words confident and rhythmic and imbued with meaning.

> Nor dare I chide the world-without-end hour,
> Whilst I, my sovereign, watch the clock for you,
> Nor think the bitterness of absence sour,
> When you have bid your servant once adieu;
> Nor dare I question with my jealous thought
> Where you may be, or your affairs suppose,
> But, like a sad slave, stay and think of nought
> Save, where you are, how happy you make those.
> So true a fool is love, that in your will,
> Though you do anything, he thinks no ill.

Nikolai's grin had spread from ear to ear, and when Douglas finished, all flaming cheeks and shy smiles but steadfastly unwavering gaze, Nikolai crossed the room, hunched down before Douglas, took that lovely, hopeful face in both hands, and kissed it. Forehead, cheek, lips. They parted for him, let him in, and Nikolai sighed into Douglas's mouth as the boy tentatively kissed him back. No passion, not yet, but it was sweet and lovely and so very *giving*, and Nikolai knew that if he were to lay Douglas down right now and ask for more, for anything at all, the boy would say yes to please him. Not out of fear, but hunger. For affection. For love. For the secret key that might let him feel those things in return. The boy was so tired of pretending; Nikolai could sense that in the manic edge creeping into the kiss. So tired of trying to fool himself.

"Soon," Nikolai murmured against Douglas's lips. "I promise you. Soon."

Douglas nodded. He knew exactly what Nikolai meant. Gods knew they'd discussed it enough, Douglas's halting, fearful, tearful questions, shame pinking his cheeks as he stumbled through one fresh admission after another. *I-I want to, but I don't and I'm sorry but I don't know how . . .* And then the last part, always the same, warming Nikolai's heart: *Please, help me.*

Yes, Nikolai would help him.

RACHEL HAIMOWITZ & HEIDI BELLEAU

He sat on the edge of the bed, and Douglas immediately shifted so that his upper body was draped over his master's lap. Nikolai ran a hand down the smoothness of his neck, down to cup his shoulder.

"Sit up." Nikolai patted the mattress next to him. "I have a gift for you."

Douglas rose to obey. There was no mistaking the tinge of fear in his eyes, but he suppressed it quickly. Good boy.

This new position, with his knees parted and his hands resting on his thighs, left his body perfectly open to Nikolai's gaze, and Nikolai took advantage of that, eyes roving over the smoothness of his chest and belly, down to his soft pink cock resting against his inner thigh. "Roger visited you with the wax?" he asked.

"Yes, sir." Barely a waver, but the remembered pain was clear on his face. Good; Nikolai could afford no moments of fondness between Douglas and anyone else but himself right now—no more than he could afford to personally do too many painful or upsetting things to Douglas during this formative time. Like waxing. Not for the first time, Nikolai was glad he could trust Roger to take on such sensitive work.

"Good. It pleases me, you know. You have a very beautiful body, Douglas. Firm and strong, but still slim enough to edge just this side of feminine." For a moment, distaste—outright *offense*—flashed plain as day on Douglas's face, but the boy schooled himself quickly, and Nikolai chose to let the fleeting bad manners go. For now. "Which ties in with part of today's gift. Go fetch the bag on the table." Douglas stood, a bit on the graceless side, and Nikolai grabbed his wrist and held him back. "Careful, Douglas. Your master's eyes are upon you; don't bound up like a newborn giraffe. Elegance, Douglas, in everything you do. Grace. Subdued power. Sit and try again."

Better this time. The boy was no dancer, lacked the hyperaware control over his body that his brother possessed, but at least he was meticulous this time, spine straight, head up, motions smooth and unwasted. He paced over to the table with the same self-conscious deliberateness. Picked up the bag by the handles without even trying to glance inside, though surely he was burning to. Nikolai could see it on his face, guileless as the boy was—curiosity, fear, apprehension. When he reached the bed, he held the bag out for Nikolai. Nikolai didn't take it.

"Is that how I've taught you to present things to your master?"

A brief flare of panic, quickly stifled; it'd been long enough since Nikolai had hurt him that he'd begun to trust it wouldn't happen again so easily. "N-no, sir," he said, eyes dropping to the carpet, knees following a moment after. "I'm sorry, sir, I forgot . . ." He ducked his chin, raised his arms, held the bag out in both hands like presenting a knight his sword.

"That's all right, Douglas." An uncommon kindness, true—normally he *would've* punished the boy—but not during this crucial, trust-building time. He took the bag and drew out the wrapped gift box with its big red ribbon. He set it in Douglas's outstretched hands.

"Wow, it's actually a present," Douglas said, mouth falling open into a sweet little O. "Thank you, sir."

Nikolai smiled. "Go on, open it."

Douglas tore into the wrapping like a child, although his characteristic neatness didn't allow him to scatter the paper. Instead, he carefully balled it up and stuffed it back into the shopping bag before pulling the lid off the gift box.

He looked up, clearly confused, yet cautiously hopeful, as if he understood what the gift might mean. "Sneakers, sir?" He reached into the box, cautious as if a snake might be hidden under the shoes, coiled and waiting to strike. Still expecting punishment, the poor thing, but this little show of generosity should help set him to rights.

"And more," Nikolai said, gesturing for Douglas to keep exploring his gifts, feeling strangely vulnerable at the idea that the boy might not like them. He had never seen Douglas dressed in anything beyond a collar, so he had no idea about the boy's tastes. He'd simply gone to a high-end shop for young men and asked the saleswoman to pick out everything he needed. Cradled now in Douglas's hands were shiny black leather sneakers with clean, bright white soles and a small alligator embroidery. Still in the box, a pair of slim-cut gray-blue jeans, and under those, a bright blue cashmere sweater, the color chosen to bring out Douglas's eyes and the fabric so soft to the touch that Nikolai would have a hard time keeping his hands off the boy.

"Clothes, sir." Douglas's voice was soft, shaky, *touched*, and Nikolai felt both gratified and relieved at the boy's obvious pleasure. Douglas couldn't look him in the eye. He was just . . . staring at the box and the treasures within. What was going through his mind now? Did he think Nikolai was giving him his freedom? He couldn't possibly be so naïve. Not after Nikolai had instructed him in the nuances of his service just a minute earlier.

Oh well, he'd understand that for himself soon enough. "Yes. There's just one more thing." Nikolai reached back into the shopping bag and pulled out a smaller box, just as beautifully wrapped as the first one.

Dougie tore away the paper. Pulled off the lid. Recoiled from it as if the snake he'd been afraid of before had finally struck. "I . . ." He put the box down on the floor, a little too quickly to be polite. And then, to cover up his ingratitude, said, "I think maybe the store mixed up your box, sir."

Nikolai crossed his arms and leaned back slightly. "What makes you say that, Douglas?"

Douglas didn't miss the disapproval in Nikolai's voice and body language. "I—sir . . ."

"Don't you think I double-checked my purchases?"

"But sir . . ."

"Consequences, Douglas. You're starting to make me cross, now."

Douglas fell forward, kissing Nikolai's knees and thighs in desperate apology. "I'm sorry, sir," he babbled between kisses. "I'll . . . I'm yours, sir, I know I'm yours, what I want doesn't matter, so if you want me to—" A hitch in his voice, another kiss to Nikolai's thigh. "Um, to . . . to put those on? If it would please you, sir?" He dared a glance up at Nikolai, the panic fading from his eyes at the continued lack of recrimination, but the confusion, the worry, the anxiety were all still there. "Is that right, sir? Is that what you want?"

Nikolai gifted the boy a caress, stroking his palm across Douglas's hair and letting it rest at the nape of his neck. "It is. The clothes are a gift to show you I trust you enough to give you new freedoms. The . . . other gift is to remind you of your place, even fully dressed. And to signal to you that it's time to resume your training in earnest. I'd be a terrible master if I didn't help a boy of your beauty become accustomed to such things." When Dougie grimaced, Nikolai added, "But there's no need to rush. Let's discuss this. Tell me, how did seeing my gift for the first time make you feel? Be honest, Douglas. You won't be punished for honesty, not with me."

Dougie leaned back into the hand at his neck and shut his eyes before saying, "Confused, sir."

Nikolai rewarded Douglas's unconscious quest for contact, affirmation, with stroking fingers, gentling up and down his nape. "And then?"

Douglas's brow furrowed, eyes still closed. "Unhappy. I didn't want . . . I *don't* want to wear pink lace panties."

More stroking across the boy's nape. *I'm not punishing you. I'm keeping my promise.* "Even if it pleases me?"

The furrow at Douglas's brow deepened, and even his mouth twisted down this time. Not distaste, just concern, perhaps a touch of fear. "I *want* to want to please you, sir, even if it means . . ." He opened his eyes, nodded toward the panties. "And I know you keep saying to be patient, it'll happen, but . . ." He picked up the panties, fussed at them with thumb and forefinger. "But, honestly, when I put these on, it'll be because . . . because . . ." He dropped his gaze to the panties, eyes following the motion of his nervous fingers.

When he said nothing more, Nikolai gave his neck a gentle squeeze, scratched lightly at his scalp—a soothing gesture he'd learned this past week that the boy loved. "Because?"

"Because I don't want you to be mad at me, sir," he mumbled to the panties. "I don't want . . . consequences. But more than that, I . . ."

"Yes?"

"I like how *nice* you've been lately, sir. And I don't want it to stop. I don't want you to . . ." He squirmed.

"To leave you alone, Douglas?"

The boy nodded, blushing fiercely.

"I won't. I gave you my word. Haven't I shown you that much?" The boy said nothing, and Nikolai knew he was thinking of his parents, his foster parents, his brother. He cupped Douglas's chin, lifted his head until their eyes met. "What you do or don't do won't change how I feel about you, Douglas. I'll never abandon you, and I'll never stop caring for you, even when I'm cross with you and have to punish you. Love and discipline go hand in hand." Still the boy remained quiet, worrying the panties between his fingers like a rosary. "But I'd not care to punish you, Douglas. Will you put those on for me? Not out of fear or worry, but because pleasing me pleases you. Because pleasing your master pleases you. Or at the very least because you *want* that to be the way of things, even if you don't feel it in your heart yet."

Douglas nodded, and stood, and made to step into the panties. Nikolai stilled him with a hand to his shoulder. Said, "That's very good, Douglas, you've pleased me," when the boy looked up, startled. "And when we're done with the afternoon's lessons, when you've served me to satisfaction, I'd like to show *you* pleasure in turn."

Douglas barely registered the promise of reward. "This isn't the lesson now, sir?"

"No, Douglas. Just one part of it. But you've done so well so far and I have full faith that you'll continue to do well. I don't want you feeling so much as a moment's discomfort when the time comes for me to give you the rewards you will no doubt earn. I want you to be *hungry* for it. *Begging* for it. Knowing I'll give you what you ask for because you've been such a good boy."

"Such a good boy . . ." Douglas echoed, as if in a trance. Nikolai couldn't tell if he was trying to convince himself, or psych himself up, or push away the nerves, or something entirely different. He despised being uncertain, but it was hardly the boy's fault and Nikolai would not take it out on him, not when he'd been so open and honest today.

Instead, he stood, went to the drawer where he kept the plugs, and selected a slim curving one, perhaps two fingers wide, with a flush base that would nestle comfortably in the crack of the boy's ass.

"Come here," he called, and Douglas obeyed, remembering to watch his posture, his stride. Very pleasing, the whole of it. Nikolai smiled. Held the plug up for Douglas to see. The boy blanched but didn't try to move away. "There now. I know you've come to associate these with discomfort, but that needn't be the case. Quite the opposite in fact. Come, spread your legs and I'll show you."

Again Douglas obeyed without hesitation, draping his upper body over the bed and spreading his legs out wide behind him. Nikolai lubed up the little plug and teased Douglas with it, stroking up and down his crack, pressing gently at his hole, rocking and thrusting in tiny increments until at last it breached him, slipped inside an inch at a time. Douglas gasped and wiggled, just a little, breath coming a touch faster, fingers curling in the sheet. Nikolai fucked him with the plug for a moment, just long enough to make the boy's hanging cock twitch, then seated the plug inside him fully, watching Douglas's hole clench around the narrow neck, pulling the base in tight.

"See?" he said when he was done. "Tell me how that felt."

"N-nice, sir," Douglas said, voice taut, as if the admission had been ripped from his throat. "Scary at first, but then nice."

"That's right. The plug has no inherent meaning or value. I'm sorry I had to build a negative association in you at all, but now is the time to correct it. It's just a tool, Douglas. A tool to teach you an important and painful lesson, and now a tool to teach you a pleasant and reassuring one. Because for now, no man but me will fuck you, and when I choose to fuck you, your hole will be hungry and ready for me." He grabbed Douglas by the hip and pulled him upright, then back, until he was nearly off balance. Pressed his lips to the curve of the boy's lower back. "For me and *only* me," he whispered huskily against Douglas's skin. "And lest you get too worked up before I'm ready for you . . ."

He stood, returned to the chest of drawers, and retrieved the little silicone cock cage he'd locked the boy in for so long before. This time upon seeing what Nikolai had in hand, Douglas actually did take a step back. But he caught himself, stammered an apology, and returned to where Nikolai had put him. "A-also 'just a tool,' sir?" he asked, and he looked like he was trying so hard to soothe himself that Nikolai didn't have the heart to chastise him for speaking out of turn.

"Indeed." He squatted down again, locked Douglas into the cage. Not as easy as he'd have liked, given the boy's half-formed erection. "Do you remember what happened the last time you came without my permission?"

Douglas's full-body shudder was answer enough.

"Then I've no doubt you'll be grateful that I've thought to protect you from making such an error again."

Understanding lit the boy's eyes, and he nodded. Nikolai had seen enough boys by now to know it wasn't because he thought Nikolai expected him to, but because he really was grateful. To be protected from his own weakness. To be guided so kindly to the correct behavior.

Nikolai met those big blue eyes and said, "I promise I'll not leave you locked away if you don't give me cause. Be a good boy for me today."

Douglas nodded again, but there was no missing the flicker of . . . *something* in the boy's eyes. Some darkness, some worry, some fear.

"What is it, Douglas? It's all right, you can tell me."

Douglas held his gaze a moment longer, then looked away with a mumbled, "Nothing, sir." But that was all right—that was all the time Nikolai needed to figure it out. He didn't *want* to be Nikolai's good boy. Oh, he wanted to want it, but he didn't *feel* it yet.

Nikolai clapped his shoulder and squeezed reassuringly. "Give it time, Douglas," he said. "Give it time." The boy nodded. "And get dressed. The day is wasting."

Douglas nodded again. After all the fuss he'd made about the panties, he pulled them on like they were any old pair of briefs, barely giving them a look or a second thought. Nikolai gave them a look, though: a long one, lingering over the way the frills of lace made his perky ass look even rounder and more lovely. And in the front? The sight of his caged cock and taut little balls stuffed into the tight satiny crotch—gods, it took all of Nikolai's self-control not to bend him over and fuck him right then. Rip the panties to shreds.

The jeans next, riding low on slim hips, then the sweater—ah, Nikolai had done well there; Douglas stroked and stroked at the fabric, as if surprised by how nice it felt—then the socks and shoes.

When at last Douglas straightened up, he looked stiff and vaguely miserable, like he'd forgotten how to wear clothes, or no longer felt at home in them. Nikolai had seen this reaction countless times, and it never failed to warm his heart. Such progress the boy had made in their short time together.

"How do you feel, Douglas?" Nikolai asked, mostly just to drive the point home.

"It's a little strange. But thank you, sir. Really. Thank you." He came forward, then, and at Nikolai's inviting nod and opened arms, straddled Nikolai's lap. Leaned in close, and when Nikolai simply waited, expression gentle and open, kissed him chastely on the mouth. Half real gratitude, half fake-it-'til-you-make-it. Nikolai, pleased as punch with both halves, ruffled the boy's hair and kissed him back on the tip of the nose.

"These clothes are yours to keep, my gift to you, but you must only wear them with my permission. Now, I bet you'd like some sunshine, fresh air, and exercise, yes?"

Douglas's smile of gratitude practically exploded into a grin of hope and excitement, lighting up his whole face. He bounced off Nikolai's lap, onto the balls of his feet. "Outside, you mean?"

How utterly adorable. Nikolai couldn't help his chuckle. "Everyone in this house may orbit around me, but I cannot help you make vitamin D. Yes, outside. Now come."

CHAPTER THREE

Dougie wasn't sure how long it had been since he'd last seen the world beyond his own bedroom door. He followed Nikolai now, quick and quiet down the narrow, sumptuous hall in shoes that felt strangely too heavy for his feet.

All of the clothes felt off. They fit him perfectly—of course they did, they'd taken his measurements at Madame's—but it was like his body was seeking to find fault with them. The sleeves of his sweater were too long. The fabric of his socks bunched. His jeans were too tight around his thighs. The lace of the panties scratched his sensitive, freshly waxed skin.

Really, the only things that felt normal and familiar were the plug and cage, a fact that initially filled him with disgust in himself and anger at the world, and then, conversely, hope. Hope that it meant he was truly changing into the pet Nikolai wanted him to be. The slave he *needed* to be to survive, to have any kind of hope of a life worth living.

Except that's not *a life worth living,* some part of him said. That voice he'd slammed the door on before, locked away in some dark closet. He pushed it back again. It was quieter now. Weaker. He could ignore it. He *could.*

Nikolai led him up a staircase, into a richly appointed foyer, pausing only to unlock and relock the doors at the bottom and top of the stairs. So many doors. So many locks. Dougie might as well have been living in the middle of an underground maze, waiting to get eaten by the Minotaur.

Nikolai didn't give Dougie any extra time to look around, though his scenery-starved eyes took it all in with ravenous abandon: the marble tiles, the paneled walls, the rich leather and hardwood furniture. Such a beautiful place. So different from his room downstairs. Maybe, if he was very, very good, Nikolai would let him come back here. Spend time here. He refused to let it bother him, how easily he could picture himself curled at Nikolai's feet, anticipating his every need as he read on the couch or watched TV or did paperwork at his desk. So many opportunities to please. So many opportunities to prove himself. So many opportunities to get lost in the simple, fear-free, pain-free mindlessness of obedience.

The thought was almost . . . tempting. Soothing. Only a little panicky.

Nikolai paused, and Dougie realized they'd come to the front door. "Would you like me to cuff you, Douglas? Leash you to me?"

That felt like an honest question, not a test. Dougie wasn't sure how to answer.

"You're about to venture outside for the first time in weeks, Douglas. No guards. No gates. No locks. Just you and me. So I'm giving you the choice to ask for my help, if you think there's any risk of you doing something . . . impulsive."

Impulsive, like trying to run. And when Nikolai put it that way . . .

"I . . ." He glanced down at his warm clothes, his sneakered feet. They'd take him far. Far enough? Maybe not, but far. He glanced back to Nikolai—his captor, his torturer, his rapist. How easy it seemed these days, locked down in that basement bedroom, to forget those things. To forget what Nikolai had done, was doing. How he was changing Dougie. *Breaking* Dougie. But in the light of day, in the fresh air of the wide-open outdoors, well dressed and well fed and well aware of just how fast a runner he could be, of where he might go, of what he might be able to get away from, what he might be able to *go back to* . . .

No. Surely they were in the middle of nowhere. Surely Nikolai wouldn't take him out if he thought there was *any* chance an escape attempt might succeed. But now that the seed had been planted and would soon be getting sunlight, he couldn't let it go. And he knew, with sick certainty, how much it would cost him. How far he'd backslide. How *angry* Nikolai would be when he inevitably dragged Dougie back. How he'd have to start all over again, the fear and the pain and the torture and the rape, because it'd only take one single taste of his old life to sour and spoil the fragility of the new one.

He glanced at Nikolai again, who was watching him, silent, patient, and said, voice trembling, "Please cuff me, sir." He didn't want a collar and leash, never wanted to be dragged around like on the stage at Madame's again. But cuffs, those would be okay. He'd almost never had his hands bound since he'd been taken. Maybe that sensation would still be safe.

Nikolai smiled, not angry at all at the unspoken admission that Dougie needed the cuffs because he couldn't be obedient without them. "Thank you for your honesty, Douglas." He kissed Dougie on the temple and went to a side table near the door, which had a drawer that in the normal world might contain gloves or sunglasses or mail. From this one, though, Nikolai withdrew two leather cuffs, linked together by bright metal rings.

When he returned to Dougie's side, Dougie put his hands behind his back without being asked.

"I could cuff you in the front, if you like."

Dougie shook his head. "No, sir." If he had his hands, he'd have his balance. He'd be faster than Nikolai. He'd be able to catch himself if he stumbled. Too dangerous, too dangerous. With his hands behind him, he'd never forget for one second . . . A potent reminder, like the pink lace panties.

Nikolai nodded like he understood every last bit of Dougie's logic. He probably did. "I know it's hard," he said as he buckled Dougie's left wrist into its cuff. The leather was soft. Padded. Something about the snugness against his skin was almost soothing. Sensual. "I'm not taking you outside to push you, or test you, or challenge you. This is a reward for good behavior. To help you . . . acclimate." He finished securing Dougie's left wrist, started in on the right. The chain between the cuffs was long enough; Dougie felt no strain on his shoulders at all. "I'll do everything in my power to make it easy for you. Whatever you need—just ask."

"Thank you, sir," Dougie said, less because he knew he should and more because he *meant* it. The reassurance of that left him breathless; he'd been so afraid, for a moment, contemplating the possibility of freedom, that he'd broken something far too tenuous inside him, some delicate spun-glass construction he needed to live. But no. A few cracks, maybe, but the structure was still sound. "Touch me, sir," he blurted as Nikolai's hands, done securing Dougie's wrists, left his skin. Heat flooded his cheeks as Nikolai's eyes snapped up to meet his.

"I mean," Dougie added, "I mean outside. Sir. I mean . . . Please don't let go of me. I might . . ." *Run anyway.*

Nikolai nodded once and looped an arm through Dougie's, then opened the front door before any new doubt could crowd Dougie's mind.

Brisk cold air, and white-hot light that burned his eyes. Dougie flinched. Fell against Nikolai for support.

"It's a lovely day," Nikolai said, ignoring the enormity of this moment, or maybe saving Dougie from feeling like he had to express it. "Autumn is my favorite season. I love how bracing the air is."

"I always liked it too, sir," Dougie said, blinking hard as he tried to get his eyes to adjust. Blue blobs were swimming in his vision, like someone had set off a camera flash right in front of his face. "Though the seasons didn't change nearly so much in Vegas as they did back in West Virginia. Still, our morning run was much more tolerable in fall than in summer. Plus, fall was when school started."

A tug on his elbow, and they were walking, the plug shifting inside him with every step as they descended the curving stairs that led from the front door to the long gravel driveway. Dougie didn't remember the outside of Nikolai's house. He wasn't sure if he'd ever come this way. Maybe he'd gone through a garage. The hours—or maybe days—immediately following the darkness of his tomb were mostly a blur.

"You liked school," Nikolai said, leading Dougie down the drive and toward a neatly maintained trail that branched off into the woods. It was true. The air here *was* bracing, and fresh, and cold. Dougie took a deep breath, filling every last square inch of his lungs.

"Yes, sir," he said, feeling a little dizzy with all the oxygen, or maybe just with the sheer vastness of the outdoors—the mountains rising in every direction, the dense endless thicket of woods, the awe-inspiring *emptiness* of it all. *Sublime,* in the true Romantic sense of the word: stunningly beautiful and terrifying both. "It was my arena, my fight cage. The place where I could train hard and excel, the place where I could make—" He faltered, tripped over an exposed root, or maybe just his own two clumsy feet. Nikolai's hand tightened on his arm, stopped him from falling, and he leaned into the touch, paused a moment to close his eyes and let it sink in. *Cuffs. Chains. Cock cage. Plug. My master. He won't let me fall. Be good for him.*

"Where you could make . . .?" Nikolai prompted.

Dougie stared down at the path beneath his feet, at Nikolai's hand on his arm. He couldn't look ahead, couldn't look up at all that open nothingness, at the whole world spread out before him. "My future," he mumbled, nearly choking on the words, or maybe his sadness, or his shame, or the sudden emptiness inside him that rivaled the vastness of the forest around him. "Where I could make my future like Mat was making his. Except mine could *last*, you know?"

Except for the part where it turned out it couldn't. He'd never even gotten to taste it, not for a moment. Never would, either. Best just to forget about it. Focus on Nikolai's hand on his arm, on the cuffs around his wrists, on the plug shifting in his ass with every step, and the cage stopping his cock from swelling at the stimulation. On his feet taking measured steps, one after another. On not running.

"Your future *will* last, Douglas. As many years as I can provide. And your education *will* help to make that future, just not in the way you'd initially thought. But your intelligence and schooling have tempered you, made you thoughtful and acquiescent, and those traits have served you well."

Nikolai was quiet for a while after that. They walked in thoughtful silence up the trail, the path climbing a wooded hill. As they neared the top, he turned to Dougie and asked, "When you were a child, what did you want to be when you grew up?"

Dougie had to think about that, but suddenly it came to him. "A postman."

Nikolai chuckled softly. "And then?"

"A fighter, for a little while, like Mat. But then he took me out in the yard and sparred with me and really hit me once by accident and I cried for like an hour and that was that. I think I was five."

"And then?"

"Um . . . comic book writer?"

"And yet you chose to study social work and clinical psychology. Do you feel any grief for your postman or fighter dreams now?"

Oh, *that* was what he was getting at. "No, sir."

"Well then. Know that your dreams of a Ph.D. will pass from you, too. You'll mourn them awhile, and then you'll move on, create new hopes and dreams, ones more suited to the man you've grown to become."

He would. Of course he would. It would all be fine. Times changed. Dougie changed. Growing out of a dream wasn't the same as having it just . . . die.

Or be taken from you.

Shut up, shut up, shut up. Dougie slammed that door in the corner of his mind again, and locked it this time for good measure. Nikolai hadn't taken him. Nikolai was just . . . showing him a new dream.

It was fine. It was all okay. Dougie would be okay. He'd survive. Thrive, even. Nikolai would give him everything he needed to go on. "Thank you, sir," he said softly. He looked up at an old-growth poplar tree, its leaves an explosion of yellows and golds, a stunning contrast to the bright red oak beside it. Fall in the mountains was breathtaking. So different from the desert. So like his old home, back before Pattie and Mike. Back before his parents had—

So maybe Nikolai *had* taken something away, but he'd also given Dougie something so very very precious *back*. He could get used to this.

Nikolai let him, too, for a while. They meandered up and down an endless warren of deer paths and hiking trails in comfortable silence, the leather cuffs and the cock cage and the plug and Nikolai's hand a constant, grounding presence on Dougie's flesh and in his head. He let his mind wander, confident in the anchors Nikolai had provided. Finally let his eyes wander as well, taking in the world around him without fearing his own traitorous reactions. The dappled green claustrophobia of rhododendron tunnels, the wide-open vistas on the ridgelines, the soothing trickle of underground streams erupting into waterfalls across the trails and down into the verdant gulches. There was no need to speak. No need to think. Just walk. The steepness of the uphills made his breath quicken, his heart pound, but in a good way, like his morning runs with Mat, his muscles warm and straining, endorphins flowing free. And sure, it wasn't Mat beside him now, would never be Mat beside him again, but he thought perhaps he could live with that now, could learn to survive the loss if he had Nikolai, strong and steady, at his side.

That thought carried him through the rest of their walk.

As they came through the front door again, Nikolai uncuffed Dougie's wrists and gave each of his not-really-sore-at-all shoulders a tender kiss. "You did very well, Douglas. Thank you for the gift of your presence."

That surprised Dougie. "I think I should be thanking you, sir. That was great. You didn't have to do it, but you did."

"And now I have another gift for you." Nikolai put the cuffs back into the drawer by the door, and placed his hand at Dougie's lower back.

Maybe Dougie should have been afraid at the mention of a gift, especially after the panties, but all he felt was trust. Because the panties had only been bad for a moment, and the clothes and the walk and the conversation had been so very good for a long while. "Thank you, sir," he said, breathing it out like pillow talk.

"Come with me; it's in the kitchen."

Dougie let Nikolai lead him there with a guiding hand at the small of his back. Now that he'd had a moment to acclimate, he loved the feel of the sweater rubbing against his skin beneath that hand. So warm and soft. Strange how the feeling was such a treat after being naked for so long. Maybe that was all part of Nikolai's plan—teaching him to appreciate the finer things in life, even the little things in life, by stripping so much of it away for so long. Unspoiling him. Taking him back to basics.

Something about that rather appealed to him, in its way.

And made what happened next so incredibly special.

Nikolai's kitchen was spacious, modern, gleaming, all granite counters and stainless steel appliances and a handsome middle-aged man he'd never seen before, happily chopping vegetables at a center island. But what *really* drew Dougie's eye was the kitchen table, the one Nikolai was steering him right to. The one practically *heaped* with contraband.

A case of Red Bull. Snickers bars. Fresh waffle fries. Sour cream and onion potato chips. Even a paper sack from Burger King, and the smell of the hash browns hit him the moment he laid eyes on it, made his mouth water so hard he practically drooled.

"Please, sit," Nikolai said. "You must be hungry after your hike."

Dougie sat in the chair Nikolai pulled out for him. Or collapsed, more like. His knees had gone all weird and wobbly. He kind of felt like he needed to cry. Over *hash browns.* How ridiculous was that?

"I . . ." He reached out, snagged the Burger King bag with one finger and tipped it sideways. Perfect greasy little hash browns spilled out onto the table. "I don't . . ." He tore his gaze from the forbidden treats and met Nikolai's eyes. His own were stubbornly watering, no matter how ridiculous it was. He wanted to thank Nikolai, *needed* to thank Nikolai, but all he could manage was, "You *remembered*."

Nikolai beamed, leaned in for a quick kiss, and then popped a hash brown into Dougie's mouth. "Don't make yourself sick," he said as Dougie practically swallowed the salty-fatty blob of carbs without chewing, but he was still grinning so wide. "Eat. Enjoy."

Dougie did.

He demolished the hash browns, then moved onto a Red Bull, which he guzzled so fast he knew he'd get the shakes. A Snickers bar next, and then one or two waffle fries, not the entire plate. They were *perfection*—crispy outside, creamy inside, salty and rich—but even though Nikolai had only warned him not to make himself sick, Dougie felt like it was his responsibility now to be even more reserved than that. To watch his weight. Be attractive and desirable for Nikolai. And even if he didn't gain a single ounce, he also needed to not fall into a carb coma and end up too sluggish to properly demonstrate his gratitude.

And speaking of desire . . . Nikolai was watching him carefully, his chin resting in his hand as if he was pleased as punch to just be spectating.

Dougie nudged the plate of waffle fries toward him. "Um, do you want some, sir?"

Nikolai, chin still in his hand, grin still plastered all over his face, nudged the plate back. "I quite like to see you happy, Douglas. These are for you. You're too thin. Eat."

Dougie had a single surreal moment of thinking, *Fattening me up for the slaughter*, and somehow, truly, believing it. But then it passed, and he picked up another fry and crunched into it with blissful satisfaction, making sure Nikolai saw every single twitch of expression on his face. He threw in a moan for good measure. Didn't even have to fake it. Inside the cock cage, his dick was swelling, trying its damnedest to get in on all the fun his mouth was having.

He squirmed a little on his chair, driving the plug against his prostate, and tore into the bag of potato chips.

When he'd eaten his fill and then some, he fell into his old ritual of sucking the salty sour cream powder off his fingers, and that was when he realized . . . he wanted Nikolai. Wanted to thank him for the wonderful day. Wanted to share in the pleasure he was currently hoarding to himself in his full belly. Just *wanted* him. And maybe that'd been Nikolai's plan all along, and maybe all this kindness was just as devious and manipulative as all the cruelty that had come before it, but . . .

But the truth was, he couldn't bring himself to care. Maybe wasn't strong enough to bring himself to care. Certainly didn't *want* to bring himself to care, not with how good he felt right now, how sated and cared for and, yes, even loved. He locked his suspicions in the same dark, distant closet as the nagging voice from his old life, and looked at Nikolai with new eyes. New eyes that drank Nikolai in, held him rapt until they were each the other's prisoner. Shoved his salty-sweet thumb into his mouth. *Sucked.*

Nikolai's palms hit the edge of the table, rattling the cans of Red Bull. "Dismissed, Jeremy," he said through gritted teeth, and Dougie heard the sound of a gas burner being shut off and then a clatter of dishes. Jeremy, the cook, must have left after that, but Dougie didn't see him go. He only had eyes for Nikolai.

Dougie slipped out of his chair at the same time Nikolai pushed back from the table. Another first: the first time Dougie had ever gone to Nikolai of his own desire. He'd been obedient before, even maybe willing, lost, or just plain desperate, but he'd never *gone* to Nikolai like this, walked—no, slinked, the movement was sensuous and sexy—right up to him and pressed their bodies together, practically climbing into Nikolai's lap as he did. "May I, sir?" he asked, remembering his manners, even though there was no question that Nikolai wanted this as badly as Dougie somehow did. Still, explicit permission—*never touch your master without explicit permission.* The last thing in all the world he wanted to do right now was break Nikolai's rules. Upset Nikolai. Let Nikolai down.

"Yes," Nikolai breathed, and his hands found Dougie's waist, fingers slipping under his sweater. Dougie lifted his arms so Nikolai could pull it away. It felt good. As fine as the sweater was, being bare felt better. Free. Simple.

Nikolai ran a hand down Dougie's newly exposed chest, so smooth from the wax, down to cup the soft roundness of his overfull belly. Dougie didn't have abs like Mat did, and he'd always been a little ashamed of that, but Nikolai caressed him, abs or no. "Beautiful," Nikolai said. "So soft."

His hands went to Dougie's fly next, slipping the button, tugging the zipper. Dougie bit his lip and blushed, feeling absurdly like a virgin. Nikolai had never undressed him before. Nobody had. That was something men did to women, undressed them slowly, revealing the secrets of their bodies. Dougie wasn't all that sexually experienced, but the times he'd fucked, he'd undressed furtively, like it was simultaneously shameful and a race to the finish.

Now, Nikolai slowly unwrapped him like a fine chocolate, like something sweet and beautiful to be savored, sliding his jeans down his thighs to pool around his ankles. There was a bit of a struggle after that, getting out of his shoes and socks, but the whole time Nikolai kept touching him, tracing whorling patterns over his skin, fingers brushing the edge of his panties. There was no doubt in Dougie's mind how attractive Nikolai found him right now. Nothing about this was awkward or uncomfortable—not even the pink lace underwear. It was just . . . it was good. It was so good. Nikolai had made it good. Dougie could never thank him enough for that.

But he could certainly try.

"Would you like me to suck you, sir?" Dougie blushed, but he didn't feel ashamed.

Nikolai unzipped his fly and reached into his briefs, big cock springing free. "No. Not this time. Come here and straddle my legs."

Dougie tugged at the waistband of his panties in silent question.

"Keep them on. Come."

Dougie went, sliding into Nikolai's lap. Nikolai's hard cock pressed insistently against the base of the plug still inside him. Nikolai took Dougie's hips in hand, thumbs stroking the fabric of the panties, and then swept one hand down to cup Dougie's caged cock and tight, aching balls.

"Sir, please," Dougie murmured, arching his back, emphasizing the curves of his body that Nikolai so loved. He knew he had no right to ask for anything—not for his own pleasure, not even for the right to pleasure Nikolai—especially after how generous Nikolai had already been, how giving and open and loving. And maybe that was the problem; here he was trying so very, very hard to remember his place, to grow accustomed to it, be comfortable in it, and Nikolai was *spoiling* him. Making it so easy to forget what he was now. Who was serving whom.

And even though Nikolai didn't seem to mind, Dougie murmured, "I'm sorry, sir, I didn't mean— I mean, I'd never presume to—"

Nikolai cut him off with a squeeze to his balls, not punishing or cruel, but just this side of sweet. He was breathing nearly as hard as Dougie was. "If you forgot your place just now, Douglas, I do believe that's my fault."

Dougie nodded rapidly, touched, mute.

The hand on Dougie's balls slipped between his spread thighs, hooking into the crotch of the panties and giving a hard yank. The flimsy fabric tore. Fingers stroked his taint, teasing at the ring of the cock cage as if to say, *Yes, you did forget your place, allow me to remind you now by leaving this here and driving you wild.* But they didn't stay—one stroke, two, and then they skirted back, wrapped around the base of the plug and pulled. Dougie's hole clenched, not ready to give it up, even as the dragging sensation half undid him, might've made him come right then and there if his cock weren't caged. He whimpered, fisted his hands lest they clamp themselves onto Nikolai's shoulders where they so desperately wanted to go, and begged, "Please sir, may I touch you?" Still begging, yes, still asking for things. But not for himself this time. Or, at least, not *only* for himself.

"Arms around my neck," Nikolai said, and that was perfect, that was *exactly* what Dougie had been hoping for, and he felt so deliriously aligned with Nikolai, so cosmically in tune, that he didn't even stop to marvel at Nikolai knowing exactly what he wanted and wanting the exact same thing in return. He just threw his arms around Nikolai's shoulders and laced his fingers behind Nikolai's neck and let his palms rub up against the soft, thick hair at Nikolai's nape and thought, *prayed, Fuck me, please.*

And maybe they really were communicating on some other level, because that was exactly what Nikolai did. Took hold of Dougie's hips, raised him up and then pulled him back down, impaling him on his cock in one clean thrust. No need to prepare—he was still lubed from the plug, which had loosened him just enough to be tight for Nikolai, only a minor burn for himself but it was . . . *pleasant*, almost, a sweet kind of pain. He wasn't sure he was ready to contemplate that part though, even here, now, happily straddling his master.

Dougie held his breath and waited for the thrusting to begin, but Nikolai held perfectly still, and Dougie didn't dare take the liberty on his own. Didn't even dare ask what Nikolai was doing; it wasn't any of his business what his master was thinking or how he decided to use Dougie.

Nikolai wiggled his hips, just a little, seating himself more deeply inside Dougie, and Dougie let loose a gasp. Held his breath as Nikolai slid one hand down to his crotch and squeezed his caged cock. "Tell me, little pet—should I leave this in place awhile?"

Dougie's first instinct was to beg *no*, but Nikolai looked serious, not teasing or angry or mean, so the question probably wasn't a test or a punishment. No . . . no, this was just like the cuffs and chains before their walk; what Nikolai was *really* asking was, *Do you need help to behave?* Because he'd come before his master once already, and it'd been *terrible*, and this time it wasn't just consequences Dougie was worried about; he wanted to do right by Nikolai for its own sake. And yes, God, Dougie *did* need Nikolai's help to accomplish that right now, worked up as he was. Maybe would always need Nikolai somehow, and was that really so wrong when Nikolai was always going to be there?

"Please, sir," he said, nodding his head and trying very, very hard not to squirm in Nikolai's lap, on Nikolai's cock, trying so hard not to chase both their pleasure. "Thank you, sir," he added, because, God, he really *was* desperate, and he'd probably explode in seconds if not for Nikolai's generous consideration.

Nikolai nodded once and kissed him, forceful but fast, then placed both hands back on his waist and rocked up into him. Dougie had thought he'd been fully seated, taken every inch, but God, there was always more with Nikolai, wasn't there? More pain, more pleasure, more joy, more grief, more religious fucking ecstasy.

The minor discomfort of being breached by that impressive cock was gone by the third thrust beneath an onslaught of *fullnesspleasureyesexactlywhatIneedyes*, and Dougie pressed the soles of his feet against the rungs of the chair for leverage and rode Nikolai in time with the man's urging hands at his waist. Rocking his whole body, his back and chest and ass all following the curve of Nikolai's cock.

Nikolai bared his teeth in a feral grin and growled his approval, stilled his own hips but urged Dougie harder with his hands. "That's it, Douglas," he panted. "Ride me. Fuck yourself on your master's cock."

Yes, Dougie thought, or maybe he whimpered it or even shouted it, because Nikolai seemed to reply, lapping at Dougie's throat with his tongue, wetting the sweaty skin even more and then cooling Dougie's fever with his panting breaths. *Bracing, like autumn air. Clear. Cold. Death, and then comes rebirth, and I'll be his spring.*

"So good," Nikolai panted against Dougie's throat. "You're such a good boy for me, Douglas, always such a good boy, such a happy accident, so perfect..."

God, it was fucking pillow talk. Not a lecture, not a teaching moment, just sweet loving words, like they *were* lovers, like Dougie was Nikolai's precious thing, and if Dougie was a pet or a toy or a doll, he was a beloved one.

Maybe I really am.

And strange how in that moment he wanted so badly to whisper back, to say all the things he was feeling—and holy hell, he *really was feeling* them: acceptance and warmth and affection and pride in his service. All he wanted in that moment was for this to last forever, to always feel this good, to always make Nikolai this happy, to always be this useful and wanted and loved, and he could see it now, he could *love Nikolai back*, he *could*, and he gripped Nikolai's neck tighter and begged, "May I kiss you, sir?" because if he didn't, *right now*, he felt quite certain he'd wither away and die.

Nikolai didn't say yes, just let his dark hungry eyes bore into Dougie's, reached up and grabbed him by the chin and yanked him forward, crushing their mouths together like they were a couple in an old noir romance, a rough seduction in black and white and in the end everyone knew their place. Dougie lost his balance, hips stilling as he fell forward against Nikolai's chest, and Nikolai didn't seem to care, but Dougie knew better, knew it was selfish of him to just *sit* there and let Nikolai tend to Dougie's needs over his own. It was so hard to think, to focus on things like planting his feet and coordinating his muscles when Nikolai was kissing him this way.

But he forced himself to pull his shit together, drew on everything Nikolai had taught him to make it good, to be perfect, to service his master above all else, and was rewarded by Nikolai moaning into his mouth as Dougie began to ride him again. Dougie smiled against Nikolai's lips, bounced faster in Nikolai's lap, closed his eyes, and relished the friction in his own ass, sensation sparking hot and bright in all his secret places, all the parts of him only Nikolai had ever lit with passion, all the parts of him only Nikolai could claim. His cock was downright painful in its cage, pressing hard against the silicone sleeve, desperate to break free, to swell and burst like his nuts would surely do any second now if he couldn't find release. But he trusted Nikolai to give it to him when it was time, when it would most make *Nikolai* happy, because that was the only appropriate time for Dougie to feel pleasure now. Because Nikolai's pleasure *was* Dougie's pleasure. And when the time came for their pleasures to entwine that way, Nikolai would make it fucking mind-blowing.

For both of them, it seemed, judging from the breathy little pants and words of encouragement spilling from Nikolai's lips. That praise caressed Dougie as surely as Nikolai's hands on his skin, lips on his jaw, cock in his ass. Made him feel just as good. Better, even. He closed his eyes again, let his head tilt back, let Nikolai's words vibrate against his throat. "Gods, you feel *so good*, Douglas, so good, look at you, you're so ready for me, so eager—" *Yes, all those things, I'll be everything for you, I'll give you everything, I'll be everything you desire.* "Such a nice tight little hole."

Hole.

Not *you have* but *you are*, and hadn't Nikolai said Dougie *wasn't* a hole? And Dougie had *believed* him—because he'd wanted to, desperately so, *needed* to because he was trapped here and that little piece of humanity Nikolai had gifted him with was all he had now. Because he *was* a person, and maybe Nikolai hadn't even meant it that way—*hole, hole, hole*—but there was nothing stopping the anxiety that ratcheted Dougie's stomach as he realized what a *fool* he'd been, how fucking much of Nikolai's Kool-Aid he'd drunk, how powerfully and totally he'd *lied* to himself about who he was, *what* he was to Nikolai.

Hole.

Hot bile choked his throat and every muscle in his body seemed to clench, and all it did was make Nikolai moan—no, fucking *roar*—as he pounded up into Dougie's ass and used that weight and leverage on Dougie's hips to slam him down, and Dougie knew Nikolai was coming, his nails digging into Dougie's skin and his teeth marking Dougie's shoulder in primal dominance as he flooded Dougie's ass with hot seed.

Just a hole to be used, a dog to be fucked and bred and owned, because if Nikolai wanted willing submission he could find guys like that, but he didn't, he wanted a pet of his own making, wanted the thrill of absolute fucking domination, of asserting himself, and that was what Dougie was. All that was left for Nikolai to do was throw him to his hands and knees on the floor and bite his fucking neck and knot in him like a dog and this horrible ritual would be complete.

Nikolai pounded up into him again, teeth sinking past pain into Dougie's shoulder, and God but he must've been a *good* little hole to make Nikolai lose such control. Nikolai had styled himself to be some kind of god above it all, some new evolution of man, and he was—*ha!*—he was a fucking animal, just as driven by need and lust and instinct as everyone he looked down on. It took Dougie to bring that out in him, just as it took Nikolai to bring out the scared, submissive animal in Dougie.

You can't let him know.

For a moment the thought froze Dougie—*He'll realize you're faking, he'll be furious, he'll hurt you, he'll* hurt *you all over again, all of it, right back to square one*—but then the panic rushed in behind it and mobilized him. *Fake it 'til you make it*, he reminded himself, even if he'd never been farther from making it in his life. He plastered on his smile, his look of desire, his false eagerness to please. Squirmed in Nikolai's lap as Nikolai rode out the aftershocks. Returned Nikolai's fervent kiss—*believe me believe me nothing's changed believe me*—even as fear gnawed desperately at his guts that he could backslide like this, lose every scrap of progress he'd made toward becoming Nikolai's good boy. And all because of a single careless syllable spilled from Nikolai's lips in the heat of his passion. It seemed he couldn't move forward, and he'd kill himself before he let himself move back again. So where did that leave him?

God help him, where did that leave him?

Nikolai will know. Nikolai will help you. Just be honest with him. Tell him. He wants to help you.

But no. No. He was too afraid. Too many *consequences*. And he wasn't so sure he believed anymore, either. If Nikolai really *could* help him, why hadn't he already? He'd been here *forever* already. And if Nikolai really was as good as he claimed to be, why was he still kissing Dougie like a proud teacher, murmuring praise into Dougie's ears as he pulled out from Dougie's ass, reaching down to shove the plug back in to stopper his cum? Couldn't he *see*? Didn't he *know*? How was it that this master trainer of men couldn't read the turmoil, the fear, the despair screeching through Dougie's head?

Well, maybe that wasn't such a bad thing, after all. There'd be no consequences if Nikolai didn't realize something was wrong. Lest Dougie give himself away, he slunk down to his knees—the action completely calculated this time, as rehearsed as dance choreography—and gently nuzzled against Nikolai's musky groin. Lapped the taste of his own (thank God, clean) ass off of Nikolai's cum-sloppy, half-hard cock.

The position made him think back to that first day he'd met Roger, when Roger had laid his head in Nikolai's lap and told Dougie how happy he was, how in love and fulfilled. Had that all been a lie? Was Roger screaming inside like Dougie was now? Was that all he had to look forward to for the rest of his life—pain and suffering and fear and degradation and a perfect mask to hide it all behind, as placid and flawless as the one Nikolai had worn in the audience at Madame's?

God, *all of this* hinged on the fact that if only Nikolai helped him, then one day Dougie would be *happy*. Would live every single day steeped in that sweet, simple joy of service he'd tasted, just for a moment, this afternoon. Share that look Roger had worn on his face as he'd sucked Nikolai's cock, that feeling Dougie had felt when he'd climbed into Nikolai's lap and kissed him.

But what if it was all a lie?

Roger would never say. Dougie couldn't blame him; he wouldn't tell either. Couldn't bring himself to say anything even now, alone with Nikolai, even after Nikolai had shown him so much patience and kindness, had urged him repeatedly to open up, be honest, share his weaknesses and fears so that Nikolai could help him conquer them. Who would open themselves up to a relative stranger with unseeable motives when they couldn't even talk to Nikolai?

There was no way to know. No way at all. The years here would pass, and either Dougie would become the happy pet Nikolai had promised him he would be, or he would become an empty shell, hating himself and smiling all the while.

And the worst part was, he wasn't sure he had any say in the matter. Maybe nothing he tried or didn't try, did or didn't do, mattered. Maybe the one man—the one self-proclaimed *master* of men—who thought he could save Dougie was as delusional as Dougie had been to believe he could ever be saved.

CHAPTER FOUR

Nikolai combed half-numb fingers through Douglas's silky hair. The repetitive motion, combined with the soft lapping of Douglas's tongue on his balls, nearly lulled him to sleep. He could sleep, if he liked. He was the master, after all, and it was his right to use his boy's ass to his satisfaction and then leave him wanting.

But no.

Douglas did need to learn that lesson, needed to learn the hard way that his pleasure could be an inconsequential thing to his master, but today was not the day for that. Today they'd shared such affection and joy and sweetness and had fucked like the happy lovers they were, and Nikolai wanted to carry that lesson and that glorious feeling through to the end of the day.

Not here, though. He pushed Douglas off him, noting the glassy look in Douglas's eyes, the flush on his face and the dazed droop of his lip, and stood. Tucked himself back into his trousers—a little bit of lube stained the fabric; he'd show Douglas how to hand-wash the spot tomorrow—and patted Douglas's head. "Come along now, boy."

He strode out of the kitchen, not needing to confirm that Douglas was following, and headed for the staircase that led up to his private rooms. Not down, not tonight. His well-fed little pet had truly earned his right to the warmth and comfort of Nikolai's bath and bed. And Nikolai didn't fancy being alone tonight, not after what they'd shared. He wanted to go sleep with his perfect new boy, and wake up beside him tomorrow morning for another round. Bliss. Nikolai had earned it. They both had.

Douglas especially when Nikolai happened to look over one shoulder and saw that Douglas was not only following, but doing so on his hands and knees, crawling up the stairs with such adoring and complete submission it made Nikolai's heart squeeze. Nikolai hadn't commanded that, hadn't asked for it, had barely even trained the boy to it; Douglas had given it to him like a gift.

He was having some difficulty keeping up, though. No wonder—they'd had themselves quite the long day, full of excitement and challenge, and his boy's exhaustion was stamped in every line of his body. Not to mention his unsated desire. Nikolai debated scolding him for his slowness—any other master would, or worse, and Douglas needed to learn that—then debated simply telling him to rise, but in the end he merely slowed his own pace, let the boy show his devotion as best as his weary body allowed.

You're too soft, Nikolai.

He half grimaced, half smiled at the familiar voice of his mentor in his head. Yes, perhaps he was. But he always got the job done, and done exceptionally well. Perhaps a touch of softness was an asset in this line of work. Or perhaps he was just rationalizing away his faults. Ah well.

Nikolai's bedroom door was already open, the curtains drawn, the bed neatly made, one window cracked an inch or so to the crisp autumn air—precisely how he liked it. The whole room smelled of falling leaves, and vaguely of Roger, who hadn't spent the night here in days but who came in to clean and straighten each morning. It was a comforting scent, one Nikolai had come to associate with *home*. Soon Douglas would feel the same.

Nikolai strode to the bed—four posters, of course, and an open canopy for all the binding points a man could ever desire—and the boy crawled along behind him, breathing hard, flushed and a little sweaty. *Beautiful.* And clearly exhausted, but that wouldn't matter to his future master, so Nikolai couldn't let it matter to him.

"Up you go, Douglas." Nikolai patted the edge of the bed, and Douglas climbed up, grimacing. Clearly relieved to be off the hardwood floor. "Up on your knees, back straight, facing the headboard."

Dougie arranged himself as ordered, more or less, arms hanging limp and exhausted at his sides. Nikolai put a hand over his spine and used his other hand to force the boy's shoulders back. "Be proud in your service, Douglas. Sit tall."

Again, Douglas obeyed, staying in place when Nikolai took his hands away. But he looked strained, too focused. Nikolai had pushed him hard today. And would push him harder still. A necessary lesson. One they'd have to work at again and again until the boy regained his stamina.

"Stay, just like that," he said, then turned to fish a bottle of lube from his dresser, watching as Douglas tried to observe him from the corner of his eye without moving his head. "Eyes forward," Nikolai ordered, because cute as it was, it simply wasn't appropriate behavior. Douglas's gaze snapped back to the headboard like an overstretched rubber band. Fine tremors ran through his shoulders and thighs. Frightened? Or merely straining to keep his balance on the soft mattress? Or perhaps he was simply cold; the room was on the cool side, and sweat was drying on his skin. "That's good, Douglas," Nikolai said as he stepped in close again. "No need to be afraid. I only wish to make you feel good." A well-earned kindness. The boy sighed out his relief.

"Thank you, sir," he murmured, eyes drifting momentarily closed, then opening again, pupils wide in the fading afternoon light.

"Don't thank me yet." Nikolai reached down and slowly twisted the plug free of the boy's ass, heat flaring up in his sated cock at the sight of his cum drizzling down Douglas's inner thighs. Such a primal, animalistic thing, to feel so satisfied at the sight, some leftover urge to breed and mark. He swept his fingers through the smear of cum and lifted them to Douglas's lips. "Open," he said, and Douglas did, eyes still distant as he licked and sucked away the stickiness from Nikolai's fingers. No complaint, but no joy yet, either. "I love seeing you full of my cum," he whispered into the boy's ear, trying to bring him the rest of the way.

"I love making you happy, sir," Douglas murmured back. He sounded so dazed. Still trembled softly.

"Is that so?"

"Yes, sir. More than anything, sir." He didn't sound dishonest so much as absolutely exhausted, wrung out, and Nikolai felt pity curl through him again. Too soft, indeed. Well, knowing his own weaknesses as a master simply meant he could adapt for them. He could walk the line, be both understanding and firm at the same time.

"Take this, then." He picked up the discarded plug, sticky with lube and cum, and gently nudged it into Douglas's mouth, pushing until the boy gagged and his nostrils flared. "I'm doing you a favor, understand? No need to talk anymore. No need to beg or apologize or explain yourself. Just let yourself take the pleasure I give you.

Now . . ." He reached around, opening up the boy's cock cage with practiced fingers. Gave the newly freed cock a slow pump.

Nothing. Flaccid.

If the boy could talk, Nikolai knew he'd be saying, "I'm sorry, sir, I'm just tired, sir, please let me rest, sir." Instead, he whined and twisted. The effect on Nikolai's mood was the same as if he'd complained aloud. "Douglas," he warned. "I know we've had a long day, but being too tired to perform is a privilege not afforded to slaves like yourself."

Douglas nodded, but still his cock didn't rise.

How very disheartening. He'd never had trouble getting or maintaining an erection before, not even when he was new.

"Too much 'contraband,' perhaps? Sugar crash?"

Douglas mumbled something around the plug that sounded to Nikolai like *I don't know, sir*.

"You must learn discipline, Douglas. Stronger self-control."

Another mumble, longer than the last. The boy clearly wished to make something known, but Nikolai had no intention of permitting excuses, not now.

"If ever I deign to treat you again, I expect you to know your limits and stop before you make yourself useless."

No mumble this time, just a nod. The boy hung his head, the gesture contrite, but kept his shoulders squared and his back straight. Nikolai felt his irritation fade a little at that.

"You'll push through it, Douglas. It's bad enough you're letting it show; I should punish you for it."

A shudder. It looked like he'd started to shake his head, to beg, but then stopped himself. Lifted his chin, set his jaw. *Yes, sir*, that expression said. *I deserve it, sir. I'll submit and be grateful.*

Gods, Nikolai couldn't stop himself from loving the boy. Wasn't sure he even wanted to. "Shhh now. Shhh." He stroked Douglas's back. "I'll help you. Do you want help to obey?"

A quick, fervent nod, and were those tears in the corners of Douglas's eyes? Nikolai leaned in to kiss them away, tasted salt and exhaustion and . . . sadness? "I'm here for you, Douglas," he murmured against the boy's temple. Stroked Douglas's cheek, then pulled the plug from his mouth and laid it on the bed beside them. "Talk to me. Tell me what's wrong."

Douglas sniffed back his tears, licked at sore lips, cleared his throat, and shook his head. "N-nothing, sir, I'm just . . . You've been so *good* to me and I'm letting you down and I'm sorry, I don't want to let you down, sir, please . . ."

Nikolai waited for Douglas to finish his thought, but the boy fell silent, lips pressed tightly together, chin wobbling.

"I'm not angry," Nikolai tried.

"T-thank you, sir. That's m-more than I deserve." Lips tight again. Chin still wobbling. Not fear, then. Was he truly so upset at his failure to perform for his master? So early in their training? Could Nikolai be that lucky?

No. Probably not. And whatever this was, it seemed unlikely to be a problem kindness could solve. There'd been nothing *but* kindness today. A firmer hand, perhaps. Nikolai stepped away, turned toward his walk-in closet. "No more tears, Douglas," he said as he opened the closet door, rummaged through the shelves for what he needed. "You'll make me think you're unhappy to serve me. We wouldn't want that, would we?"

"N-no, sir." The boy's watery voice drifted in on another sniffle, but then he took a deep breath, let it out slowly, loudly. Nikolai found what he was looking for and took it back to the bed.

No more tears had fallen in his absence. Even more pleasing, the boy was still holding position, arms tense at his sides and legs trembling with effort, but back still straight, eyes still forward, not tracking Nikolai's movement—though the tension in his shoulders and neck made it clear that he wanted to. Nikolai opened his mouth to praise Douglas for his discipline, then thought better of it. It was time to be stern now. He laid the toy in his hand at Douglas's knees—pleased again to see Douglas not trying to peek—and picked up the plug again. Lifted it to the boy's lips and held it there, barely touching. Douglas unclenched his jaw and opened his mouth wide without needing to be told, even though he clearly took no pleasure—yet—from sucking on the silicone. "No more tears," Nikolai reminded him as he swallowed hard around the plug, adjusting to its presence. The boy shook his head minutely.

Nikolai picked up the other toy, held it where Douglas could see it. "Do you know what this is?" The boy studied it, blue eyes wide and still shining with wetness (and now fear, Nikolai was sure of it), and shook his head.

"It's a penis pump. Nothing to be afraid of—it should feel good. A bit strange, perhaps, but good. It will make you erect for me. Now be still."

He leaned in close to Douglas's groin, lubed the boy's cock—not the slightest stirring of interest at his slick touch—and placed it inside the tube. Twisted the tube a few times to form a good seal against the boy's freshly waxed groin, careful to keep his balls out of the way. Then he squeezed the pump once, twice. Douglas made a little startled noise around the gag, and his hips twitched, but he checked himself and went still and silent.

"This is a onetime free pass, Douglas. You must *always* be ready for your master, no matter how tired you are. If ever I need to make you ready again, there will be consequences, do you understand?"

The boy nodded, mumbled what Nikolai assumed was a *yes, sir* around the plug. Nikolai squeezed the hand pump again, one eye on Douglas's filling cock and the other on the pump chamber's pressure gauge.

Sweat pricked up Douglas's face, and he blinked rapidly, obviously in an effort not to wince. Good, at least he was trying.

"Some masters buy slaves to use their cocks, but you probably will never be one of those. That doesn't mean a master won't want to see you hard or give you pleasure. Just remember that if he does, that act of giving is not selfless. He wishes to *see* your pleasure, take visual enjoyment from you. And you must perform." Another slow squeeze of the hand pump. Douglas's cock was swelling nicely, turning a deeper shade of red than its usual bright, healthy pink. "Tonight you'll show me you understand. You'll show me you're stronger than your exhaustion. I'll give you the gift of your pleasure, but you must unwrap it. Take it. Be active. And never forget who it's really for."

Douglas nodded again, but he was blinking too much, fingers clenching nervously at his sides. "Hands behind your back," Nikolai snapped. The boy hastily obeyed. "If you can't be still, I'll bind you. You won't like it." Nikolai gave the pump another squeeze. Up to 4 inHg, and Douglas's cock was bigger than ever, flush with blood, no doubt achingly hard. Enough for a first-time pumping session. The big question, of course, was whether it'd stay hard when the pump came off. Nikolai could warn the boy of the consequences of failure, but that might spark erection-withering fear or nerves. Then again, Douglas needed to learn to perform through all sorts of distress. Might as well start now.

"You'll stay hard when this comes off," Nikolai ordered, "or you'll be punished. Understand?"

The boy's nod this time was half frantic. He squeezed his eyes closed, clenched his teeth around the plug. As if he meant to hold his erection through sheer force of will. Gods knew it was possible. Hopefully the boy wouldn't disappoint. Nikolai very much wished to see his face in orgasm tonight; he had less than no desire to turn the boy over his knee and stripe him red.

But he would if he had to.

Fortunately, he didn't have to. He disengaged the pump, and Douglas's erection sprang free, proud and leaking.

"Beautiful," Nikolai said. "Absolutely beautiful. What a good boy."

A lovely pink flush came to Douglas's face that. Flattered? Nikolai hoped so. He meant it.

"That's a cock I'd love to suck, but I think I've spoiled you enough for today. Time to perform for your master."

Douglas nodded, the motion making the engorged cock between his legs bob.

Nikolai retrieved the bottle of lube from the bed and slathered both hands with it. "Good. I'm going to put my hand behind you, now. Three fingers out. You're to push back, find those fingers, and fuck yourself on them." He could have done this more easily in the bathroom, with a big dildo suction-cupped to a wall or the floor, but he wanted the intimacy of it being his hand. The dildo would have to wait. "And make it good for me."

The alternating threats and encouragements seemed to have done the trick. Still with his hands clasped and his back rigidly straight, Douglas bent at the knees and waist and thrust his ass back, seeking Nikolai's hand. Nikolai waited, palm up, until his fingertips brushed against that sweat-slick skin.

"That's it. Just about there," he coaxed, and after a little bit of slipping up and down, Douglas finally pushed back, Nikolai's middle finger hitting his hole first and breaching easily.

A slow stretch, and the other two fingers followed.

"Make it good for me," Nikolai reminded, and Douglas moaned on command, the sound muffled and sweet and just a little bit frightened, which gave Nikolai an extra thrill.

The second knuckle. The third. Nikolai's hand was flush with that perfect, stretched ass, now. Another moan, and Douglas began to move, timidly at first as if he were afraid of losing the fingers so painstakingly found, and then faster, especially when Nikolai gently crooked his fingers.

"Sit up, back straight," Nikolai ordered, and Douglas lifted carefully from his crouch, still holding Nikolai's fingers in his ass as he returned to his old position. Nikolai curled his free hand around Douglas's lube-slicked erection, squeezed, gave the boy a nice tight hole to fuck. And he would fuck it: Nikolai wouldn't be jerking him off tonight. Douglas's moan at the contact was much louder than the others, free of artifice. Sweat popped on his flushed skin again, giving him an enticing glow. He fucked forward into Nikolai's hand, back onto his fingers. Back and forth, from pleasure to pleasure like a quick game of tennis. Panted hard. His thighs trembled. Behind his back, his fingers clenched and tangled around each other, white-knuckled. He bared his teeth around the plug, screwed his eyes shut. Exhausted as he was, he looked ready to blow any moment.

But he didn't.

And for a time, Nikolai took advantage of that fact, basking in the sight of his boy toiling for him, working so hard to earn his pleasure, moaning and arching and fighting so valiantly against his own exhaustion and his base need to climax. It wasn't just enjoyable to watch, it was downright intoxicating. There was nothing like this, nothing like this power. This power to give and withhold pleasure, this power of watching a man bend his will to your own, all in a desperate bid for a scrap of your approval.

And just now, Nikolai approved wholeheartedly. He ached to draw the scene out longer, keep his boy on the edge until his needy, pleading whimpers filled the whole house, but even he had to admit that Douglas had given enough today. If he pushed the boy any harder, he'd fail through sheer exhaustion, and that would be just as much Nikolai's fault as Douglas's.

Time to let this end, then.

"You can come whenever you're ready Douglas. Your master gives you permission."

Two strokes after that, and Douglas was done, coating the inside of Nikolai's palm and sobbing with pleasure as he rode out his orgasm.

Or *was* it pleasure? Nikolai withdrew his hand from the boy's clenching asshole, grabbed his shoulder, and turned him. Tears streaked his face, big fat ones, and snot ran down from his nose. Nikolai's first urge was to slap the boy—he'd said no more crying, said it *twice*—but there was clearly something more at play here, and until he knew exactly what it was, he'd be a fool to act in haste. So he withdrew the plug and offered up his hand to be cleaned. Douglas cried the whole way through licking up his own hard-won cum.

"Tell me," Nikolai said, softly, and combed his newly clean hand through the boy's hair.

Douglas hiccupped in reply. Shook his head. "Nothing, sir, it's nothing. I'm just tired."

"You're lying, Douglas," Nikolai said flatly, and didn't even bother to voice a threat. The boy shuddered at the tone, or perhaps the naked truth of Nikolai's words. Clearly terrified, yet he gave no answer to the accusation, just shook his head slowly as if to himself. Nikolai began a silent ten-count; if the boy took longer than that to resolve the battle in his head, Nikolai would put violent end to it himself.

Eight seconds later, Douglas finally choked out, "I'm scared, sir. I—I'm so, *so* scared."

Nikolai nearly struck the boy anyway, tired of all that *whining* that unbroken slaves felt so entitled to. But then Douglas added, "I'm scared I'll never be happy, sir. Y-you were so good to me today and you've *been* there for me and you've never lied to me and I can see how you feel about me, sir, you m-make me feel so *special* and for a minute there I thought it would all be okay, you know? But then . . ." He crumpled forward, fell prey to his tears, sobbing and hiccupping too hard to speak, though it seemed he was trying. Nikolai tucked Douglas's face to his chest, rubbed soothing circles on the boy's back, and waited with much more patience than he'd felt a moment ago. Douglas wasn't complaining after all; he was baring the wounds of his soul. These things took time. Nikolai understood.

"And then?" he prompted gently when Douglas's sobbing eased.

Douglas disengaged from Nikolai's arms and met his gaze, eyes swollen and streaming and shining with fear. "A-and then it wasn't okay and I . . . I'm scared I'll never . . ." He broke eye contact and mumbled into his lap, "I'll never l-love you the way I want to."

The way I want to.

Nikolai gathered him up into his arms again and kissed his face, gentle, sweet kisses as he laid them down together in bed, Douglas cradled shivering and sniffling like a child against Nikolai's shirt. "Shhh," Nikolai murmured. "You will, Douglas. I promise you will. We don't learn to love overnight. But soon—you'll see. Soon."

Douglas shoved away—Nikolai was so shocked by the sudden vehemence that he let go—and shouted, "You keep *saying* that! You keep—" He sat up and tore a hand through his hair, looking vaguely horrified by what was spilling from his mouth but too angry to care. Nikolai couldn't decide if the fury was a step forward or a step backward from the hopeless despair it had followed. "You keep saying be patient, wait, it'll happen soon, but it's not . . ." Both hands now, shoving the hair from his face, clenching at the crown of his head. He squeezed his eyes shut, sending tears down his cheeks; he did not, Nikolai noted, move out of arm's reach. "It's not *working*! How long am I supposed to just . . . to *trust* you? To *kid* myself? I can't! I *can't* . . ."

Nikolai sat too and took hold of Dougie's forearms, tugging gently until the boy stopped trying to rip his hair from his scalp and allowed Nikolai to hold his hands. He wouldn't meet Nikolai's eyes, but clearly now was not the time to force the issue. To force *any* issue but the matter of trust, which could not be had by force in any case. "Listen to me, Douglas." The boy sniffled, breath hitching, and Nikolai felt his attention upon him. "I know how this seems to you. How it feels like we've made no progress. And I'm sorry I can't push things along any faster, but this is delicate work, you know that—you of all people know that."

The boy sniffled again, nodded, gaze still cast to his lap. A tear dripped from his chin and splashed onto his knee.

"But look at us. Look at where we are. At where *you* are. Expressing your fears not with anger toward the goal but with anger toward *failure* to reach it. Do you see how momentous that truly is? How far that means you've come?"

Another sniffle, but accompanied this time by an upward glance, a momentary locking of gazes. The hesitant beginnings of understanding bloomed in those tear-stained eyes. Nikolai resisted the urge to fill the silence, and instead simply let the boy process, stroking his wrists as the tension slowly leeched from his shoulders.

At long last, the boy nodded his reluctant acceptance.

"Good, that's very good, Douglas." Nikolai lay back down, pulled Douglas along with gentle tugs on his wrists, tucked him back against his chest. No resistance at all anymore; the boy went where he was placed. "Now rest, and know that I'll be here watching over you, and taking care of you. I won't let you be unhappy forever, Douglas, I promise."

Douglas sobbed afresh and wrapped both hands around Nikolai's forearms, holding him close. No telling if the boy believed Nikolai's promise, but it was clear he wanted to, and that . . . well, *that* Nikolai could work with.

MAT

M at had been a fighter long enough to know that bruises faded and fractures knitted back together, but some injuries never went away. Like brain damage that got worse and worse and worse until there was nothing left of you but a shell.

And this pain? The one he was feeling now? Was the kind that festered and grew by torturous inches until it killed you.

Well, fuck that. Because Mat didn't have to stick around for it. He was a monster anyway; the world would be better off without him. *Dougie* would be better off without him. At least then Nikolai couldn't trick him into hurting Dougie anymore.

He opened his eyes and turned his face away from his pillow for the first time in what felt like weeks.

Couldn't *be* weeks, though, because he wasn't dead of starvation yet.

A tray sat on the mattress beside him. Toast. Broth. Bland food meant not to upset a long-empty stomach.

He pushed it to the floor. Let it clang and splatter. Roger would come in and clean it later—had done it a dozen times before. The fact that Mat couldn't bring himself to care enough about making the poor SOB clean up unnecessary messes to actually stop making them in the first place was just one more sign of what a terrible person he'd become. How *useless* he'd become. How callous and empty and awful.

He couldn't understand why Nikolai wasn't punishing him for it. Wished he would. Maybe then he'd feel better after. Maybe even during, if it would take his mind off the betrayal in his brother's eyes, the hurt he'd let happen, the screams he hadn't lifted a finger to end, even for a single second. Better the serum than the knowledge of what he'd done to the one person left in this life who'd loved him. Who'd trusted him. Whose heart he'd snapped clean in two.

But no. Only one thing would put a stop to that particular highlights reel.

Lifting himself up onto his elbows made his arms shake with exertion, and actually sitting up and getting his feet on the floor was even worse. But he was determined, and *nothing* stopped him when he was determined. Bracing himself on the wall, he stood, and stumbled to his exercise shorts hanging over the handrail of his treadmill. Gritted his teeth and pulled them on. He wasn't going to do this nude. Roger wasn't going to find him naked. That was the best he could hope for now.

The jump rope, next. The heavy leather one.

He wondered why he'd never thought of this before, why he'd spent all this time fantasizing about fucking safety razors and self-starvation. Maybe because he hadn't ever *wanted* it this much before. His shaking hands made tying the knots particularly difficult, but he managed it somehow.

He threw the noose over the chin-up bar and thought, *Good-bye, cruel world.* Then snorted—truer words, etc. etc.—and forced trembling fingers to tie the final knot.

There was that determination, again. Too bad he couldn't apply it to getting himself the fuck out of here.

Well, he supposed he was, in a way. Just not the exit he'd been hoping to make.

Oh well.

THE FLESH CARTEL

SEASON 3: TRANSFORMATION

CARTEL

EPISODE 8: LOYALTIES

CHAPTER
ONE

After Dougie's revelation in Nikolai's bed, after Nikolai had shushed him and held him until long after his tears had stopped, he led Dougie back down to the basement bedroom Dougie had been calling home for the last however long. Dougie wasn't sure how he felt about that. Part of him desperately wanted to be wrapped back up in Nikolai's arms, in Nikolai's private inner sanctum, borrowing Nikolai's strength and conviction and basking in his love. But another part of him knew he needed this alone time to think, to process, to deal on his own. He wasn't helpless. He needed not to feel helpless. Had to know he could cope, at least a little, on his own.

Nikolai sat him on the bed with a lingering kiss to the crown of his head and a whispered good-night. He closed the door behind him, but he didn't lock it.

A show of good faith, no doubt. Of trust. Dougie wasn't sure if Nikolai wanted him to take advantage of his freedom or not, but he suspected there was no wrong answer here. Felt confident enough in that, at least, not to add fresh fuel to the banked fire of his panic. Besides, he was certain as certain could be that all the doors leading up to the ground floor were locked—Nikolai knew better than to trust him *that* far—and there wasn't a single thing in the basement he wanted to see.

Mat. Mat's down here somewhere.

Not a single thing.

His new clothes were folded in a neat pile atop the dresser on the far wall, his sneakers beside them, cleaned of the dirt and leaves he'd tracked through this afternoon. Someone had done that for him and he didn't even know who. He thought briefly of putting them on. Thought equally briefly of throwing them away. All they meant, all they represented . . . it was too much to trust him with right now. Left him feeling too much like his old self. Maybe he should tell Nikolai

that. Ask for his help—ask him to take them away so he wouldn't have
to think about it again before he was ready.

He stared at them for a long time. Until his eyes felt dry and he
realized he'd forgotten to blink, even long after he'd stopped thinking
of anything his conscious mind could access. Overload. Maybe even
shock. Too much to wrap his head around. Too much to wrap his
heart around. Best, then, just to put this whole day behind him. Sleep
on it. Maybe he'd wake up with answers tomorrow.

He didn't, though. Woke, instead, to a tentative knock at his door,
and blinked into the darkness, wondering who that could possibly
be. Nikolai never knocked, didn't *need* to knock; this was his room
and his pet inside it. Couldn't be Mat—Dougie disgusted him, and
Nikolai wouldn't let him wander free besides. Nobody else ever came
to see him here.

Another knock, just as soft as the last one. Dougie sat up in bed,
groped for the light switch. Blinked against the too-bright flood of
full-spectrum bulbs and mumbled, "Come in?"

The door cracked, and a face peeked around its edge. Handsome.
Open. Familiar. What was his name . . .?

"Roger?" Dougie rubbed sore eyes, pulled the covers a little
higher up his lap. It'd been forever since he'd thought to be shy, but it
was hitting him now, powerful enough to heat his cheeks.

Roger nodded, smiling a bit sheepishly. "Mind if I come in?"

"Um." Dougie made himself let go of the blankets, gestured a
little awkwardly. Strange how quickly he'd forgotten how to talk to
people. How to behave around them. "Sure?"

Roger let himself in, closed the door behind him. He was dressed
more casually than Dougie remembered him being the first time
they'd met—a lot like how Nikolai had dressed Dougie yesterday,
actually: washed-out jeans and a soft forest-green sweater with the
sleeves pushed up to his elbows. He was balancing a tray in one hand.
"Brought you breakfast."

"Um, thanks." He tracked Roger with his eyes as the man sat on
the edge of the bed, placed the tray between them, lifted the lid. Yogurt

and granola and fresh fruit—perfect after yesterday's overindulgence. His stomach grumbled. Was it okay to just dig in? Should he offer to share?

"Go on," Roger said, nudging it forward. Added, "I already ate, so don't mind me."

Dougie took that for the permission it was and started mixing granola and strawberries into the yogurt. Took a bite. The sugar, or maybe just the pleasant tang of it, woke him up a little, cleared his head. He realized Roger was still sitting on the edge of the bed. Watching him with that soft, inviting smile on his face.

Was still watching him when he'd scraped the last of the yogurt from the bowl. It wasn't unnerving so much as just plain strange. If Roger wanted something, why wasn't he *saying* something? Dougie put the bowl back on the tray a little harder than he'd intended and said, "What?"

Roger made a sort of half-shrug, and his smile turned rueful. "The master thought you might find it helpful to talk with me." When Dougie said nothing to that, he added, "Seeing as I've . . . you know. Been where you are."

He looked a little uncomfortable. Dougie hadn't seen very much of Roger, but he'd never seen him even *hint* at unsteadiness. Did Dougie remind him of something he didn't want to think about? Was he worried that he couldn't give Dougie what he needed because he'd been faking it for the last twenty years or however long he'd been stuck here? Oh God, was he—

Dougie flinched so hard from the hand landing on his knee that he almost knocked the tray off the bed. "Hey," Roger said. "Hey, it's okay, you don't have to talk to me if you don't want to."

Dougie was panting, could feel his pulse pounding at his temples and throat. And Roger's hand, stroking soothing little circles right above his knee. "Sorry," he mumbled. "I . . . Sorry."

"It's all right." Roger's hand stopped stroking, patted Dougie once. "I'll just . . ." He hooked his thumb toward the door, began to stand.

Dougie lunged forward and grabbed his wrist. "No!" He was on his knees somehow, his blanket-shield fallen away, the empty tray clattering on the floor. Completely naked in front of this stranger, making a mess of everything, and he didn't even care. "No, I mean . . . please, stay." He didn't know why he wanted that so much—*needed* it so much—but he did. He did.

And thankfully, Roger sat back down. Offered him that patient smile again. Not patronizing, not condescending, not even mad about the mess on the floor. Just . . . kind. Understanding, too.

I've been where you are.

Dougie let go of Roger's wrist, settled himself back against the headboard, pulled the blankets back up to his waist. All easier things to do than giving voice to any one of the jumble of questions rushing to the forefront of his mind. But he could only fidget for so long while Roger sat patiently by, and who knew how long Nikolai would let the man stay. So Dougie sucked in a deep breath and forced himself to start talking before he could overthink himself into a corner. "What, um . . ." His eyes darted to Roger's—pretty, bright green like the kind you read about in romance novels but never see in real life—and back down to the blanket bunched in his lap. Had Nikolai chosen him for those eyes? The rest of him wasn't so bad, either.

Off topic, Dougie. Stop stalling.

Yeah, okay. "When you . . . *before*, I mean, you know, before . . ."

"Nikolai saved me?" Roger offered.

Dougie nodded, desperately searching for the sincerity in that statement, for any hint of artifice. He found none. "What was it like? I mean, what did you want to be? What did you dream about? Who did you love?"

"Ah." Roger said nothing else for a long moment, but that *Ah* spoke volumes. Like he knew the question Dougie was *really* trying to ask—*How did you leave it all behind?*—but wasn't brave enough to articulate. "It was . . . confusing. Messy. Not very nice." Roger shifted, tucked one leg up beneath him and scrubbed a hand through his dirty blond hair. It stuck up endearingly—still cute, even at his age. And since when had Dougie started to think about other guys as *cute*? "My mom died when I was little. I don't remember her at all. My dad . . . well, he loved me, but he wasn't very good at the whole father thing, you know?" He looked down at his hands, examining his knuckles. Did he have his father's hands? "He worked a lot. We never had much. He drank. I was fourteen when I ended up in foster care."

Foster care. Just like Dougie had been.

No point to thinking about it, though. Trying to puzzle out the reasoning behind his capture was the action of a man still wishing to be free.

Roger, oblivious to Dougie's revelation, went on. "I decided then and there that I wasn't going to be like him when I grew up. I studied hard. I got into college. All I wanted was to be a cop. Not just any cop, either; I wanted to make detective. I didn't realize until after I came here that all I'd *really* wanted was to not feel helpless anymore. Not feel afraid, you know? I wanted to learn how to take care of myself because there was nobody else in the world who would do it for me. Nobody else I could lean on. And I was scared all the time, even if I didn't *realize* it at the time. The mast—Nikolai, Nikolai helped me. Took care of me. Taught me how not to be afraid anymore."

"I don't want to be afraid anymore either," Dougie said. "Not even of Nikolai, or what might happen to me a week from now. I'm even afraid of myself, of what I might do." *To* Nikolai or *for* Nikolai, he couldn't say.

"My advice? Let it go. Just let it go. Give it to Nikolai. Let him carry that burden for you. He wants to."

Dougie nodded. He believed that every bit as much as Roger clearly did, but it was still way easier said than done. "I wanted to be a therapist. A psychologist." He paused, shut his mouth with a click of teeth. Why had he *said* that? Why even talk about his old life? And why to Roger, of all people? It wasn't like Roger had been expecting him to respond. Talking about his own past and expecting the same in reply was the action of a man with ulterior motives, and no way was Roger the type. He was too . . .

God, he was too *pure.*

"I know. Nikolai talks to me about you." He put up a hand before Dougie could respond, before the flash of jealousy Dougie felt at that knowledge—Nikolai *confides* in Roger—could fully form, let alone be analyzed. "Nothing too personal, I mean, nothing you'd be ashamed of me knowing. But where you came from, I know that. We're alike in that way. That's why Nikolai chose us: we want so badly to serve. I wanted to serve the law, serve my community. You wanted to serve people's mental health . . . which I guess serves the community, too.

But the kind of service we were striving for? It's a losing battle, and we'd have burned out and the world would have eaten us alive. Even worse, it's not what we *really* want. It's just . . ." He shrugged. "A Band-Aid. A symptom of a deeper disease, of a pain we'd never have figured out how to heal on our own, one we were trying so desperately to guard against feeling again. But *this* kind of service . . ." He gestured in a way that encompassed the room, Nikolai, even some unknown new master waiting in the future. "This we can do. Nikolai won't let us fail. And Nikolai *healed* me."

Roger met Dougie's eyes, and Dougie was shocked to see them shining with wetness, with a kind of devotion he himself had never known, never understood. "Nikolai will heal you too, if you let him."

Dougie swallowed hard, and thought about school, and studying, and his old dreams of a practice, of rescuing Mat from a life of fighting, rescuing himself from . . . from what? Maybe Roger was right. Maybe he *had* been trying to rescue himself from a life of misery and fear. Maybe he'd picked psychology not out of passion but out of self-preservation. If he could master the human mind, if he could master the art of therapy and healing, then maybe he could heal himself. Was that what he'd been doing all that time? Chasing futilely after some panacea for his wounded soul and inadvertently making himself even more miserable in the process?

Could Nikolai really help him stop running from himself?

Looking into Roger's earnest, open eyes, he dared to hope the answer was yes.

CHAPTER TWO

Mat adjusted the rope around his neck, wishing he knew how to tie a noose instead of a simple slipknot. The ceilings weren't high here. The chin-up bar was even less high. When he stepped off the chair, his toes would be only inches from the floor. He didn't want to screw this up, didn't want to give his instincts a chance to kick in and fight.

Knot over the carotid. He spun the leather, placed it carefully. Just like a sleeper hold. He'd be out in seconds. Dead in a couple minutes. And with any luck—any at all—it would be Nikolai who came in and found him, Nikolai who'd first get to see the fruits of his twisted efforts. Would he look at Mat's limp body and see a *person*? A life lost? Or just a waste of a million dollars and several weeks of his time?

No. Don't think about Nikolai. Not now. Don't give him that.

Happier thoughts. Happier. There'd been a time when he could call up such memories so easily. Everything seemed so far away now, so out of his grasp.

He curled his toes into the seat of the chair. Pressed a palm to the wall. Smooth and cool beneath his fingers. Tried to ignore the touch of the leather around his throat. *Focus.*

The taste of homemade lemonade.

The day Knockout had stumbled, hungry and wet, onto their porch, stared warily at Mat, and started meowing. *Can we keep him, Mom?* Never any question she'd say yes.

Christmas with Dougie, the year they'd gotten a Super Nintendo and played it so obsessively that their mother had to lock it away.

His first kiss. The taste of cigarettes—the forbidden stacked on the forbidden—sticking to his lips.

His first state championship, Mom and Dad and Dougie cheering wildly from the bleachers when the last bell rang.

His first KO in a pro MMA fight, just forty-five seconds into round two, Mom and Dad and Dougie hugging and fist-pumping from the front row.

The look on Dougie's face when he'd opened his acceptance letter to his first-choice undergrad school—the letter he'd left unopened for four whole days so he could do it with Mat instead of Pattie and Mike.

Dougie's college graduation, Mat sitting with Mike, so full to bursting with joy and pride he didn't even care if the whole crowd saw him cry.

Yeah, he'd had a good run. Right up until the end, almost, despite everything that'd happened. He could let go now. He wouldn't be hurting anyone. Not anymore.

"I wish you wouldn't do that."

Mat whirled around so quickly he almost fell off the chair. A moment of sheer panic as his hand shot out, found the chin-up bar to steady himself, chest heaving, heart thrashing. He blinked down at Roger's open, wounded expression, at his half-outstretched arm nearly close enough to touch Mat, and felt a laugh crawl up his throat at the absurdity of it. He'd been preparing to step off the chair on purpose; why so much fear at falling accidentally?

And how had he not heard Roger come in?

"I really wish you wouldn't do that," Roger repeated. He sounded like he meant it, too—not for Nikolai, but for *himself*, like he'd miss Mat, or maybe took it as a personal affront that Mat would choose to leave him.

Or maybe as a failure. Maybe he thought he hadn't taken enough care of Mat.

Which was bullshit. The way he'd come in every day, morning, noon, and night, with fresh food and bandages and antibiotics and painkillers and soft hands and softer smiles and more patience than any one man had a right to. The way he'd picked up after Mat's hurled trays and hurled insults without complaint, without so much as a squinty glare. The way his mere *presence* had shouted, day after day, *I understand. I care. It's all right.*

"Yeah," Mat said, but it came out on a croak, like the leather jump rope was already strangling him, so he cleared his throat and tried again. "Yeah. All right."

He didn't know why he was saying that. Hadn't meant to. Didn't seem to have any control over his fingers, either, as they reached up to his throat, loosened the slipknot, pushed the rope up and off himself. Lost control of the rest of himself as his legs and feet took him off the chair. Something bloomed hot and tight in his chest, as thick and choking as he imagined the rope would've been. Pain, maybe. Definitely. But something else, too.

And then he fell into Roger's arms.

He hadn't meant to do that either, really. Maybe the shock or the adrenaline had weakened his knees, or maybe he was just feeling sappy from all the reminiscing, or maybe some part of him was happy to have survived and wanted to share that primitive joy with the only kind person left in an increasingly cruel world.

Roger didn't say anything. Didn't back away and leave him cold. Just enfolded Mat against his big solid body and . . . held him. God, *held him*. Mat hadn't realized how much he'd missed being touched by someone who wasn't using that touch to hurt him. Or to lull him into a sense of false security just to hurt him more.

None of that. This touch was comfort and understanding, and all the things Mat once used to seek in the arms of men.

"You're all right," Roger said, gruff voice full of masculine tenderness, and *that*, after everything that had happened today, the last few weeks or months, was what finally broke Mat.

He clutched at Roger's shoulders, pressed his body to Roger's, and slammed their mouths together in the most desperate kiss of his life. He *wanted* this. Wanted this connection, wanted to know there was something left to live for. Not Roger himself, but what Roger symbolized: the freedom to love and touch and need and be needed, and to do it of his own free will. Not that Roger wasn't a good outlet for those urges—he was kind and handsome and kind and strong and kind and had a gentle smile and beautiful green eyes. Out in the real world, it wasn't completely out of the question that Mat might have picked him up at a bar.

He wondered what Roger had been like before he'd come to this place. Would there ever be any chance for them to meet outside these walls? Would it be *real*? Or had this place tainted everything, *ruined* everything, twisted them both around so hard they couldn't even tell what they were looking at anymore? He'd backed Roger all the way across the room, backed him into the wall, had his hands tangled in Roger's soft blond hair and his tongue shoved halfway down his throat and his cock grinding hard into the line of Roger's hip and thigh and this was a man who'd tied him down against his will once upon a time, *I don't have permission to feel sorry for you*, stood by and watched as he'd been raped and beaten and raped again and how was it that Mat couldn't even bring himself to care about that now, to care about anything but the slight minty taste of Roger against his tongue and the softness of his lips and the firmness of him beneath his need—

But apparently Roger cared. It finally got through to Mat that Roger was trying to push him away. Not panicked, not even struggling, not really. *No, of course not, how can you rape a fuck-toy?* Just . . . insistent. Firm, but gentle. Mat wondered how often Roger had the option of refusing sex, and God, giving him that had to be just as important as him giving Mat the option to *choose* sex.

Mat pulled off with a gasp. "Sorry," he panted, wiping at his mouth and stepping away, giving Roger as much space as he could. "Sorry, I . . . I don't know what—"

"Shush." No rancor, though. All kindness. Mat noticed that Roger hadn't bothered to wipe *his* mouth. That Roger's full cock was pressing hard against the confines of his jeans. Breathless relief at that, that he hadn't forced him, hadn't hurt him. Roger took a step forward. Another. Re-closing the distance between them. "It's all right." He was in Mat's space now. Reached out and touched Mat's arm. "But I love someone else, you know that. And even if I didn't . . ."

Roger cast his eyes down and to the side for a moment—not so much sad or even resigned as just . . . habit, maybe. He didn't finish his sentence, but Mat knew anyway: *I belong to someone else. This body isn't mine to give.*

"I'm sorry," Mat said again, horrified that he'd even *tried* to take something he knew Roger didn't own, couldn't offer. But he'd needed it, God, he *still* needed it. "I'm sorry, I'm sorry." Now that he'd let himself say it, he couldn't seem to stop saying it. "Please just . . ." Forget it? Forgive me? Hold me? He didn't know. He shook his head, stepped into Roger's space in a silent plea, and of course Roger's arms came up around him, so warm and giving. "I'm sorry," he mumbled again into the side of Roger's neck, feeling the tears well without knowing where they were coming from or how to stop them. "I'm sorry, I'm sorry..."

Roger shushed him gently, walked him backward until his knees hit the mattress and he tumbled over, Roger beside him, still holding on as if he knew Mat would fall to pieces without him. Fuck it, Mat was falling to pieces anyway, and all he could do was hold on, and he didn't know whether he would hang up his noose again or if he would starve himself or if he would finally give in to Nikolai's demands and become a man like Roger. Whatever it was, what was one more day of it? He'd suffered so much already, and anyway it wasn't like he didn't deserve to suffer, not after what he'd done, and maybe he couldn't have anything down here but at least someone was holding him with love as he cried. One more day... What was one more day?

He'd let himself die tomorrow, if it came to that.

Roger, brilliant thing that he was, had talked Mathias out of hanging himself. After that, Nikolai kept a close eye on the camera feeds for Mathias's room, and though no more suicide attempts were forthcoming throughout the day or night, the man also didn't make any moves toward recovery. He still wasn't eating. Still wasn't getting out of bed. His beautiful muscular body had begun to waste away this past week and change. And yet Nikolai knew there was nothing he could *do* to that body that would cause Mathias more pain than he was feeling right now. No way to motivate him by shouts or threats or punishments. How to motivate a man through pain when it was pain that he craved the most?

Fortunately, he'd long since put his contingency plan into motion by introducing Roger's care and affection to Mathias. It was quite the shame he actually had to go through with its final stage, though.

He took a walk to clear his head and focus his resolve, sun shining bright above but cold wind howling through the trees. He stayed out in it longer than was comfortable—his own little taste of self-flagellation, perhaps, for what he'd have to do next.

Roger was waiting for him when he returned to the house, standing in the foyer, a chastising smile on his lips and a mug of hot chocolate—homemade, of course, not the powdered trash—cradled in his hands. He held it out wordlessly and Nikolai took it, warmth blossoming in his heart along with his stomach as he took a first, careful sip. Not too hot to drink. He took a longer sip. Stared at Roger over the rim of the mug. So beautiful, still, even after all these years. So *perfect* in very nearly every way. Nikolai felt near to bursting with pride. Affection. And yes, love.

Regret, too, for what was about to come.

He allowed himself one last sip of his drink, then set the mug down on the table by the door. "I'm afraid it's time," he said.

Roger's smile fell a little, but he wasn't afraid, and he didn't pull his gaze from Nikolai's. "I agree, Sir." He swallowed hard, once. Held Nikolai's eyes.

Nikolai thought of taking Roger up to his bedroom for this, but he didn't want to do it there. Didn't want to pollute that sacred space with the memory of what was to come. On the other hand, he wanted Roger to be as comfortable as possible. His den, then, where Roger had happily spent so many hours curled on the couch beside him or at his feet beneath his desk, head resting on his thigh.

He led Roger there with a caressing hand at the small of his back. Roger began to undress the moment Nikolai had closed the door behind them. Folded his clothes so neatly, took so much care. The same care he showed with everything—and everyone—in his life. A natural nurturer. Nikolai was blessed to have found him.

When Roger was totally naked, Nikolai sucked in a deep breath and unbuckled his belt. Pulled it from its loops. Wrapped the ends around his fist. He took two steps toward Roger but then stopped. Just took him in in all his beauty, his openness, his honesty, his devotion. Stunning. *Breathtaking.*

"It's going to work, Sir," Roger assured him. How could he be so calm in the face of what was coming? "It *will*. I've spent enough time with Mathias these last two weeks to know. I'm sure of it, Sir."

Nikolai took another deep breath, forced himself to close the final distance between himself and Roger. "I know," he said. He believed it, too. He wouldn't be doing this if he didn't. He huffed a dull laugh, flashed a dull smile. "That doesn't mean I have to like it."

Roger smiled back, not dull at all. "No, Sir," he agreed.

Nikolai took one more step, until he was close enough to see the pulse fluttering hummingbird-quick at Roger's throat, belying his outward calm. Close enough to feel the heat of him. He cupped Roger's face with the hand not holding the belt, leaned in slowly, and kissed him. Gentle, no tongue, just . . . affection, gratitude, love, strength. Roger sighed into his parted lips, and Nikolai murmured, "I'm sorry," against the man's mouth.

Roger pulled back just enough to meet Nikolai's eyes, and said, "I'm not." *For you, Sir. Anything for you.*

Nikolai nodded once in acknowledgment, stepped back, and swung the first strike.

CHAPTER THREE

There were no windows down here, but Nikolai had kept Dougie to a pretty regular schedule for some time now, and his body had adjusted to the new rhythm. Plus, Nikolai had brought him an alarm clock last week—*Always be ready for your master in the morning*—and he'd taken to setting it for 6:30, getting showered and shaved and tidied before Nikolai's arrival with breakfast an hour later.

But it was 8:15 now, and he'd been kneeling at the foot of his neatly made bed for forty-five minutes, and all he had to show for it was stiff shoulders and a sore back and knees and a tingling in his feet that told him they'd both fallen asleep. No Nikolai. No breakfast.

I hope he's okay.

Dougie shifted minutely, trying to restore circulation to his toes without breaking position. Realized with a jolt of warmth—no, more than that: hope, triumph—that his unbidden thought for Nikolai's welfare had been genuine. Was still genuine. And Dougie *genuinely* missed him. Not just because he was hungry and sore and accustomed to a certain routine, but because he missed just talking with Nikolai, talking to him and spending time with him. Not necessarily the sex, but everything else, and with that Dougie could almost believe that missing the sex would follow too. In time.

Forty-five minutes he'd been kneeling here, weeks he'd been in Nikolai's care. From the moment Nikolai had pulled him from the dark living death of his tomb and given him water, to the day he'd punched his own client to protect him, to the morning of Dougie's first nature hike when Nikolai had been watchful enough to protect Dougie from himself—he'd never, ever let Dougie down. Never left him to fend for himself. Never left him alone. He wouldn't now, either, Dougie was sure of it, and that thought brought with it a new jolt of warmth and hope. He could do this. It was happening. Nikolai was helping him to make it happen. And he didn't hate himself and he didn't hate the world and he *certainly* didn't hate Nikolai. No disgust, no self-recrimination. Just a strange sort of peace, of patience—a carefree, worriless existence the likes of which he hadn't known since the day his parents had died. It was all happening exactly the way Nikolai had promised him it would way back at the beginning. All he had to do now was wait. All he'd ever needed to do was wait.

For Nikolai.

Mat rose hesitantly from sleep, woozy and still tired. The overhead lights were on—why hadn't he turned those off before he'd gone to bed? He blinked against them, wondering what time it was, how long he'd slept, if anyone would care if he went back to sleep, why his face felt so sticky and his eyes so sore. Like he'd been crying. Like—

Roger. Suicide attempt. Kissing him. Sobbing like a baby in his arms.

The memories came back slower than they should've, shamed him less than he thought they would. His stomach cramped and rumbled incessantly. He ignored it like he had for the past God-knew-how-long. Closed his eyes again. Thought of Roger's arms around him, Roger's kind words and understanding, his gentleness and generosity. Of what might've—no, *would've*—happened yesterday if Roger hadn't shown up when he had.

No surprise, then, that he wished Roger were here now. Practically *burned* with it, in fact. It wasn't healthy, couldn't be. But it was all he had.

He sighed, rolled from his right side to his left. The effort wore him right out. How that would've scared him before Baseball Bat Guy—the weakness, the helplessness, the way his body was shutting down. Now it was almost . . . reassuring. Meant it wouldn't be long now until the final bell, even if he couldn't bring himself to commit a decisive act to end things.

In the meanwhile, he'd take his punches and wait.

His thoughts drifted for a while, his mind as dull and untethered as his body felt. He might've slept. Or maybe he just passed the hours staring at the far wall. Didn't matter. Only mattered that nothing hurt when he drifted like that, that no stray unpleasant thoughts wafted through his skull. No thoughts at all, really. He liked it that way. Easier that way. Barely even felt the stomach cramps.

At some point, his door opened, and someone shuffled inside. He didn't move. Didn't turn his head to look. Couldn't really even be roused to care. Nikolai, probably, come at last to force him out of bed, to force him to eat, to fight. Or to fuck him, or to punish him for lazing. Whatever, let him try. Hard to hurt a dead man, after all.

But what if it's Roger?

No. Roger would've said something. Roger *always* said something. *Good morning* or *Hello* or even *Do you mind if I come in?* Roger treated him like a human being. Roger wouldn't be inviting himself onto Mat's bed like his current visitor was doing. So Nikolai after all, then. Or maybe a guard. No difference—they all wanted the same thing. They could have it. Mat was too weak to fight even if he'd wanted to.

He rolled over onto his stomach, then hefted himself up onto wobbly elbows and knees. If Nikolai or whoever wanted to fuck him, they could pull his blanket the rest of the way off themselves.

But nothing happened. The person sitting on the bed just sighed. "This has to stop."

Roger.

"I wish it would," Mat replied, bitterly, then felt bad for using such a cruel tone with Roger, who didn't deserve it.

"*You* have the power to stop it, Mat."

"Don't fucking say that to me—" And then his voice cracked, trembled on the edge of tears, and he managed to gasp out, "Not you too."

He realized how much it suddenly hurt to see Roger siding with Nikolai, even though Roger always *had*. Right from the first moment he'd been Nikolai's man, but he'd been the only kind person in Mat's life here and God, Mat wanted more from him, wanted him to be more and do more. He knew it wasn't fair to Roger, but fuck-all was fair down here, so why should *he* have to be?

A tentative hand cupped his shoulder, and it was the sheer gentleness of the touch that finally made his own arms give out. He flopped back to his stomach, squeezed his eyes closed. Roger's hand followed him down, rubbed between his shoulder blades. "I meant you're the only one who can stop blaming yourself for what's happening

RACHEL HAIMOWITZ & HEIDI BELLEAU

here. To you. To Douglas. I know you can't . . . you can't *transform* like Douglas is, that the master can't let that happen. But you can't fight this, either, not really. So either you choose to keep hurling yourself against a brick wall, or you choose to save your strength for when it matters. And that too is a choice only you can make."

Mat scoffed, jerked his shoulder until Roger stopped touching him. The only thing that made him madder than hearing this shit from Roger's mouth was the fact that Roger was *right*.

Which was why he was lying here waiting to die. Because *nothing* mattered anymore. Nothing ever would again. So what was there to save his strength for?

Winning.

God, how long ago had it been that he'd written that stupid fucking list? And everything Nikolai had predicted had come to pass. Was the list any less true now than then?

Get out of here. Burn this place down. Save Dougie and himself.

"Nikolai told me once that you wanted to help people."

But Dougie hated him now.

I can still save him.

"Can't even help myself," he growled into his pillow.

Roger, the persistent bastard, laid a hand back on Mat's shoulder. He wanted to shrug away again, but he didn't have the energy for it. Which was fine, he supposed—it gave truth to his words, truth Roger would have to listen to.

"Of course you can. You've just chosen not to."

Strength returned in a rush of righteous fury—*How fucking dare he!*—and Mat lurched up and spun around, fist following the momentum in a hard right hook that smashed into Roger's cheek and sent the fucker tumbling clear off the bed. Mat started after him, feeling pretty fucking proud of himself for managing such a clean blind strike just by following the sound of Roger's voice—*starved half to death and you still got it, baby*—but as Mat rolled (okay, sort of fell, more like) off the edge of the bed, he caught his first good look at Roger's face. Or rather, the bits he could see of it around the hands pressed to Roger's cheek. Like the fresh black eye that could under no circumstance have formed in the last five seconds. Or the barely healed split lower lip. Or the defensive bruising and welts on Roger's bare forearms.

And he knew in an instant, with a certainty that made his very empty stomach try to turn itself inside out, that somehow this was all his fault.

"Oh God . . ."

"That bad?" Roger asked, and then he fucking *laughed*.

"N-Nikolai?" Mat managed to get out, so furious, so confused, so terrified, so fucking empty and plain old *sad* he couldn't form a sentence.

Roger shrugged and picked himself up the floor, helping Mat up in turn. "He's my master. Our master. He told me to nurse you back to health, and I let him down. Did you think you were the only one who had to face consequences?"

Why wasn't Roger upset?

No, Mat knew the answer to that. The guy was a fucking mess. Could Mat really hold him responsible for that fact? Nikolai had half broken Mat, probably *destroyed* Dougie by now—with Mat's cooperation, Jesus—and they'd only been here . . . well, Mat didn't know how long. Roger had been here for *years*. He was fucking helpless, and here Mat was making his life hell and then punching him in the face for his trouble. "I'm a selfish asshole, aren't I?"

Roger rubbed at the redness just above his jaw, but Mat didn't think he intended to chastise with the gesture. "A little, yes. But that's normal, on the outside. I was too, before I came here." Not angry at Nikolai for hurting him, not mad at Mat for causing that hurt. The guy was a saint. A stupid saint. The human equivalent of a kicked dog that kept getting abused and abused and just loved you more for it, worked harder to make you love it even half as much in return.

And Mat had the man's welfare in his hands, and he'd completely fucked it up. His stomach tried to crawl up his throat again. First Dougie, now Roger . . . God, was there anyone he *hadn't* hurt? Maybe Roger's injuries weren't so bad. He had to know; maybe he could find a way to live with himself if they weren't so bad. Find a way to redeem himself. Maybe . . . "Let me see."

Roger sat back on the edge of the bed and gave Mat a sort of narrow-eyed look that said *Are you sure?* and *Don't be stupid* and *What the fuck for?* all at once. Now that Mat was paying attention, it was easy to see how gingerly Roger was moving. His face and arms were probably the least of it.

My fault. This happened because of me. Roger did everything *he could. He did* take care of me.

"Let me see," Mat said again, and maybe Roger felt sorry for him, or maybe he was just reacting instinctively to the edge of command in Mat's voice. Whatever the case, he grabbed the hem of his T-shirt and pulled it over his head.

This time, Mat actually *was* sick. Just bile—not even any water in his stomach—and it burned like lemon juice in an open wound as it came up and he fucking *deserved* it, Jesus, the poor guy was a mess, looked like Nikolai had taken a belt to him for hours and then kicked him when he'd gone down. The damage blurred, and Mat realized he'd begun to cry, silent and insidious but utterly unstoppable, and he could make out just enough of Roger's expression—*sympathy, the stupid fucker,* he's *sorry for* me!—to be glad for the obscuring scrim of tears.

"I'm so sorry," he choked out, and when Roger just put his shirt back on and shook his head and went to fetch a towel to clean up the mess Mat had made of the floor, the feeling got so much worse that it ripped a sob clean from his chest. "Tell me how to make it right, Roger. Please."

Roger turned to face him, a sad little smile in place as he sat back down and laid a hand on Mat's knee, held his gaze. "You already know how to make it right, Mat. You've always known. All you have to do is make the choice. Stop hurling yourself against brick walls. Live."

Mat blinked at him, tears overspilling and dripping off his chin into his lap. He lifted one shaky hand and laid it atop Roger's where it rested on his knee. He'd been selfish. He'd been a fucking moron. Worse, he'd been a *quitter*. He'd let Nikolai turn him into the one thing he'd never abided in his life. So Dougie hated him. Call the fucking waaaaambulance. He could still save Dougie. He could even save Roger. But first . . . first he had to save himself, and yes, he could sure as fuck do that too. He *would* do that too, pain be damned. Nikolai could knock him to the mat, but he couldn't make him stay down.

He nodded—mostly to himself, but partly to that hopeful, breathless question in Roger's eyes—and felt a sudden, powerful urge to kiss Roger, just as strong as yesterday when he'd come down off that chair. But he knew better than to give in to it this time, settled instead for bringing his free hand up to Roger's head, cupped the cheek he'd reddened and ran his thumb ever-so-gently under Roger's eye. Roger didn't flinch, held his gaze, and his smile softened beneath Mat's hand. Mat's breath caught at the mere reflection of Roger's devotion for Nikolai in that gaze.

Lucky bastard. Mat averted his eyes, cleared his throat. "I, uh, I'm hungry," he said.

Roger stood, Mat's hand still grasped in his own, leaned in and kissed Mat on the cheek. "I'll go fetch you a tray."

Dougie was still kneeling two hours later. His whole body was aching, but he couldn't let himself break position. It had become something of a test for himself, as if each passing minute proved his dedication and loyalty.

Which meant he was rewarded when the door finally opened and he was still holding strong.

He beamed up, proud of himself and excited to see Nikolai—to show Nikolai how good he'd been, how obedient, how eager to please—but his face fell when someone else strode through the door. Jeremy, the cook, the one Nikolai had sent out of the room after their first foray in the woods.

"Get up," Jeremy said with an impatient little wave of his hand, like he couldn't be bothered with Dougie's earnestness. "The master's busy today with Roger and isn't to be disturbed, but he asked me to come collect you. I've got some lunch upstairs for you, and after that I'm to put you to work."

Dougie struggled to his deadened feet, using the edge of the bed to help himself up when he faltered. Even his legs had gone numb. But none of that was as bad as the strange tingling tightness in his chest where he'd been holding so fiercely onto thoughts of Nikolai all morning, where Nikolai's absence buzzed and burned in a way he wasn't sure how to explain but knew *mattered* somehow. It was a good pain, though—it had to be. It meant he was . . . how had Nikolai put it? Transforming? Yes. It meant he was *transforming*.

Finally.

"Oh, I almost forgot. He said to plug yourself for him. He said you'd know what to do. I have stuff to do upstairs, so just come up when you're done. I'll be in the kitchen. I'd *suggest* you don't get lost on the way there."

"Understood," Dougie said, not sure whether to call the man "sir" or not. He was a slave, Dougie thought, but his mannerisms were so . . . in control. Maybe even in service, men got to be themselves. Roger was kind. Dougie would be earnest and sweet and a little nerdy, just as Nikolai was encouraging him to be. Just as he'd always been, but better.

Still himself. The thought made him smile.

He was still smiling after Jeremy left, as he opened the drawer with all the plugs. The heaviness in his chest was fading. He hoped Roger was okay. Maybe he'd gotten sick or maybe he'd hurt himself and Nikolai was taking care of him, like he always took care of Dougie, like he seemed to take care of everyone else in his charge. A good man. Like a father, almost. Strict, but loving.

Dougie eyed the wide array of plugs, and his smile faltered a little. *He said you'd know what to do.* Except Dougie *didn't* know what to do. What was the plug for? Did Nikolai want him distracted while he worked? Happily distracted or uncomfortably distracted? Or did he just want Dougie ready to be fucked when the time came? In which case, stretched to Nikolai's exact specifications . . . The thought made Dougie's cock chub up a bit and he gave it a stroke. He liked the thought of that, wearing a Nikolai-sized plug. It would edge on uncomfortable, but he'd be full and thinking of Nikolai. Uncomfortable *and* happy.

Except, this wasn't *about* him, was it. No, it was about Nikolai. And maybe Nikolai would want Dougie's ass to be tighter when he breached him, which would mean a smaller plug. And, wow, he should really stop touching his cock, shouldn't he, because *that* was all about Nikolai, too—it was Nikolai's cock now, and his pleasure was Nikolai's decision to make. He pulled his hand away, surprised at the flush of guilt heating his cheeks. Maybe if he admitted to Nikolai what he'd done, how he'd accidentally touched himself thinking about being ready for Nikolai . . . Well, maybe Nikolai would go easy on him and maybe he wouldn't, but either way he had a sneaking suspicion he'd feel better about himself for the confession. And surely *that* meant he was transforming, too. A good sign. All good signs.

But he still didn't know what Nikolai wanted. And if he got this wrong, Nikolai might . . . might *beat* him. He'd warned Dougie about that, after all. Just as bad, Nikolai would be unhappy with him. And he might be transforming and growing and getting better, but he still felt enough of his old self to know how *fragile* all that was, and he wasn't sure he could handle Nikolai being unhappy with him right now. Was afraid of how he might react. Was afraid he'd backslide in the face of Nikolai's disapproval.

He didn't want to start fighting Nikolai again. He *had* to get this right.

So what would Nikolai want?

Tight. Ready. And really, with how kind he'd been, would he want Dougie in pain? No, pain was for punishment. The plug was a tool, a way to make sex more convenient, a way to help Dougie remember his place. He stared at the plugs, estimating measurements, eventually finding one that looked the same size as Nikolai's cock—girth and length—and because they were neatly arranged by size, selected the next one down the line. Just a little bit smaller, almost not even noticeable, but for Nikolai it would feel different for sure.

It was bright blue and curved and soft to the touch, and Dougie shivered with anticipation as he drizzled it with lube, using a little extra to make sure he'd be nice and slick inside for Nikolai when the time came.

If the time came, he reminded himself. Nikolai was busy today, after all. Nikolai was Dougie's first and only priority, the center of Dougie's universe, but Dougie couldn't be the center of Nikolai's. Nikolai loved him, he knew that, but he was a man with responsibilities, with people who depended on him, and that meant that Dougie would have to put his own needs and wants aside when they didn't coincide with Nikolai's needs and wants.

And be happy for it.

Besides, the fact that Nikolai felt he *could* leave Dougie alone for a day was just one more in a long list of signs that Dougie was getting closer and closer to what he needed to be. To what Nikolai was grooming him to be. Transformed. His best self. After so long spent afraid of never reaching that point no matter how hard he tried, it was finally happening, and all he'd had to do was trust Nikolai, give himself over. Nikolai trusted him. Nikolai trusted him to make this decision. Nikolai trusted him to please his master.

The joy of that filled his chest to bursting.

He didn't think he could possibly feel happier, but then he was pushing the plug into his body, a little discomfort but no real pain because Nikolai had so patiently taught him how to relax. He fucked himself with it teasingly just as Nikolai had done, picturing that it was Nikolai's cock inside him, that Nikolai was fucking him and he was so tight and willing, and Nikolai would be so happy. So happy.

And Dougie was happy too.

Roger shifted against Nikolai's chest, settling a little lower between his legs with a contented sigh. The bed was comfortable and Roger sleepy and warm in his arms, the skin of Roger's stomach smooth against the palm Nikolai had slid beneath the hem of his T-shirt. He had one eye on the laptop balanced atop the comforter in Roger's lap, but the other firmly on Roger, who'd so willingly given so very much in service to him yesterday. Who'd more than earned this day of pampering—they both had, truth be told—of lounging in bed with lazy snuggles and unhurried affection.

And a laptop. But then, some responsibilities could simply not be shirked. Anyway, Roger actually seemed more interested in the new pets' camera feeds than Nikolai was. He supposed the man had earned that too—he'd certainly been instrumental in their growth these last days.

Nikolai pressed a kiss to the side of Roger's head, then another—and then one more, why not?—as Roger flipped the primary feed from Douglas's room (the boy had been staring at his collection of plugs for what seemed like hours now) to Mathias's.

"See, Sir?" Roger said—practically purred, in fact, as Nikolai indulged in another nuzzle, this time to that sensitive spot behind Roger's left ear. Roger shivered and pointed at the screen, and lo and behold, Mathias was *out of bed*. And more than that, he was *eating*. Nothing too heavy, just broth and apple juice, but still the first nourishment to pass his lips in ten days. Looking grim and determined, too. "I told you it'd all be worth it."

"You did," Nikolai agreed—out loud, anyway. Secretly, he still wasn't so sure; certainly, they'd achieved their ends, but the means had come at a steep price. "What would I do without you?"

"Waste away and die, probably."

Nikolai laughed at the playful tone, but stilled himself with a mental kick as Roger hissed. He must've jarred something particularly painful. "Are you sure you wouldn't like a stronger painkiller, Roger? Morphine? I can give you something to take the edge off the nausea too. You can rest."

Roger wiggled a little, settling himself more firmly in Nikolai's lap, ass rubbing hard—but so briefly it might've been unintentional—against Nikolai's crotch. "You're the best painkiller of all, Sir." He wrapped both hands around Nikolai's forearms where they rested on his belly, and added, "I'd hate to—"

Nikolai wondered for a moment how he meant to finish that sentence, but then Roger blushed clear to the tips of his ears and Nikolai understood: *I'd hate to fall asleep through one second of this.*

"I'd still be here when you wake up," Nikolai tried. He hated knowing that his own workaholic habits had made moments like these so rare and precious that Roger would rather suffer to have them than not suffer and risk missing them. Nikolai might be a good trainer—the best, even—but the hard truth was that he wasn't a very good *master* sometimes.

Roger made no reply to Nikolai's attempt to sway him, and Nikolai allowed the silence. He buried his nose in Roger's freshly washed hair, inhaled deeply, and went back to watching the monitor over the top of Roger's head.

Despite refusing the stronger painkillers, it didn't take long for Roger's breathing to even out and his fingers to go slack on Nikolai's arms. Nikolai was sure he was sleeping, but then Roger murmured, half-slurred, "Look, Sir," and pointed vaguely toward the picture-in-picture.

Nikolai had been watching Mathias—he'd practically licked his tray clean and then dragged his ridiculously stubborn ass onto the treadmill, even if it was only going at a slow but grueling walk—so he'd failed to notice Douglas finally picking out a plug. He couldn't quite tell which one it was from the tiny picture, so he hit the key to flip the images around just in time to see something curvy and blue disappearing into the boy's ass. There were only two blue plugs in Douglas's room, and one of them was far too large to have slotted in so neatly without preparation. Which meant the boy had chosen the mid-sized one. The one just half an inch shorter and a sliver thinner than Nikolai's own cock. The one that would leave him well prepared for Nikolai, but not so loose as to be disappointing.

Nikolai felt a grin spread clear cross his face.

What a good, bright boy you are.

Even poor sleepy Roger seemed to perk up a bit, watching him.

Nikolai slid his hand back up beneath the hem of Roger's shirt and stroked warm circles on his bare stomach. "Would you like to have him?" he offered. The mere thought of watching Roger and Douglas together made his cock firm against Roger's ass.

Roger expertly non-answered with, "If it would make you happy, Sir." And then, when Nikolai's hand stilled—a clear warning he wanted truth, not pandering, "He's very, very pretty, Sir. And clever. A thoughtful boy. He has a good heart." Nikolai started stroking again, and Roger added with a shrug, "But, he's not . . ."

You. He's not you, Sir.

Nikolai's heart (and other crucial parts of his anatomy, truth be told) swelled so hard at that he couldn't help himself—he cupped Roger's chin, turned his head to the side, and kissed him.

Roger opened so fast beneath him it was as if the man had simply *melted*, all lips and tongue and breathy little moans of *want* and *need* and *please, yes, Sir*, and this time when he squirmed back ass to crotch, there was no question at all of his intent.

Time to put a stop to this. He didn't want to hurt Roger.

"Be still," he said, and pulled away, and Roger whined but fell obedient, didn't chase after his lips or wiggle his hips again. But oh gods, those *puppy eyes*. Had he been anyone else, Nikolai would've slapped the attempt at manipulation right off his face. But it *wasn't* anyone else. It was Roger, his sweet, beautiful, selfless, loving Roger, and the man *wanted*, and he was damn well entitled to want after all he'd been through for Nikolai this week.

"Be still," he said again, and then he toggled the microphone on his computer and called down to the speaker in the kitchen, "Jeremy, when the new boy gets there, send him to my room."

He just hoped he and Roger wouldn't have to wait long.

CHAPTER FOUR

"There's been a change of plans," Jeremy said without turning when Dougie arrived, flushed and buzzing with excitement, at the door to the kitchen. "You're to go straight up to the master's suite. Lucky little shit."

Dougie blinked, not sure whether to apologize or what. Had Jeremy meant to say that last bit aloud? Was it okay for him to talk that way? Would Nikolai approve?

"Don't think you're getting out of chores though, little favorite. I'll be saving my dishes for you. Better hope you don't have sensitive skin; the last boy I had on dish duty got chapped hands and the master spanked his ass twice as raw for it." Jeremy may not have been facing Dougie, but Dougie could *sense* his cruel grin. He wouldn't be surprised if he found out the guy had been spitting in his food while Nikolai wasn't looking.

Not that Dougie hadn't eaten worse at times. Maybe a little spit wasn't so bad.

"Don't just stand there," Jeremy said, and the knife in his hand was big enough to send Dougie stumbling back a step. *Vegetables. Just chopping vegetables.* "Or should I tell the master you decided to keep him waiting?"

Dougie turned tail and ran.

Well, half ran. Kind of waddled, more like. The plug up his ass might not've been quite as big as Nikolai's cock, but it sure as heck didn't make walking easy. He went as fast as he dared. Stumbled once halfway up the stairs. Paused on the landing for a moment trying to remember which one of the many closed doors led to Nikolai's bedroom.

Left. Definitely one of the doors on the left. Which narrowed it down to . . . three. Great. He'd only ever been up here twice, and the first time he'd been incoherent. The second time, he'd been on his hands and knees.

Which, actually, didn't seem like such a bad idea now. He dropped to his knees, where the hallway looked more familiar. He remembered crawling fifteen, maybe twenty feet last time. *Second door, then. Has to be the second.*

He popped back to his feet again to close the distance. No reason to crawl without Nikolai here to enjoy it. Besides, it'd only make him slower. Keep Nikolai waiting. And that was simply unacceptable.

When he reached what he hoped was the right door, he knocked politely, trying to imitate the perfectly unobtrusive rapping that Roger had mastered.

"Come in, Douglas," Nikolai called softly from inside. He didn't sound angry. In fact, he sounded quite happy, genuinely at ease, and the thought of being called to him under these circumstances filled Dougie with sweet pleasure. More than that—warmth, pride, *want*. His cock stiffened, tall and proud as the rest of him, as he opened the door and quietly stepped inside, then shut it behind him. This morning had been a test, then—the waiting, and more waiting, and Jeremy's brusqueness, and the vague order about the plug, all of it—and he'd done well. He'd chosen correctly at every turn. Anticipated his master's needs. And now his master was rewarding him with his company. Maybe, if he was very lucky, his master would reward him further with a good hard fuck. Permission to orgasm. A kiss and some kind words.

He couldn't ask for more. He smiled demurely at Nikolai, tucked his arms behind his back, and presented himself.

From his place on the bed—on the bed with *Roger*, with Roger *in his lap* and Jesus, they were *cuddling*—Nikolai smiled. Dougie's own smile almost faltered at the sight of the two of them being so intimate, but he forced down the surge of jealousy and disappointment—*Roger's a good man, he deserves Nikolai's love too and I'm just an untrained pet I don't deserve* anything *stop acting like a spoiled child*—and froze his expression in place.

"Don't you look lovely and well rested, Douglas. Roger and I were just talking about how very attractive and pleasant you are. What was the word you used, Roger?"

Roger shifted lazily, casting a soft smile at Dougie that made him burn simultaneously with desire and shame for ever being jealous or resentful of this kind man. "Pretty, Sir."

"I believe you said *very* pretty," Nikolai corrected, and reached out to crook a finger in Dougie's direction. Dougie walked toward them both, feeling a little like a mouse caught between two cats. At Nikolai's nod, he climbed up onto the bed at their feet. "And thoughtful, wasn't it?"

"Yes, Sir. Clever, too. Good heart."

This close, Dougie could see that Roger's face and arms were covered in a mottled pattern of bruises, livid and fresh, like they'd still be hot and raised to the touch. Had he been disobedient? Had Nikolai punished him? They certainly didn't *seem* like there'd been any falling-out between them. But then, maybe Nikolai was quick to forgive, not the type to carry a grudge once the consequences of a bad choice had been delivered. Or maybe it wasn't Dougie's place to question and he should just stop thinking about it at all.

"Roger's been very loyal, Douglas, and deserves a reward. However, you may have noticed he's a little too tender for the kind of fucking I like to give my slaves. And since I'm a little busy playing chair for Roger right now, I've devised a suitable alternative." He paused, staring at Dougie expectantly.

Oh God, he means me. He means that I should suck Roger's cock. And why wasn't that thought as disgusting as it should have been? Wasn't Dougie straight? And he hardly *knew* Roger. The thought of having to pleasure a near-stranger—a *male* near-stranger, made his heart race and his throat tighten.

But it was a good fear, he realized. Like riding a roller coaster. Exhilarating and terrifying, but ultimately safe.

Because Nikolai was here, and this was what Nikolai wanted, and what Dougie wanted was to make Nikolai happy. And if this was all it took—Roger was a kind, giving man, and he was undeniably attractive—Dougie could pleasure him. Of course he could. It'd *almost* be like pleasuring Nikolai directly, wouldn't it? And he'd practically been daydreaming about that all morning.

"Yes, Sir," he said. "I'd like that."

Nikolai shifted, subtly spreading his legs. He ran one hand up Roger's stomach, rucking his T-shirt up to expose hairless abs barely softened by age, and the other down to cup a hard, heavy cock inside Roger's gray sweatpants. Roger threw his head back onto Nikolai's shoulder and moaned, spreading his legs until he'd hooked his calves over Nikolai's own. Utterly wanton. Trusting. Hungry.

Beautiful.

Dougie couldn't take his eyes from where Nikolai's lips and teeth had latched onto the exposed tendon of Roger's neck. If he focused hard enough, he could almost feel that moist heat and pressure on his own skin.

He *wanted* it to be him. Really, honest-to-God wanted it. The gleam in Nikolai's eyes as they met his told him that Nikolai knew, too. Knew he was transforming. Was pleased with it.

Douglas crawled up the bed, wiggling his plugged ass as he went, insinuating himself like a cat between both men's legs.

"Very pretty," Nikolai said.

"Very pretty," Roger agreed, though his head was back and his eyes were closed as Nikolai laved at his neck. Dougie fixated on that patch of wet skin again, surprised to realize that no matter how much he wanted it, he didn't begrudge Roger for having it instead. At least he got to watch. That was generous enough. Nikolai hadn't forgotten about him, hadn't left him out. Nikolai had specifically *sought* to include him. He could have given Roger his pleasure and reward all on his own, but he hadn't. He'd called for Dougie.

Little favorite. That's what Jeremy had called him. Dougie was starting to believe it might even be true.

"Show me how you undress a man you're to service, Douglas."

Douglas dropped to his elbows and crawled in as close as he could. He craned his neck to reach the swath of skin Nikolai had bared, brushed a kiss across Roger's abs. Then another when Roger made a breathy little gasp and the hard muscle twitched beneath Dougie's lips. Added some tongue this time. Worked his way down to Roger's waistband with his mouth while he crept one hand up Roger's thigh, featherlight in deference to the bruises that might be hiding beneath the fabric. It wasn't like kissing Nikolai, not exactly, though they both had the same lean bodies that yielded so beautifully beneath a heartfelt caress. Certainly the noises he made were as generous as Nikolai's when Dougie pleased him, as full of praise and promise, and over Roger's shoulder, Nikolai's breathing had sped up too, so it was easy for Dougie to close his eyes and pretend this was Nikolai's stomach he was mouthing, Nikolai's crotch he was palming.

And it *was* Nikolai he was pleasing, no question about it. Roger was collateral, just as Dougie was. It was all about Nikolai, and that made all of this okay. Better than okay. Perfect, almost. Their master. They'd work together to please him.

"That's my good boy," Nikolai murmured, the sound muffled against some patch of Roger's skin and how he wished it were *his* skin those words were sinking into, but they were a caress nonetheless, and he set his mind back to the task at hand, to making the act of undressing as sensuous and pleasurable as what would come after. Nikolai hadn't told him not to tease, or at what pace to proceed, and yeah, okay he was maybe still a *little* jealous so he chose to drag it out as long as Nikolai would let him (and anyway the longer he was here, the longer he was with Nikolai, right?), painting every inch of Roger's skin with lips and tongue and little love-nips as he exposed it, millimeter by millimeter. Drawing Roger's sweatpants down with such agonizing slowness he knew he'd have been half out of his head by now in Roger's shoes, and frankly, he was half out of his head even in his own shoes, with the plug filling his ass and warm skin in his mouth and his cock bumping against his stomach and Roger's leg and occasionally the bedspread as he moved. But he could do this all day if given the chance, worship at Nikolai's altar, prove his studiousness and his intent and his worth.

One more tug at the elastic waistband, and Roger's cock sprang free. It was . . . God, it was *thick*. Thick enough that Dougie wouldn't be able to wrap a hand around it comfortably.

Thick and hard and a deep, dark color, the head straining out of a stretched-taut foreskin. Dougie tore his eyes from it, looking to Nikolai for permission.

"Do you like my man's cock, Douglas?" Nikolai asked with a wicked smile.

Not as much as yours. "Oh yes, Sir," Dougie purred. Even if he wasn't exactly sure what to do with it, how that foreskin would come into play in the pursuit of Roger's pleasure. It didn't seem *too* different, and anyway he had one of his own, didn't he? *Just touch him the way you like to be touched, that's all.*

Except, no touching at all until Nikolai gave him the go-ahead. Roger might be a slave too, but Dougie sensed he was an avatar today, a virtual extension of Nikolai's own flesh. And you never, ever touched your master's cock without permission.

So he leaned in close instead, licked his lips and took a tentative sniff. Partly to encourage Nikolai to let him begin pleasuring them both in earnest, but partly for his own curiosity as well. Roger didn't smell like much, though—he was freshly washed, smelled like Nikolai's soap with just a hint of warm skin and salt and sex beneath, leaking fresh from the slit of his very hard dick.

"Tongue out," Nikolai said, his own hands working Roger's nipples, tweaking them gently and making Roger grunt. Dougie stuck his tongue out but didn't touch, not yet. If Roger could sit so still and patient beneath his master's stroking fingers, Dougie could wait too. "Now lick," Nikolai ordered, then amended, "Just the tip. Taste him. Nothing more."

Dougie closed the final inch between them with a gratified moan, and licked one shallow stripe across the crown of Roger's cock. That earned him a little gasp from Roger and Nikolai both, and Roger's cock jumped nearly up to his stomach.

"Good," Nikolai breathed. Dougie pulled his eyes from Roger's crotch and sought out his master's satisfied smile, the sparkle of pleasure in his eyes. "Just like that. Again."

Dougie obeyed, looking at Roger just long enough to find his target, then turning his eyes back on Nikolai as he teased Roger's cock with the tip of his tongue. *I'm sucking his cock but it's only for you. Only for you.* He sighed happily.

"You must learn to pleasure an uncut man. Run your tongue under his foreskin."

"Can I touch him, sir?"

Nikolai nodded.

"Thank you, sir," Dougie and Roger said, nearly simultaneously. Dougie wrapped a hand around the thick base of Roger's cock, and just like he'd predicted, his fingers and thumb didn't touch. So thick. Unbidden, the thought of that girth stretching his hole flooded his mind and made him blush. Was that what'd first caught Nikolai's eye when he'd bought Roger?

No matter. He was thinking too much. He *always* thought too much. Less thinking, more doing.

Pointing Roger's cock at his mouth, he tilted in and traced his tongue along the line of Roger's foreskin, teasingly slipping underneath that ridge every so often as he went.

"Now. Roger's foreskin is quite tight to his cock, especially when he's fully erect. In fact, sometimes it pulls back so far that he doesn't appear any different from a cut man, although I think you'll agree he *feels* much different in the hand. Some men have much more give and the heads of their cocks are only revealed if you purposefully draw the skin back. They may want this. They may not. Uncut men can be very sensitive, as I'm sure you know."

"Yes, sir," Dougie said.

"The foreskin itself can be a source of pleasure, too. Suck it into your mouth, worry it between your teeth—gently, of course—or slide your tongue underneath it as you're doing now."

This time, Dougie only nodded because his mouth was too busy for a reply. Sucking, licking, working that circle of exposed head that, yes, was so *very* sensitive. Or maybe Roger had just been that well-trained to perform for his master whether things felt amazing or not—he was squirming and panting in Nikolai's lap, hands fisting the sheets beside Nikolai's legs as Dougie worked his cock and Nikolai worked his nipples. It didn't *seem* like he was faking it, though, not with all the pre-cum leaking onto Dougie's tongue and the way his cock was twitching in Dougie's hand. Dougie gave it a little pump, and the foreskin glided over the shaft so smoothly it made Dougie's own dick twitch with jealousy. He had a hand free, wanted so badly to touch himself, but he didn't dare. Didn't even dare to ask. The best he could do was look up at Nikolai—who was too busy nuzzling Roger's neck to look back at him—and whimper.

Nikolai didn't acknowledge the needy little noise at all. Maybe hadn't even heard it. But Dougie was too chicken to try again.

He turned his focus back to Roger's cock instead, wrapped his lips over his teeth and nipped up some foreskin between them, sucked very, very gently and swiped his tongue across the flesh. Roger thrust up into his hand and mouth, a short, abortive motion like maybe he wasn't supposed to be moving at all, and Dougie grinned to himself and repeated his nip-suck-lick, delighted at the thought that he was doing something right enough to make a man like Roger—possibly the best-trained and most devoted slave in the world—lose control.

Nikolai was teaching him well. Was he making Nikolai proud? He cast his eyes up again, hoping to draw the man's attention, but Nikolai was still busy working a mark onto Roger's throat. And yes, it was hot—God, was it ever hot, both their faces nearly *transcendent* with love and pleasure. But it also made Dougie, for one agonized moment, want to do something *stupid*, like maybe bite Roger's cock. And then that moment passed and he was left with nothing but the burning desire to prove himself.

He redoubled his efforts, twisting his grip on Roger's cock as he pumped and sneakily giving Roger's foreskin a downward tug, exposing that sinfully sensitive head. Roger was starting to squirm in earnest, pushing forward into Dougie's mouth and grinding back against what was no doubt Nikolai's hard cock nestled up against his ass. If Dougie could make this good enough—draw it out long enough and make Roger move enough—maybe he could get Nikolai to come too. Like a secondhand orgasm. A chain reaction. Dougie's hands and mouth getting them both off.

Roger whimpered, biting his lip, and his hands left the mattress, snaking up to curl around Nikolai's arms. Much to Dougie's surprise, Nikolai's hands abandoned their torment of Roger's nipples to twine with Roger's fingers, and they clung to each other through their pleasure, hand in hand like real lovers.

No, not like *lovers, they* are *lovers, just* look *at them.*

The thought crushed something small and delicate in Dougie's chest, but then he reminded himself he could have this too if he tried hard enough, was patient enough, good enough, trusting enough. He could be a lover to Nikolai. They could share moments like Nikolai was sharing with Roger. He just had to earn it first, that was all.

He tore his eyes away from their joined fingers and set about to earn this and more. Freed the arm he was propped on so he could take Roger's balls in hand, cup them both and press his middle finger between them like Nikolai had taught him. Dougie almost didn't hear Roger's gasp over his own at the shocked jolt of pleasure he felt as he laid out flat on the bed and his cock pressed into the mattress. He knew it was wrong to chase that—this wasn't about him and Nikolai hadn't told him he could—but listening to Nikolai and Roger, watching the two of them together . . . God, he *needed*, and it wasn't like he was neglecting Roger at all, could totally multitask here, and Nikolai probably wouldn't even notice—

A sharp crack echoed in his ears, and half a second later, an equally sharp sting bloomed across his left ass cheek and he yelped, pulled back from Roger's cock, glanced up at Nikolai with wounded eyes to see a crop in his hand and a . . . a *smile* on his face?

"Naughty boy!" Nikolai chided, but he didn't seem angry, not at all, even if the warning was clear in his eyes—*Do it again and I really will be mad.* Maybe he was willing to give Dougie a little leeway after how well he'd served him today. Or maybe he was just feeling too good right now to get too worked up about anything as minor as Dougie humping the bed without permission. Whatever the case, Dougie wasn't going to push his luck. He stilled his hips and put his hands and mouth back to work.

"Got carried away, did you, boy? My little pet?" Nikolai grunted as Roger ground back against him, Roger's cock bumping the roof of Dougie's mouth as he did. God, Nikolai really was going to come. He wasn't instructing, he was *dirty talking*. "My sweet fuckable little boy, so turned on by the big plug in his tight ass and the big cock in his slutty mouth . . ."

Turned on? Yeah, actually, he really, really was. Well, maybe more by knowing how good he was making Nikolai feel than by the feel of a cock stretching his mouth, but still, tomato, tomahto, whatever.

"I should beat you for taking liberties," Nikolai panted, and Dougie's whine at that was pure instinctive fear, but of course it felt great against Roger's cock and Roger just ground against Nikolai harder. "But I think—" Whatever he was thinking, Dougie (well, Roger) drove it right out of his head for a moment. "—I think you'll learn your lesson well enough by the time this day is through."

Dougie didn't want to think about what that meant, but at least it seemed to mean that Nikolai *wouldn't* beat him, so he counted that as a win and pushed it out of his head. No room in there for stray thoughts anyway, not between all the focus he was putting into making Nikolai (and Roger) come and all the focus he was putting into keeping himself from fucking the mattress. God, Nikolai looked so gorgeous like this, simultaneously completely in control and completely fucking losing it.

And right in the middle of that moment of adoration, Nikolai's brow stitched together. "Don't look at *me*, Douglas. Look at the man you're servicing."

Yes, sir. Dougie forced himself to tear his gaze from Nikolai's flushed face, down to the cock in front of his nose, just like the good little pet Nikolai wanted him to be. Knew that he was already.

Someone's hand came down on the back of his head then—he didn't know whose, didn't really matter—and drove him down into Roger's crotch, chin to balls, Roger's fat cock filling his mouth and his throat and his fucking nose and sinuses and brain pan and everything else and he choked around it but didn't panic, *didn't panic*, because he'd done this enough now and Nikolai had taught him well and as unpleasant as it was, he knew Nikolai wouldn't let Roger hurt him and he wanted to be good be good *be good*. The hand fisted so tightly in his hair it brought tears to his eyes, and from above him he heard Nikolai growl, "Come on his face," and Roger panted out an eager, "Yes, Sir," and then the hand was yanking his head back and Roger's balls were pulling up beneath Dougie's fingers and that thick cock filled his vision and blew all over his nose and lips and eyes.

He was surprised to discover that he didn't mind it at all. Even poked his tongue out to lick at the cum dripping down his lips. It wasn't the cum he *wanted* to taste, definitely wasn't the cum he wanted soaking into his skin, but Nikolai had asked for this, wanted it, was so hot for it he was grinding out his own orgasm right now against Roger's ass as Dougie's tongue lapped at Roger's jizz, and for that, Dougie was happy to be blinking the stuff out of his eyes.

Maybe next time, if he was lucky, Nikolai would stripe Dougie's face instead.

He cast Nikolai a hopeful look, and had to bury another surge of jealousy when he realized that Nikolai was still fawning over Roger, kissing him now, hands stroking Roger's bruised face, turning him to just the right angle for Nikolai to fuck Roger's mouth with his tongue.

But that didn't mean Nikolai didn't love Dougie, or even necessarily that he loved Roger more. Because maybe this was all just a test, a chance for Dougie to prove that he could function on his own, that he wouldn't fall apart without Nikolai supporting him every second of the day, that he knew his place in the hierarchy and wouldn't ever push for more than he was entitled to. And if it *was* a test, he damn well meant to pass. So, as unobtrusively as possible, while Roger and Nikolai were still fucking each other's mouths like a pair of teenagers, he licked Roger's cock clean and then shimmied Roger's sweatpants back up his hips. He couldn't reach Nikolai, which was a shame because Nikolai was probably feeling pretty gross in his cum-drenched pants right now. Was it okay to go get a warm washcloth for him? Or shouldn't he leave the bed? It wasn't like either of them was paying him the slightest attention right now; would they even miss him? What was he supposed to *do* here? Why hadn't Nikolai prepared him better?

He only realized he was starting to freak out a little when a hand landed on his shoulder and he jumped half out of his skin. "Easy now, little pet," Nikolai soothed. His hand rubbed at the tense muscles in Dougie's neck. "It's all right. You've done well." The strain in Dougie's body eased at those words, and he darted a glance up to Nikolai, no longer lip-locked with Roger. No, now that mouth was turned to Dougie, formed into a swollen but approving smile. Dougie's muscles went downright noodly at that. His jaw and wrist were sore. He hadn't even realized. "Tell me, Douglas, what I've taught you to do after you service your master."

A simple question he could answer. His mind settled at that. Cleared. No more panic. "Clean and attend him, sir." Nikolai nodded, but said nothing more, and the panic began to creep back in. "But . . . But you were . . . I mean, I didn't want to—"

"Interrupt?" Nikolai punctuated his question with a kiss to Roger's earlobe. Roger's eyes drifted shut.

"Yes, sir."

"That was very smart of you to realize. No man wants to be pulled from kissing to answer a slave's questions. If you find yourself in such a position in the future, where it's clear you're not needed for the moment, you may go to fetch a washcloth and fresh clothes for your master without waiting for permission. But don't dawdle; if he wants you and turns to find you're not there, it will not end well for you."

Why did it seem like almost *everything* held the potential to end poorly for him? It hardly seemed fair. How could he know what to do when the master *might* want one thing or *might* want another thing but didn't always want the same thing and couldn't be bothered to tell him? He wasn't a mind reader. He needed *orders*. Clear, no-interpretations-required orders. He'd fill them to the last, and happily, but all this uncertainty made him downright queasy.

"Do you have something to say, Douglas?" His master's expression *dared* him to lie.

"I just— God, I'm sorry, sir, but sometimes I feel like it's just a lose-lose situation." And his unloved erection, hanging heavy and burning between his legs, didn't exactly help with that.

Nikolai shrugged. "Sometimes it is."

"Wh—"

"Sometimes it is a lose-lose situation for a slave. That's the nature of your place in the world."

My place. Dougie couldn't help it, he shuddered at that. Because *his place*, which had seemed so comfortable, so *safe* just a moment ago, suddenly seemed so fucking *terrifying* again. And even worse than the fear of being beaten for no fucking reason at all at any fucking time without any fucking way to predict or stop it was the fear that that fear might make him backslide. That it'd strip the thin veneer of civility and comfort from the life he was building here and remind him afresh of the ugliness underneath. And sure, he *knew* there was ugliness, but he'd been finding ways to live with it, hadn't he? Ways to be *happy* with it, even—or at least happy despite it. But it was fragile, still— so fucking fragile—and he didn't want to lose it. *Couldn't.* Getting it back again would be too hard.

Nikolai studied him as he processed, as the fear in his head no doubt disseminated across his features. Roger was watching him too, silent and sharp. Nobody was judging him, he could tell that much, but beyond that, he couldn't read either of them, and that uncertainty in the men who were supposed to be his rocks, his anchors, just made everything worse.

It was Nikolai, of course, who finally broke the silence. "But consider this: if a master is of a mood that he wishes to punish you for something you couldn't predict or prevent, then perhaps taking the punishment is the best way to serve him, after all?" Dougie had no idea what to say to that, wasn't really even sure what to make of it. But Nikolai took pity. "Think, Douglas. Haven't you ever been so angry or so frustrated or wound so tight that you just wanted to *hit* something?"

Ah. Yeah, that made all kinds of sense. Just, a normal person threw their pillow at the wall, not their fist at a slave's face. But the kind of men who owned men, well, they weren't normal people, were they?

"Sometimes your master will be looking for an excuse to let out that aggression, perhaps without even knowing for himself that that is what he really wants. You will give in to him, and you will serve him, as happy in your suffering as in your pleasure when he takes your ass."

Dougie nodded, trying to ignore the shame he felt at the wetness in the corners of his eyes.

"Just look at Roger."

Roger leaned back into Nikolai's chest, sated eyes closed, completely oblivious to the seriousness of the conversation going on around him. His expression and posture were so at odds with the horrible markings all over his body. The bruising. Brutal.

"He doesn't enjoy being beaten, Douglas. He isn't a masochist. But he is a *good* slave, so when I needed this from him, he undressed without being told to and stood still for me, and he did it with a kiss. *He* comforted *me*. And look at him now—look at *us* now. Look how happy we both are. Look how well I'm taking care of him."

Dougie studied Roger again, who *did* look undeniably happy. Didn't even seem to be in pain, though like Mat or anyone else who made a living being hard on their bodies, he'd probably just learned to not express it or pay it much mind. Then again, he had just gotten an expert blowjob, if Dougie did say so himself. And was lounging in his master's arms, a whole day of tasks and orders replaced with affection and pleasure. A day he'd probably only earned *because* he'd taken some random punishment like a champ.

Still, that did little to ease Dougie's fears. He needed *rules*. Needed logic and order in his life, needed to know that if he followed those rules he'd be fine, not just punished arbitrarily. How could he serve his master well if he was constantly afraid the next beating might be just around the corner, totally unavoidable? And could he really ever endure one with such grace? Be *glad* for it? Nikolai seemed to think so, and Dougie trusted Nikolai, knew he needed to trust Nikolai. But maybe Nikolai didn't realize how paper-thin the membrane was between his old life and his new one. How easily damaged. And how much might spill from one side to the other if someone punched even the tiniest little hole in it.

"S-sir . . ."

Nikolai raised his eyebrows—*Go on.*

But Dougie didn't know what to say after that. Hadn't meant to say even that much. He ducked his head, desperate to escape Nikolai's probing, expectant gaze. Desperate to string his thoughts together in a way that would make sense to Nikolai without upsetting him, without making Dougie sound like a selfish child. *I need you to reassure me. Hold my hand. Make it all better. Help me.*

"Can you . . . I mean, I need . . ." God, was he *really* trying to ask Nikolai to beat him so he could see for himself how this would all make sense? It kind of seemed like he was. And surely Nikolai would, now that he'd had the audacity to practically demand it of the man.

From the look on Nikolai's face, it was pretty clear he thought Dougie was overstepping, too. "Need me to prove it? Guide you? Show you?"

Yes. Yes, God yes, please. Please, Master, yes.

Nikolai very deliberately turned his face away from Dougie and buried it in Roger's neck. Dougie felt his heart sink clear to his toes at that, couldn't even breathe for a moment. "No. I've had enough of you now, and you've served your purpose. Back downstairs with you, and find Jeremy. Make yourself useful."

"Sir—"

"*Dismissed*, Douglas."

Somehow, Dougie managed to choke out a "Yes, sir, I'm sorry, sir," and back himself out the bedroom door, though he felt so numb with disappointment and dread and sadness and fear and a million other things that he couldn't feel his hands or feet.

He was halfway down the stairs, completely unaware of how he'd gotten there, before logic started crowding its way back into his head around the riot of emotion. There had to be a reason for Nikolai's refusal to help him. Nikolai had *never* refused to help him before. And

Nikolai didn't make mistakes, at least not with things like this. Which meant Nikolai had a plan, knew exactly what he was doing, and it was *Dougie* who was wrong somehow. Or maybe Nikolai cared about him too much to beat him for no reason, trusted him enough to believe— no, to *know*—that when the time came for Dougie to take a random beating, he'd take it with pride and grace. Nikolai *trusted* him; he just needed to trust Nikolai in return.

Except, this time, he really wasn't sure he could.

Fake it 'til you make it, Dougie.

Yeah, okay. He could do that. Walk down the stairs and into the kitchen and take orders from Jeremy, and with any luck, get lost in some endless series of mindless chores that would let him take his mind off punishments and random violence and disappointing masters and being afraid and that cool, hard look in Nikolai's eyes when he'd said *I've had enough of you.*

He didn't mean that, not really. Couldn't have meant that. Enough of me for today, *maybe, but . . . not . . . not* forever, *right?*

Right?

Great, now he was crying. He didn't want to cry in front of Jeremy.

Too late, he was already in the kitchen. Jeremy gave him a quirked eyebrow and a cruel sneer. "Learn your place in the world, new favorite? You'll get used to licking Roger's ass eventually." He pointed at the sink. "Dishes."

Dougie went to them, shocked at the huge stack that had swallowed up the entire counter.

"Got a lot of guys to feed. Guards. Staff. Others like us. Your fucking brother with his ten-page list of nutritional requirements."

Dougie nudged the tap with his wrist to get hot water going and hit the automatic soap dispenser. "Others like us." He'd never seen *anyone* else around the house. Not even guards, not since he'd been brought here. "How many?" He didn't know why he was making small talk with Jeremy, seeing as Jeremy was a fucking asshole and he was still on the verge of tears, but then, maybe that was exactly why. He could trust Jeremy not to mince words.

Jeremy shrugged, whisking at something in a big mixing bowl. "Maybe a dozen buybacks. He picks up one a year or so, his old favorites, when their masters get tired of them. Most of them work the grounds, don't stay in the house. Master's got over a thousand acres to maintain, after all, even if most of it's forest." He put down the bowl, grabbed a smaller one with dry ingredients and started folding them together, one eyebrow raised at Dougie. Dougie took the hint and grabbed a pot to scrub. "But there's me in here, of course. And Tim, who cleans the place, though the guy's like a fucking ghost. And Roger. Roger was the first, you know. First one Sir ever trained without Master Edgar's help, that's why he's so fucking spoiled. Not that I'm jealous of him today, though." A low whistle. No mistaking what that was about. The bruises, of course.

"Do you mean to tell me you were ever a favorite of his?"

Jeremy laughed. "Smartass fucking kid, I should kick that big plug up your ass, see if I can get it to pop out your mouth like a Pez dispenser. But no, I was no fucking favorite. Not as a slave, anyway. Just as a cook. My parents died when I was thirteen, fourteen? I got put in this shit-fuck boys' home with some pervert director. Ran away, got a job as a busboy, then as a potato peeler, and on up to cook until suddenly some asshole was hitting me with a Taser and lugging me off to some torture cell to get my ass raped some more."

An orphan in the system.

"And then Nikolai bought you? At an auction?" Dougie was beginning to piece together the story. The details varied, but the plot was always the same. Little Orphan Assrape.

"Nikolai *saved* me. Trained me in this very house, then sent me on and I thought I'd rather fucking die, but after eight years of misery— my new master never let me cook, didn't buy me for that, you see—I was back home again with Nikolai." Jeremy's gaze went misty, and then snapped back again. Whatever ingredients he was folding, he was apparently happy with it, because he clattered around a cabinet full of baking pans for a moment and then pulled one out, started pouring the batter into it. "I was lucky. You might not be. Nikolai does the whole buyback thing because he's a sentimental fuck, for all of his master-of-the-universe talk, but sometimes he doesn't get to us in time. And plenty of us just plain aren't worthy enough of his attention, not even after he's finished training them. The guy leaving as I was coming in, I never saw him again. I imagine his body got dumped for a John Doe in some fucking river, or maybe he's still making his master happy, who knows." He scraped out the bowl, then pointed his spatula at Dougie. "You—you I expect to see again. That is . . ." He shrugged, dumped the bowl on Dougie's heap of dishes left to do, "if you don't fuck this up. You've got a good thing going here, kid. Got the master's eye. Don't ruin it by acting like some spoiled two-year-old who throws a tantrum every time daddy spends the day with his older brother. Cos daddy don't put up with bullshit like that. He'll spank your ass and send you away. I'm sure after a few years in the system, you know all about getting sent away, don't ya, kid?"

The corner of Dougie's mouth trembled. Yeah, he did. "So . . . so what, he buys us and trains us and sells us, and if he likes us enough, he buys us back again?"

"Yep. That's generally how the whole business works . . . well, except for that last part. Somebody finds you, somebody grabs you, somebody sells you, somebody buys you and trains you, somebody buys you again. Well, some sorry fucks don't go to professional trainers like Nikolai. Some masters, they got a taste for breaking people themselves so they buy direct, whether they know what the fuck they're doing or not." Dougie shuddered to think of it, being with someone cruel, without Nikolai's finesse and caring. Like if one of Madame's guards had purchased him for day-in-day-out torture and humiliation, fucking him until he died. Jeremy continued on, unawares. "But Nikolai's clients just want the finished product, all polished up and ready to suck dick like pros."

God, it all sounded so crass and awful when he put it like that. They were doing something beautiful here, something *special*, bringing out his best self. Weren't they?

"And he always sells us?" Dougie wrung the sponge in his hands, just to squeeze something, just to hold something and imagine never letting it go. The water ran free and clear and uncatchable over his hands and through his fingers. "He never . . . he never just chooses to *keep* someone?"

"Aw, do you think the master's gonna keep you all for his own? Dumbass fucking kid, you're as bad as a girl with a crush, still in pigtails. Of course he's going to sell you on. Don't get me wrong, he likes you, likes you more than most if I'm honest, but you're still a fucking meal ticket in the end. One day, you're gonna walk out those doors and wind up at the feet of another man, and you're gonna spend five, ten, maybe fifteen years there missing Nikolai for every fucking second of it, like your heart's torn out of your goddamn chest." If it was possible to cut vegetables bitterly, Jeremy was doing it, slamming his knife against the cutting board. "But you stick it out and do your damn job as best you can because you know he wants you to and you promised him you would and you'd *die* before you'd disappoint him. And maybe, if you're real lucky, your new master reminds you a little of him and maybe even loves you a little like Nikolai did and maybe you even love him back a little like you love Nikolai. But of course it's never the same. And then at the end of it all, when you're too old or too tired or just too plain familiar and boring for your master and he's had enough of you, Nikolai might buy you back on the cheap, or maybe your master'll take you out back and Old Yeller you for kicks. Or worse. So like I said, don't screw this up, kid. You give Nikolai *everything*, and then you give your new master everything, and maybe when it's all over, Nikolai will give you everything in return."

Maybe. So many possibilities for a bleak and empty future if he wasn't careful. Dougie didn't want to picture it. Didn't want to picture what Jeremy must know about it. He stared down at the sink, scrubbing furiously at a stubbornly filthy brass pot and trying not to cry.

"Oh! Master!" Jeremy said. "We were just talking about you."

Dougie didn't want to turn around.

Dougie wanted to turn around more than he'd wanted anything else in his life.

"I heard." Nikolai's voice was soft and calm, and those two words were punctuated by the sound of a chaste kiss. A kiss for Jeremy. Dougie's shoulders stiffened, waiting for his own greeting, but it never came. "Roger's asleep now. I told him to call you on the intercom when he wants lunch. And we'll *both* be taking dinner in bed tonight."

"Of course, Sir. Luke killed one of the chickens today. Freshly plucked. I could roast it."

"With stuffing?" God, Nikolai sounded so *affectionate.*

"Would I ever serve you a chicken without stuffing, Sir?"

"There was that one time you gave me wild rice." Dougie could actually *hear* the good-humored crinkle in Nikolai's nose. He glared at the pot in his hands. That fleck of stuck-on whatever didn't budge, so he scrubbed it harder.

Jeremy laughed, a pure sound without any of his usual bitterness. "You're never going to let me live that down, are you?"

"You wouldn't love me if I did," Nikolai countered flirtatiously.

"I would *always* love you, Sir."

Dougie's stomach clenched. Why the hell couldn't he get this damn pot clean? Why couldn't he do this one simple fucking thing?

A hand fell on his shoulder, gently cupping it. "Hello, Douglas."

Oh Master, thank you. Dougie wanted to fall to his knees at Nikolai's feet and just cry and cry and cry, beg Nikolai to forgive him, to let him stay, to love him like he loved these other men, and if he could have that, God, he'd be good, he'd be so good, he'd do anything, he'd let Nikolai beat him every day. "Hello, sir," he finally choked out, his voice rough with unshed tears.

"How are you feeling now, Douglas?"

Like I'm afraid you'll send me away. Like I don't want to go.
Like I love you so much, but I don't know if you really love me back.
Like I don't know where I stand.

"Like I don't know what I mean to you, sir." He braced himself for a swift punishment, a kick or a slap—what he meant to Nikolai was none of his damn business, and of no import besides—but it never came. The absence fucking *hurt.* "And I'm just . . . I know I can't ask anything of you, and that this isn't the kind of relationship where I ask you to tell me you love me and we can't go steady like teenagers and I guess I'm just confused, sir."

"But you know your place."

"A slave, sir. I'm nothing, sir." And why did admitting it hurt now, instead of filling him with that calm peace and acceptance he kept grasping and losing again? Damn it, he wanted what Roger had, what even Jeremy somehow fucking had.

"That's right. Whose slave are you, Douglas?"

I don't know. I just don't know. Yours, temporarily, and then?

"I want to be yours, sir."

"So why don't you know what you mean to me? Why are you confused?"

His hands stilled in their scrubbing, and he *itched* with the urge to turn around, to confront Nikolai head on with his answer. "Because," he said, and this, surely *this* would get a rise, a punishment, a beating, painful in its truth as it was. "Because you tell me you love me in one breath and talk about selling me in the next!"

No punishment came. Again. Just a breath on his ear, a warmth against his back, a hand lightly pressing on his throat from behind, threatening to choke him. "You *think* too much, Douglas. You say you know your place, but you don't. It's not your place to worry about the future, and it's not your place to ask questions, and it's not your place to wonder about your place. In the world. In this house. In my heart. Your place is just. To. Accept." The hand on Dougie's throat tightened, and his mouth fell open, trying to pull in air that just wouldn't come. "If only there was a way for me to remind you. An easy way to put your restless mind at ease, to express to you in *no uncertain terms* that you are mine, and that your body and your fate are all mine, and all you need do is . . ." The lack of air was starting to hurt, to burn, and now there was another hand sliding down Dougie's side, down to cup Dougie's ass, weighing the flesh in a thoughtful palm. "Accept."

Punish me.

A reminder that he was Nikolai's, that Nikolai owned his body and his mind, and that he would gladly give: even things he didn't want to give, even things he was afraid to give, even things that were unpleasant to give. The same way Jeremy and Roger and all the others had gone to their new masters, given up their happiness and their security with Nikolai, because that was their fate, because that was what Nikolai chose, and all they had to do was trust in his wisdom and know that he would one day bring them home.

Punish me and bring me home.

My body, my life, my sex, my pain. Let me give myself to you.

When he tried to speak it, only a strange whistle came out.

"What was that?" Nikolai said sweetly, crushing Dougie's windpipe one last time and then the hand was gone and Dougie was gulping down air, burning air that made spots like soap bubbles pop in front of his eyes.

"Punish me," Dougie croaked. "Punish me, sir. Hurt me like you hurt Roger. I can take it, sir. I deserve it. I want to give it to you."

"Good boy," Nikolai said, and ripped the plug from Dougie's ass.

Dougie *was* a good boy. A *very* good boy: he'd chosen just the right plug, big enough that Nikolai didn't need to prepare him but small enough that it still burned and stretched when Nikolai's erection claimed his ass.

Dougie was a good boy. He gave his master his ass, gladly took the rough pounding, even though it meant getting a horizontal counter-edge bruise right across his belly and hips, even though it meant sobbing out his pain with Jeremy standing *right there*, watching through the corner of his eye, watching Dougie crying and being fucked, because this time Nikolai hadn't cared to send Jeremy away, and it wasn't Dougie's place to ask for privacy.

Dougie was a good boy. When Nikolai grabbed him by the hair and jerked his face forward and told him not to neglect his chores, he picked up his sponge again and he picked up the stubborn pot and resumed scrubbing, the motion of his shaking hands across the bottom of the pot following the rhythm of Nikolai's strokes inside him.

Dougie was a good boy. He kept on washing even when Nikolai grabbed his cock and jerked him hard, bringing him off so fast his head spun and he had to cling to the counter's edge just to stay upright so Nikolai could continue chasing his own pleasure inside Dougie's abused ass. And Dougie held still for that, even through post-orgasm sensitivity that set his teeth on edge every time Nikolai's cock drove over his prostate—a pleasure so raw, so far past *good* it might as well have been the punishment he'd been begging for.

Dougie was a good boy. When Nikolai finished with him, filled him with seed and plugged him up again and told him to clean up the mess he'd made, Dougie knew he wouldn't be needing the sponge.

Dougie was a good boy. He licked his master's cock clean, and then he turned and did the same to the cupboard doors, lapping up his own dripping semen with a happy, sated hum.

Dougie was a good boy. He knew that his master hadn't punished him upstairs, even though he'd deserved it, because it was only through denial that he'd learned the *value* of that punishment.

A reminder of who was in charge. Who was owner, who was owned. Who did the thinking and planning and worrying, and who accepted his fate with dignity and humility.

Yes, Dougie had forgotten that. Been bad. But Nikolai had guided him in ways he hadn't even begun to be able to see, and now he was back on steady ground and a good boy again, and Nikolai had rewarded him with punishment *and* pleasure, had given him what he'd needed and then what he'd wanted, and this time when Nikolai had finished with him and left him alone with Jeremy again, Dougie didn't mind, not even a little.

Because Dougie was a good boy. And he'd *stay* a good boy, and one day Nikolai would come back for him and keep him and love him forever.

CHAPTER FIVE

M at was eating an austere lunch of toast and jelly and applesauce—but hey, solid foods, big step in the right direction—when he heard the key in the lock of his door. He put down his spoon. Shucked off his shorts and draped them over the back of his chair.

By the time the door opened, he was on his knees in front of it, legs spread and palms up, waiting.

This time, it wasn't Roger who came through the door, not that Mat had ever thought it would be. Not this time.

This time, it was Nikolai.

It couldn't have been anybody else, of course, because it was *time*, and Nikolai was never early and he was never late for anything.

Right on time.

"You've decided to live."

Mat looked up into Nikolai's eyes, giving him a hard stare to prove he still had what Nikolai wanted, that Nikolai hadn't *broken* Mat, but merely tamed him. "Yes," he said. Not *Yes, sir* or *Yes, Master.* Just *Yes.*

Mat would obey, but he wouldn't cower.

Obey, and bide his time, but Nikolai didn't need to know the second part. Or maybe he already knew the second part, but thought he could still come out on top in the end.

Yes, Mat was done underestimating Nikolai. But Nikolai had *always* underestimated Mat, and that would be his downfall. All in good time.

"I'm ready to do what you want. I'm ready to *be* who you want."

Nikolai nodded, not smiling, not showing any emotion at all, not even victory. Just acknowledgment. "Let's begin, then."

You and me. You versus *me.*

Mat nodded, too. "Yes, let's."

THE FLESH

SEASON 3: TRANSFORMATION

CARTEL

EPISODE 9: TRIALS AND ERRORS

CHAPTER ONE

"**I**'m ready to do what you want. I'm ready to be who you want."

Nikolai peered down at Mathias—the source of so much frustration these last weeks, the source of Roger's recent pain—and read the sincerity in his face. In his body, too, weakened and thinner than before, naked, a near perfect picture of submission. Not capitulation, not by any means. But obedience, at least. No attitude he could detect. No anger, either—they'd have to work on getting that back, but how hard could that be? The man looked almost casual, but for the glint of determination hardening his eyes and jaw. He suspected Mathias was trying to hide that, though, trying to appear unfazed. It was a farce Nikolai was willing to let him cling to, at least for the moment.

"If you're sincere," Nikolai said, "then your first step is to return to my good graces. I think you know what that means."

Mathias's tongue darted out to lick at cracked lips, and his eyes went to Nikolai's crotch. Then he blanked his face—*it's all good, look how cool I am with this*—and nodded. "But just so you know," he said, and the absence of the "sir" at the end of that statement was more pointed than the words he'd spoken, "I'm not doing this for me *or* you. I'm doing this, all of this, for the people it protects. Roger"—*Yeah, I know you beat him, fucker*, that gaze said—"and Dougie. So I'll *do* it, I'll be the good little slave, I'll fight when you want me to fight and I'll stop when you tell me to stop, and I'll suck your cock and take the beating I know you plan to dish out afterward, and I'll even fucking thank you for correcting me if that'll get your rocks off. But the instant—the *instant* you take Dougie away from me, I'm done. I'm outta here." He leveled his gaze at Nikolai, no forced ease now, just naked truth and angles sharp enough to flay someone on. "So you'll let me see him, you understand? And when we leave this place, we leave *together*. Or you can tell me no, and we'll find out just how bad for business it is when your client's new multimillion-dollar prize offs himself before the fucker even gets to have any fun."

Well, that was . . . not unexpected, Nikolai supposed. In fact, he couldn't help but be impressed by the fact that his fighter had such a wily little brain behind the brawn. Still, the reality of it *rankled*— he knew damn well he couldn't call Mathias's bluff, at least not now, because it *wasn't* one. He couldn't play the trump card of Mathias's affection for Roger again, either, not without Mathias wising up to their little game. And time had made it clear that nothing short of breaking Mathias for good would knock the unrelenting stubbornness out of the man. Oh, Nikolai *could* break him, could break *anyone*, but the client's requirements wouldn't permit that. Not this time.

Which meant Nikolai would simply have to outsmart him. Wear him down piece by piece and stay three steps ahead.

Fortunately, he had an idea.

"All right," he said. "But do be careful what you wish for."

Mathias thought that was bluster—Nikolai could read that clear as day on the man's face—but he'd learn the truth soon enough.

"And watch your tone in the future. You've had your say. If you ever speak to me like that again, I won't react so kindly the next time. You'd do well to call me *sir*, too. Or master." His hand drifted to his pocket, where an auto-injector was tucked away. He wasn't afraid to use it, not this time. "Honestly, Mathias, will you really make me start at the beginning again?"

The tiniest flash of fear in Mathias's eyes proved that no, Nikolai wouldn't have to start quite at the beginning. "No, *sir*," Mathias said. "Have it your way. Sir."

Nikolai curled his fingers around the hard plastic. "I've half a mind to use this anyway, given what a spoiled little *brat* you've been the last ten days. But you owe me more than that. You'll be active in what's coming to you. You'll stand still for it, and yes, you *will* thank me for correcting you."

"Get on with it, then. Sir." Mathias glared at him, stony-faced and unafraid. Which was just what his client desired, although Nikolai certainly didn't see the appeal.

"*You* get on with it. Go to the dresser. Third drawer down, there's a black case. Bring it to me. Remember to offer it to me *properly*."

Mat went to rise to his feet, and Nikolai barked, "*No*. You *crawl* before your master."

Mathias's sigh was downright theatrical, but he dropped to his hands and knees. Minute tremors ran through his arms as he shuffled toward the dresser. He'd eaten a dozen tiny meals in the last twenty-four hours, but clear juices and soft bland foods only went so far after the way he'd abused himself. He was still hungry. Still weak. Nikolai would feed him up again, have Roger oversee his exercise routine. Make him strong like before.

But first he'd have to earn it.

Crawling was way harder than it should've been. Not mentally—he barely even felt the humiliation after all the other, bigger humiliations that'd come before—but physically. He wasn't used to being weak this way, and he didn't like it one bit. Couldn't wait to get back on his feet—literally as well as figuratively. Now that he'd decided not to die, he'd need his strength. Now that Nikolai had given in and promised to let him see Dougie.

Dougie, God. Maybe, somehow, he could convince Dougie how sorry he was, get Dougie to forgive him. He'd figure out a way. He *had* to. He could scarcely believe that Nikolai had given in so easily to his demand, but since he had, there was no way in hell Mat was going to waste the opportunity.

He reached the dresser, panting a little, and lifted tired arms to open the third drawer. Saw the black case right away. It was disconcertingly large and heavy. What the fuck was Nikolai hiding in there? What would he end up having to endure to convince Nikolai he was sincere? To see Dougie again? To fix the biggest fucking mistake he'd ever made?

"Oh, and fetch the lube, as well—the bottle next to the case. You'll be needing it."

Sick fuck. Mat bit his tongue to keep from saying it aloud. There was no doubt in his mind that Nikolai would want him to keep up the argumentativeness in the long run, but not today. Today he had to prove he could be a good little slave.

So he grabbed the lube.

Crawling back with the lube in one hand and the case in the other proved something of a challenge. The floor was hard beneath too-bony knees, he felt tired enough to sleep for a week, and he *didn't want to do this*, whatever it was. Fear was an insidious thing, and if he were stronger he'd shove it away like he always did, but shuffling back toward Nikolai now, toward the man who was no doubt about to rape and beat him half-unconscious and make him say thank you for it . . . well, he figured nobody would blame him for slowing down a little bit.

Nikolai said nothing, just watched him, expression empty of all but a vague expectation, a ghost of haughty triumph, and a shade of doubt—not in himself, no, but in Mat. In Mat's willingness and ability to keep playing along.

Well, he'd fucking see. Mat would do it all, no matter how painful, no matter how depraved. To protect people weaker than himself, like Roger. To protect the only person he loved: Dougie.

He could hardly believe he'd be seeing Dougie at all. How the hell had Nikolai agreed to that? Fuck, he didn't care. Dougie was like a fever dream now, a memory as sweet and painful as their parents, but he was getting his brother back. He was getting Dougie *back*, and that was worth anything.

Unless Nikolai was lying. Just saying what he wanted to hear. Stringing him along.

But . . . no, If nothing else, Nikolai was a man of his word. As sick and twisted and horrible as he was, he hadn't ever lied—not that a man in his position needed to. Besides, what would the point of it be? He knew Mat wasn't bluffing, so why risk it?

Nikolai snapped his fingers and said, "Give me the case, Mathias," and Mat realized he'd stalled out, lost in his own weakened mind.

He shuffled the last little way and rose up onto his knees. Laid the lube on top of the case and picked up the whole shebang with both hands, held it aloft on his palms, bowed his head. "Master," he added, and managed not to make it sound too much like a sneer. Yeah, he could play along. *Woof woof, look how well I learn new tricks.*

Nikolai, the fucker, left him hanging, left the case in his outstretched hands until his arms began to tremble, then outright shake, then cramp, and he gritted his teeth and locked his elbows and tried not to hyperventilate or pass out or fall over or drop the thing as sweat formed on his brow and under his arms and between his shoulder blades and dripped down his skin.

"You've weakened yourself, Mathias. For shame."

"I'll get strong again, sir. You'll see." *Now please just take this fucking thing.*

"I'm sure I will."

But still he just *stood* there. What was he waiting for?

"Ahem," Nikolai said, a sort of half cough into a loosely curled fist. Mat twitched an eye up and saw the fucker holding back a smile. "Don't you have something you want to say to me, Mathias?"

Oh. Of *course.* "I'm, um, sorry, sir?" God, even his voice was shaking with the strain now. *Take the case. Please take the fucking case.*

"For what?" Nikolai prodded, way too fucking smug.

Which . . . good question. Just what imagined slight was he supposed to be fucking sorry for?

The case. Your weakness. Trying to escape this place and this life in the only way you knew how.

"For damaging your property, sir." Spoken with proper deference and everything, never mind how fucking *sick* it made him, because if Nikolai didn't take this fucking thing from his *damaged property* in the next five fucking seconds, he was going to drop it, and he didn't even want to *think* about what might happen then.

Nikolai nodded once, sharply, and took the case from his hands. Mat dropped his arms like lead fucking blocks and struggled to rearrange himself into some semblance of proper position, ass to heels, thighs spread wide, hands resting atop them. He couldn't quite manage the straight back and squared shoulders, but Nikolai wasn't paying any attention to him anyway. He was opening the case, rummaging around inside, up on the table where Mat couldn't see it.

He heard the click of lube, and then Nikolai handed him the opened tube with one hand and a giant black and silver butt plug with the other. Fucking *huge.* Like, size-of-his-fist huge at least, and heavy too, and there was no question about what Nikolai expected him to do with it.

He almost, *almost* said "I can't." Because, seriously, it kind of didn't even look physically possible. But he knew it was—he'd taken that expanding plug at Madame's, after all—and he *wouldn't* fuck this up before it'd even begun.

Even though he hadn't spoken, Nikolai must have seen the protest on his face, because he said, "You can and you will, Mathias. Your brother regularly plugs himself without complaint."

No, please, don't say shit like that to me. I don't want to hear it. It's not true.

God, maybe Nikolai *was* going to let him see Dougie, but when he did, would Dougie even *be* Dougie anymore?

It didn't matter. Mat would love him just the same. Always. Forever. And one day, when they got out of here somehow, Mat would help him heal. That was who he was. The big brother, no matter what. He just needed to hang on to that. Through whatever was coming.

So let's get through this thing.

"Yes, sir," he said, surprised to find himself swallowing back tears, and where the fuck had those come from? It was just exhaustion, that was all. It would pass.

He placed the huge plug on the floor and drizzled lube down onto the top of it, squeezing the bottle with both shaking hands, nearly emptying it. It was . . . different than the usual lube. Thicker.

You can do this. You should be thankful he's letting you do it to yourself, because you can take it slow. Take it slow and easy, deep breaths, just relax and let it happen.

He rose up onto his knees, spread his legs a little. Scooted forward until he was straddling the plug. No way to do this without spreading himself first, so he reached around with both hands to do just that. He hadn't been fucked in so long he wasn't quite used to the sensation anymore. It made his skin crawl. He closed his eyes.

"No," Nikolai said. "Eyes on your master. You're putting on a show for *me*. Never forget that."

So much for trying to pretend Nikolai wasn't here.

He met the man's eyes, let his mouth fall open a little and licked his lips, nice and slow. Remembered a far-off place and a far-off time when he'd pick up a fan after a match and kiss him hard, pinch his nipples, and squeeze his balls, then lick his lips just like this, just before kneeling and giving the guy the blowjob of his life, so hungry to make someone feel good after an evening spent trying to smash people's faces in.

His performance now was just a hollow imitation, almost a caricature of lust, but whatever, it seemed to make Nikolai happy. He stared right through Nikolai, held the image of the post-match blowjob in his head, spread himself as wide as he could, and lowered himself onto the plug.

The tip, slick and dripping, breached him easily, and he gasped a little at the sensation, no pain yet, not even pressure or fullness, just that first lick of once delicious pleasure, irrevocably tainted now, as twisted and disgusting as everything else here. He had to let go of his ass then and brace his hands on the floor, legs too weak to hold him suspended for long, and the last fucking thing he wanted was to *sit* on the plug, drive it into himself too far too fast with his body weight. Instead he wiggled his hips a little, reminded himself he was supposed to be putting on a show and gasped again, let his eyes flutter briefly closed before returning his gaze to Nikolai's face. He remembered the lesson Nikolai had taught him earlier about lying, about faking it, about convincing the master that Mat's pleasure was *his* pleasure too. Maybe, just maybe, if he did that well enough now, Nikolai wouldn't force him to hurt himself too badly.

Except Nikolai seemed utterly unmoved by Mat's show. No hard-on. No dilated pupils. No parted lips or speeding breaths or anything but mild interest and maybe boredom. "Faster," Nikolai said. "This is *supposed* to hurt, remember?"

Sick fucking bastard. Did you get off on beating poor Roger, too? Do you get off on hurting my brother this way?

Don't think about it. Don't think about how Dougie is suffering right now, just focus on seeing him soon. That's all that matters.

He sank an inch or two down the plug, which got hugely wide way too fucking fast, until the burn made him hiss and he had to stop for a second to breathe through it.

"Keep going," Nikolai ordered.

Fuck you. Fuck you. Fuck you, you bastard. Even in his head, his inner voice seemed to be panting with exertion. Or maybe that was just his brain shorting out. He sat back a little further, his weight driving the plug in a little more, splitting him open wider until he just *couldn't* anymore, too much resistance from shrieking muscles and he'd fucking *tear* if he went any faster, and somehow he didn't think Nikolai would appreciate that.

Or, fuck, maybe Nikolai wouldn't care. The memory of a baseball bat ripping up his insides came back so fresh and visceral he actually panicked for a second. Hard to push it aside when the plug didn't feel all that different and he was pretty sure it wasn't even halfway in yet.

"Oh, just *sit* on it," Nikolai snapped. "No more dawdling. Hands off the floor."

"I'll bleed, sir," Mat choked, blinking sweat from his eyes.

Nikolai shrugged. "You might."

God, when had he become such a fucking pussy? Since when had he gotten so afraid of a little blood? A little pain? This was *Dougie* at stake here. *Suck it the fuck up, Carmichael.*

He picked his hands up, curled them into fists on his thighs. Let his muscles relax. Sat. Screamed a little, maybe, as the plug drove in deeper, ripping him open, and he was suddenly sweating so hard he had no idea if it was blood or just perspiration he felt dripping down his taint and to his balls. The pressure and burn were fucking *unbearable*, and he growled through it, eyes clenched shut and teeth gritted, just waiting for the moment the widest part would pop through and he could close around the neck of the plug.

But it kept. Not. Fucking. Happening.

He was going to fucking pass out and Nikolai had barely even begun.

Dizzy, he pried his eyes open just in time to see the fucker folding his arms across his chest, raising a smug eyebrow—and *yes*, there *was* such a thing as a smug eyebrow—and saying, "Stuck?"

Would it ruin things if he told Nikolai where to shove it?

"If you need help, Mathias, all you need to do is ask." Nikolai took a single step forward, shrugged with one shoulder. "Well, your brother need only ask. *You* would have to beg, a little, perhaps. Convince me you mean it."

Mat gritted his teeth. Glared, blinking back the sweat that kept falling in his eyes. Shoved down on the plug again.

Nothing. Well, no movement, but plenty of screaming pain.

He gasped and panted and clutched at his stomach because it was the next best thing to pulling off the plug entirely and holding his ass like a spanked child. He was just too fucking weak to muscle anything anywhere right now, let alone a plug that big into a very small space.

Nikolai unfolded his arms and glanced pointedly at his watch. "If that plug isn't nestled flare-deep inside you in two minutes, I'm going to go spend some time with your brother, and *you* can forget about seeing him at all."

"Help me then, damn it." Added when Nikolai didn't move, "Fuck, what do you *want*?" His voice was as hoarse as if he'd been screaming. Maybe he had been.

"I want you to show me the respect I'm due. I want you to show me how well you understand that I owe you nothing, that you *are* nothing. I want to know that you'd be undyingly grateful should I deign to offer you assistance."

Do it for Dougie, Mat. Swallow your pride and just do it.

"Please, sir," he whimpered, and told himself it was all for show and nothing to do with how much he hurt. "I know I'm just a slave and I don't deserve your attention, but please, help me to make you happy."

Nikolai closed the case on the table, put it on a chair instead, and then came over to stand beside Mat. He was so slippery with sweat that when Nikolai grabbed his arm to haul him upright, the man nearly dropped him. Nikolai adjusted his grip, the plug mercifully sliding free as Mat was dragged to his feet and shoved face-first onto the little table, ass up, feet barely touching the floor. Short reprieve, though; Nikolai's hands left him, and a moment later they were jamming the plug up inside him with so much force that the table lurched across the floor. Mat screamed, pride be damned, clutched at the table's edge with both hands and thumped his forehead against its surface, hard, over and over as the pain built and built beneath Nikolai's relentless pushing.

Well, at least he's having trouble with it too.

But Nikolai had far more strength and stamina than Mat did just now, and after a few more rough thrusts and jabs and ripped-out screams, the fucking thing finally, *finally* slid home.

Not that it was much improvement, as it turned out. He was beyond full, felt like he had to shit and piss and throw up all at once.

"Now, wasn't that so much better than living by your foolish pride?" Nikolai asked with a fatherly pat on Mat's sweaty, raised ass.

Mat dragged his nails across the table and balled his hands into fists. "Yes, sir," he said through clenched teeth, hoping Nikolai would read his tone as pain instead of fury. "Thank you, sir."

"Stay," Nikolai said, and then went to rummage in the case again. It was on the side Mat wasn't facing, and he couldn't be bothered to turn his head to look. Didn't want to know. He heard Nikolai place something on the table. Then Nikolai was jiggling the flare of the plug, and Mat whimpered. For all the pain he was in, the fucking thing was so big it couldn't help but stimulate his prostate. He was half-hard against the table edge. Fucking mortifying. At least Nikolai wasn't providing any of his usual commentary.

"Sit."

"What am I, a dog?" Mat bit out as he fell into the chair Nikolai had pulled out for him, then yelped as the plug drove in deeper on impact.

"I wouldn't do this to my dog." Nikolai reached between Mat's legs, and Mat flinched back, unable to stop it. But Nikolai wasn't going for his junk, he was going for . . . wires?

Oh, shit. The blood left his face so fast he could *feel* it draining.

"What, no more sarcastic remarks?" Nikolai found the ends of the two leads, plugged them into the little black box he'd placed on the table. The one with the dial turned all the way up to ten and an ominous red button. "Finally remembered your place, did you?"

"Yes, sir," Mat said, because he did *not* like where this was going. He curled his fingers around the edges of his chair, ass spasming around the plug. Those silver stripes on it, they weren't for decoration, they were *metal*. And that weird lube wasn't lube, was it. Some kind of conductive gel, probably. God, who manufactured this shit? What the fuck *for*?

Hell, maybe this whole human slave operation was big enough that they made their own tools. What a nightmarish thought.

Doesn't mean I can't still bring it down. Get out of here, shove this thing up Nikolai's *ass until he spills every name he knows, and then kill every single one. Just get through this. Get through this. Fix your fucking mistakes.*

"Give me your hand."

It took all the willpower Mat had not to spit in his palm first, but he managed it. Gave Nikolai his left, just in case the fucker planned to break it or something. Not that he really thought he would, but it wasn't a chance he was prepared to take.

Nikolai folded Mat's fingers down until only his index finger was still extended. "Here's how this is going to work, Mathias." He moved Mat's hand until his finger was touching the red button. "You're going to push this button. While this unit can be used to create some rather remarkably pleasurable sensations, I think you'll find that not to be the case at this particular setting. You will thank me for it anyway—*Thank you for correcting me, master.* Go on, practice. Say it."

In the face of such unbearable smugness, it was hard to remember why he was bothering with any of this. But then he thought of Roger, of that terrible beating he'd endured for Mat's choices, and of Dougie, who was maybe already more like the man Roger had become than the boy Mat knew, and he smiled up at Nikolai saccharine-sweet and said, "Thank you for correcting me, master."

There was nothing but hatred in Nikolai's eyes. Or maybe anger, but the guy was too in control of his emotions to flip out and yell and whale on Mat. There was something boiling under the surface, though, something that made his jaw twitch and fine lines appear between his brows.

"You will do this fifty times—I think that's enough even for *you* to learn your lesson and be sorry." Nikolai fiddled with his watch a moment, then took it off and laid it on the table next to the machine. "You have an hour. If you don't finish by that time, the *privilege* I have recently—and very generously—bestowed upon you to visit with your brother will be taken away. You won't see him again until after you've left here, and you won't leave here until you've proven your worth. Understood?"

"Yes, sir. Let's get on with it, sir."

"Ah, such bravado. There's my fighter back." Nikolai reached out and ruffled Mat's hair, then started the countdown on his watch. "Begin."

RACHEL HAIMOWITZ & HEIDI BELLEAU

Mat didn't hesitate for even a moment. He jabbed the button.

And jerked so hard he fell off the damn chair.

Holy *fuck*. That . . . was not fun.

"Get up," Nikolai said. Calm, but no mistaking the edge in his voice. He'd lost his patience with Mat but good.

Mat climbed back into the chair. The second he was sitting again, Nikolai knocked his legs apart and checked the leads on the plug, jiggling it miserably against still-spasming muscle. Fuck, he was so fucking raw already.

"I'm waiting," Nikolai said, but when Mat moved to press the button again—much more hesitantly than last time—Nikolai actually smacked his hand away.

Oh. Right. It was probably a good thing he was in a little too much pain to roll his eyes. "Thank you for correcting me, master."

Nikolai nodded and gestured toward the box.

Dougie, Mat recited to himself like a prayer, clenched his jaw against the scream he knew was coming, and pressed the button.

The dog had tenacity, Nikolai had to give him that.

Shock after shock, and he took each and every one, even after his muscles began to twitch involuntarily, even after he bit his lip until blood welled up, even after his face was soaked with tears. He'd pick himself back up and cast his eyes to the timer with grim determination, do some calculation in his head—*twenty seconds to rest and recover, twenty more to catch his breath and his pride enough to say thank you, ten to build up the courage to push the button again*—and keep going.

Nikolai's little fighter. His champion. Half of him wanted to throttle the man for the measures he'd forced him to take, the concessions he'd forced him to yield. But the other half of him simply *marveled*.

He'd begun to resent the fact that he couldn't break Mathias properly, that he'd had to go against everything he knew and believed about his work and its purpose, but this hour had done much to convince him that this kind of alternate training might be the only way to do a man like Mathias justice. A modern gladiator, meant to bow only under the whip and die in blood and glory.

If only that fate didn't require Nikolai to make compromises with regard to Douglas.

No matter. Mathias would get his meeting, and Nikolai would get his use of it. Perhaps it wasn't the way he'd initially planned to advance Douglas's training, but it would suit that all the same—it might even be more effective than his original choice—and it would suit Mathias's, too, for all that the man thought he was winning something here. After all, Nikolai was an artist, not a factory worker. Artistry required improvisation.

Go where the clay leads you.

When Mathias's punishment was finally over and Nikolai had been thanked, breathless and tear-choked, for the fiftieth shock (with an impressive three minutes to spare), he kissed Mathias on the forehead with renewed appreciation and helped him to his bed.

Removing the plug proved a challenge, thanks to Mathias's still-spasming muscles, but they managed it together, and afterward Nikolai sat on the bed, stroking Mathias's sweaty back as he shuddered and moaned into his pillow.

"I'll send Roger to help you bathe and bring you more food. When you have your strength back—then and only then—I will let you see your brother."

"Thank you, master," Mathias murmured, and though the response was probably just rote by now, for the first time ever, Nikolai detected not a single trace of insincerity in those words.

CHAPTER TWO

The next month passed in blissful peace, everything according to plan and pattern. Mathias dutifully tended himself, appetite rushing back and strength soon following. He worked harder than Nikolai had ever seen him work before, and though sometimes Nikolai worried he might be pushing too far too fast, the man did seem to know what was best for his own body. Nikolai, for his part, enjoyed the show. Loved sitting on the man's bed and watching him jump rope or run or attack his punching bag with single-minded ferocity. There was an animalistic fierceness in him, but also a uniquely human resolve that carried him through the more mundane or unpleasant tasks Nikolai gave him, through the myriad of domestic and sexual service chores he trained Mathias in each day. Whether fighting or fucking or simply folding his master's clothes, Nikolai loved to watch the play of his muscles, his broad shoulders and tight, hard ass and powerful legs. Still a bit leaner than when he'd been acquired, but getting there. All in due time.

His brother, on the other side of the coin, got softer and sweeter with each passing day. He took well to his chores, and always smiled and flushed and lowered his lashes when Nikolai passed him in the hall or the kitchen. Nikolai still hiked with him each morning—no need for hobbles or cuffs, not anymore—and often sent for him when he needed his back rubbed, or when he wanted someone to read aloud to him while he lazed in bed. Douglas took remarkably well to service: to cooking and cleaning, of course, but also to piano and poetry, and showed no evidence of his former heterosexuality when he worshipped at his master's altar. In the shower. In bed. In front of Roger. With Roger. The boy had learned his place so well now that Nikolai never even bothered to lock his door anymore. Instead he let Douglas come and go as he pleased—and was continually delighted to see that every choice Douglas made was made to please his master.

But no honeymoon could last forever, and as much as Nikolai hated to say it, it was time to move on to the challenge and drudgery of marriage. Time for Douglas to prove he was committed enough to make this work in the long term. To take the bad with the good. To perform even when the performance was distasteful or downright painful. He'd need to arrange for the boy to prove his dedication to service with a man not his rightful master—a cruel and unhygienic one, to be specific. And then there was Douglas's debut to consider, although that wouldn't be for at least another month, depending on the boy's performance. There was also, of course, the final severing with his old life. In that, at least, Nikolai could kill two birds with one stone.

He'd begin, then, with the most challenging test. Well, he had never been a timid man.

Dougie liked these quiet moments best.

He liked nearly everything, lately, but if he had to pick a favorite, this would be it, just sitting quietly at Nikolai's feet, letting his mind wander where it would, while Nikolai above him handled everything important and stressful and demanding. He could barely remember what it felt like to be stressed, to be thinking about money and deadlines and assignments and scholarships and Mat's fights and the job market. That life was a fading dream . . . No, it was a *nightmare* Nikolai had woken him from.

Nikolai's cock in his mouth was soft but heavy on his tongue, a constant warm weight that he happily took on. He'd suckle on occasion, or steal a swipe with his tongue, and Nikolai would chuckle and let him, or sometimes if he was trying to concentrate, flick him on the ear or pinch his cheek, but never cruelly. If Dougie was very lucky, Nikolai would harden and lengthen in his mouth, and if he was *very* very lucky, Nikolai would let Dougie bring him off, right there in the keyhole of his desk while he worked, and then let him swallow a big gratifying mouthful of cum. The petting and praise that'd inevitably follow was nearly as satisfying as knowing he'd been responsible for Nikolai's pleasure.

For now, though, Nikolai stayed soft, and that was just fine, too. Dougie lounged between his master's legs, head pillowed on his master's thigh, and mentally rehearsed piano exercises to the clack of Nikolai's rhythmic typing. Sometimes on days like this, when Nikolai's work went long and he didn't want to be disturbed even for a moment, the soft cock in Dougie's mouth would fill his throat with something entirely different from cum. No pleasure, no warning, just a hot bitter flow, endless and choking. (God, the first time he'd vomited, and Nikolai had been so angry that Dougie was *glad* he'd beaten him.) But Dougie was a good boy, and after that first time, he'd learned to endure because it was his duty, and performing that duty made Nikolai happy.

Not today though, luckily. Today was lazy and long and Dougie was warm and safe and happy, drifting yet still anchored.

It was because of this drifting that it took a moment for him to realize Nikolai was speaking, and he flared with panic and self-recrimination—*What if I missed something important? How could I let myself lose focus on my master?*—but Nikolai didn't sound angry at all.

"—special planned for you today, Douglas. A challenge. I'm afraid that you may not like it, but I have full faith that you'll make me proud." A hand reached down, gently stroking Dougie's hair, which had grown floppy. He'd never worn it long before, but then, he'd never worn women's underwear or played cock-warmer before, either. "Because you're my good boy, aren't you Douglas?"

Dougie hummed around the cock in his mouth and leaned his head into Nikolai's stroking hand. *My good boy.* They were the sweetest, most joyous words he could ever hope to hear, and yes, of course Dougie would perform, of course he'd make his master proud. He'd be absolutely brilliant. He'd do so well that Nikolai would never doubt him again.

Even if, sometimes, in the darkest, most quiet hours of the night, he occasionally—maybe a little—still doubted himself. That soft insidious voice he couldn't quite silence, the one he thought of as "Before" Dougie, the frightened, lonely, aimless child striving desperately, futilely, for everything Nikolai gave him so freely. But like most children, its voice was shrill when it was angry, when it demanded attention, when it shouted words like *Stockholm Syndrome* and *he trusts you now, use it to your advantage and run away before it's too late.*

He tapped frantically at Nikolai's thigh, and the hand in his hair tugged gently back, giving him the permission he'd sought to speak. "It's happening again, master," he whispered the moment Nikolai's cock left his mouth. He missed it already, wanted to chase it back, but this was important, and Nikolai would fix it; he always did.

Nikolai pushed his chair back. Then a second hand came down to cup Dougie's face, urged him forward out of the keyhole and tilted his head back until he was looking up into Nikolai's eyes. "Shhh," his master said. Stroked his hair, his cheek. He didn't want or deserve this kindness; he wanted, *needed* Nikolai to turn him over his lap and punish him until his screams were louder than that damn *voice.* "Fight it, Douglas. Use your logic. You're too smart to let it mislead you."

No, no, he wasn't, not right now with that gaping chasm of *doubt* the voice had dug in his chest. He couldn't think, couldn't focus, couldn't bring his hammering heart under control. He clung to Nikolai's pants, closed his eyes, and tried to narrow his world to the feel of his master's loving hands on his face, the warmth of his master's body, the residual taste of his master's cock on his tongue.

"This challenge I've planned for you will help, Douglas."

Challenge. Test. Oh God, how could he perform a test right now? He'd fail. The voice would rise up and distract him and make him doubt and he'd *fail.*

"Easy, Douglas, easy." Fingers stroking at his hair, thumbs caressing his cheeks. "I'll give you a correction afterward, if you still need it. But not now." *Yes. Now. Please.* "Now I need you to find your center on your own. Prove to me you can."

Dougie squeezed his eyes tight, clenched his hands into hard fists until his trimmed fingernails dug into the skin of his palms. *My master's hands. My master's warmth. The taste of my master's cock. You're a good boy, Douglas, such a good boy . . .*

His breathing slowed. His heart calmed. Nikolai believed in him, and if his master believed in him, then he could believe in himself.

"There, there, good boy. That's a good boy," Nikolai recited, hands gentling Dougie down. Once Dougie's cheek was to Nikolai's thigh and his breathing had quieted, Nikolai said, "Now. Today you're going to learn to perform with another slave for your master's pleasure."

Well jeez, that didn't sound so bad at all. Had the real test been Dougie's reaction to hearing his master say that it was a challenge Dougie wouldn't like? It was true that Dougie liked sex with his master best, but he could do anything just so long as he knew Nikolai enjoyed it. Besides, Dougie had done plenty of performing with Roger already. Maybe the test this time would be to perform with someone like Jeremy? Even that wouldn't be too bad; Jeremy was difficult to get along with, but he and Dougie had a pretty good working relationship by this point. Dougie was sure he could handle taking that relationship to another level.

"You will find some things about this slave . . . distasteful."

Oh. Was he . . . was he ugly, maybe? Dirty? Dougie could handle the first one—*just think of Nikolai, no trouble*—but the second one made him apprehensive. Still, if he could swallow Nikolai's urine, he could suck sweaty cock. But what if it was worse than that? What if Nikolai wanted him to rim the guy and he was . . . he was . . .

"You're starting to hyperventilate again, Douglas. Your master needs you to be calm."

Calm, right. He could do that. He *could*. No point in working himself up over something that might or might not even happen, after all. Just trust Nikolai, and wait to see what his master wanted of him. Stop second-guessing. Stop *worrying*. Nikolai would take care of him. He always did.

"That's better." Nikolai reached a hand out to draw Dougie to his feet. He tapped the intercom on his computer and said, "Roger? Is everything ready?"

"Yes, master," came through the laptop speaker.

Hmm, maybe it was Roger, after all. Well then, that wasn't bad at all. Dougie liked Roger. The only way he'd ever be distasteful to Dougie was if he'd rolled in shit or something. Which, oh God, maybe he had—

No. Don't think about it. Just trust.

Before he could get too worked up again, Nikolai stood too and guided him out the door and down the hall. To the stairs that led nearest to Dougie's bedroom. Down into the basement. His heart picked up pace again. He didn't like that; his bedroom was supposed to be a safe space. This whole *house* was supposed to be a safe space. He hated being afraid of it, of any of it.

When they reached his bedroom door—which was closed; he hadn't left it that way this morning—Nikolai took him by the shoulders and maneuvered him in front of it. Kept his hands on Dougie, nice and firm, and Dougie had to stop himself from leaning back into the touch even as he couldn't help but think that Nikolai was standing this way to stop him from fleeing when he saw what was behind that door.

"Go on," Nikolai said. "Open it."

It's just Roger. You're psyching yourself out with all this second-guessing.

Dougie's sweaty palm slipped on the doorknob.

"I'll be right behind you," Nikolai reminded him, and that was all Dougie needed.

The door swung open.

The bed was empty.

A chair by the table . . . was not.

Dougie smacked hard, face-first, into something solid, and only then realized he'd turned and fled and run right into Nikolai.

"This exercise isn't optional, Douglas."

"No. No no *nonono* please master, you can't, you *can't,*" Dougie blubbered, because it wasn't Roger tied to the chair, wasn't Jeremy, wasn't a man covered in shit and piss, wasn't even a fucking *dog.*

It was *Mat.*

His *brother.* His brother who hated him and, oh, by the way, was his *brother.* Tied and gagged and naked and struggling and *his brother.*

Nikolai grabbed Dougie by the shoulders, *hard,* and forcibly turned him to face the horror at the center of the room. Someone—Roger, presumably—had sat Mat in that chair and tied his wrists to the back legs and his ankles and knees to the front legs and fitted a cruel black gag into Mat's mouth—the one with the little penis that reached all the way to the back of your tongue and made you choke if you weren't careful, Dougie recognized it from his own early days here and it was awful, awful—so that all Mat's noises of protest, mirroring Dougie's own, were reduced to drooly grunts and whines.

Dougie planted his heels and clutched at Nikolai's hands on his shoulders. "Please, please master, *please*, I don't even want to see him. Please just let's leave. I'll do anything you want, you'll see, anything at all but *this*. *Please*."

Nikolai was unmoved. His hands tightened painfully on Dougie's shoulders and shook, rattling his head on his neck. "*This* is what I want. You need to learn to service a man you hate. You need to learn to service an *unwilling* man. And more than anything, you need to learn to let go of all your silly, stupid morality, all the trappings and judgments and pointless rules of your old life."

Mat howled, jerking so hard at his restraints that he was making himself bleed. Dougie whined for both of them, "No no no, please, please, he's my—he's my—"

"Douglas." Nikolai's voice was artificially calm, a raging anger rising underneath, an anger Dougie had never seen before. *Just punish me. Punish me and be done with it and then we can be happy again, I'll be good, I'll do anything else, anything.* "He's nothing to you now. You're not the broken man you came to me as, you're something new. You're mine and mine alone now, and you *have no brother*. This slave is nothing to you. Nothing but a means to please me, to prove yourself to me. There's lube on the table. Kneel in front of this slave and prepare yourself. When you're done, you'll use your mouth—just your mouth—to get him hard. He will get hard, Douglas, he's very virile. When you're done, you'll ride him for me. And then the test will be over and that voice in your head will go silent for good. Sever the last thread that ties you to your failures, Douglas. Prove to me you're ready to be mine."

I don't have a brother. I don't have a brother. I'm Nikolai's boy now, not Dougie Carmichael at all, and this man isn't my brother, he's just a slave, he's just a slave and he's not my brother and I'm Nikolai's boy, I'm not Dougie Carmichael, I'm Douglas Petrovic, Douglas Petrovic, Douglas Petrovic.

He sucked in a huge, wet breath and stepped out from the sheltering force of Nikolai's grip. Toward Ma— *No, the slave in the chair, just some slave in a chair.* Toward the bound slave. A foot closer. Another foot. Nearly there now. He was crying. Powerfully, helplessly, endlessly. Didn't matter. He'd performed through tears before; he could do it now. The tied-up slave was crying too, but silent, stoic, like Dougie wished he could be. Just tears and tears and tears, soaking his trembling cheeks and jaw. His teeth were bared around the penis gag. He wasn't making any more noise. He looked . . . resigned. Sick. Helpless. All the things Dougie had put behind him—forever, he'd thought. This slave was an animal. Untrained, wild. Dougie wouldn't be like him, not again. Never again. He *wouldn't*.

He dropped to his knees between the slave's bound-open legs. Stared at the soft cock resting, forlorn, against the firmness of his left thigh. Uncut, like his own. Of course it was, they were broth—

No. Shut up shut up shut up don't think about it he's nothing to you he's nothing he's nothing he's nothing.

Dougie picked up the lube in one trembling hand. Fought with the cap. Lost. Felt a sob overtake him, and next he knew, somehow, he'd thrown himself into Mat, chest on his lap, cheek pressed to his stomach, arms around his waist and the chair back, sobbing and sobbing and wishing Mat's hands were free so he could shove Dougie away (*stroke your hair*), show him how much he hated him (*hug you back*), how vast the differences between them had become (*he's still your brother, always your brother, nothing will ever change that*). But Mat's hands *weren't* free, of course, and Dougie's master was looming over him now, and the anger was coming off him in waves. Anger, but also disappointment, which was so much worse, God, but as much as Dougie wanted (*don't want at all, you fucking monster*) to please his master, he couldn't. He couldn't do this to Mat. He'd take the punishment, he would. He'd take the punishment for both of them, he'd take another baseball bat up the ass, he'd even bear Nikolai's disappointment and go back into the dark room alone and slowly starve to death. He'd let himself be sold to a master who'd castrate him and break his feet and make him crawl every day for the rest of his life.

"Douglas, you have one more chance to please your master. Get back on your knees *right now* and put that slave's cock in your mouth. Consequences, Douglas. Worse than you've ever known, do you understand me?"

Mat arched his back, bumping their chests together, as if trying to knock Dougie off him. "*Hws*," he grunted through his gag, the sound so high-pitched there was nothing it could be but "Please."

Oh god, he wanted to, he *wanted* to. Wanted to obey, to make Nikolai happy, to show him he was a good boy, such a *good boy*. Wanted to throw himself at Nikolai's feet and beg, plead, kiss and cling and suck his cock and let Nikolai beat him until he bled, until he couldn't stand, couldn't think, couldn't *screw up* so badly anymore, until he'd never, ever question or doubt Nikolai again. But he just . . . couldn't somehow. Found himself—half to his utter horror—tightening his grip on Mat instead, pressing his cheek to Mat's chest and listening to the sound of his hammering heart. His brother's heart. His brother's blood pumping through his brother's veins. The same blood. There was nothing that could overcome that, not even Nikolai's most complex psychological machinations. Not even his own disgust at how pathetic it was to be clinging to someone who'd discarded him, especially when Nikolai, sweet good loving Nikolai, was *right here*.

But look what he's making you do. If he really loved you, would he ask this of you?

Yes, he thought. *Yes. It's a test. A coming of age. Hard love, but love all the same. Important. Necessary.*

And yet still his body betrayed him, his mouth opening, his tongue forming words his mind railed to keep inside. "I'm so sorry but I can't, sir. I won't. I won't do this to Mat. Anyone else, *anyone*, but not Mat."

"Fine."

Oh thank God. Thank you, master. Thank you.

"The two of you can stay here, then, until you decide for certain where your allegiances lie, Douglas. I'll give you the night to make up your mind and will return in the morning to hear—and to see you prove—your answer. Just know that if you choose wrongly, both of you will suffer the consequences, and the consequences will be *dire*."

Yes, punish me, punish *me, I've been bad, I don't want to be bad, I want to be a good boy,* your *good boy.*

"Yes, master," Dougie sniffled, ear still pressed to Mat's chest, awash in his heartbeat. Mat had gone still, perhaps seeing the futility in trying to dislodge Dougie. "I'm sorry, master, I'm sorry, I'm so sorry . . ."

"We'll see how sorry you are, Douglas."

And with that he took his leave, closing the door behind him, softly as ever but the *click* of the latch in the strike plate sounded so horribly *final* somehow this time. Dougie couldn't let it be. He *wouldn't* let it be. He just needed some time, that was all.

Time, time . . . He glanced at the clock. Not even six yet. That meant he had nearly fourteen hours to get his head on straight, fourteen hours to figure out a way to silence that fucking *voice* and do what his master ordered. He pulled himself away from Mat—easier, now, that Nikolai wasn't standing over him with his demands; he didn't feel so cornered anymore, so needful to hang on—and put some distance between them. Mat made a noise at that—*Thank God*, probably, though Dougie's "before" voice told him it was *No, come back*. Well, even if that were true, it was probably just because Mat felt so alone that he'd settle for Dougie's company despite his hatred. Or maybe because he was jealous that Dougie belonged to Nikolai now, even though Mat didn't like him, didn't want him, thought him a burden. Dog in the manger and all that. Well, fuck him. He didn't get to just throw Dougie away and then expect Dougie to come back to him at the slightest hint of bitter affection. Dougie was stronger than that now. He didn't need Mat anymore.

He backed up to his bed and very deliberately didn't let himself look at Mat's face. Too hard to get his thoughts in order while watching those silent tears fall. Mat made another noise. And another, more desperate than the last, as Dougie continued to ignore him. "Just *shut up*," Dougie snapped. "I need to think. Please. Just . . . stop."

Mat stopped.

"What do I do," Dougie moaned, putting his face in his hands. "I hate this. I *hate* this. I hate *you*." His "before" voice shouted in his head, made him add awful, awful lies: "I hate Nikolai. I hate myself."

Mat moaned, mournful. Or maybe encouraging. Dougie couldn't tell, wasn't willing to look at him to find out. "I said shut up," he said instead.

He almost wished Mat wouldn't, because every reason he could think of for why Mat *would* do as he asked just complicated the situation even more.

Screw this. Dougie couldn't be in the same room with the man, not right now. Couldn't stand to be reminded of his old life *or* his catastrophic failure in his new one. He stood, paced to the door, had his hand on the knob before he realized he couldn't face *anyone* out there right now, not while he was still being a *bad boy*, not until he'd been punished for it, punished *but good*, forgiven and taken back into the fold.

Which just left the bathroom. Dougie went inside and slammed the door behind him. Turned on the shower. A good hot soak always did help him think, and at least with the water running, he had no chance of hearing those awful little noises Mat might make.

CHAPTER THREE

For one long, horrible, vomit-inducing minute, Mat had actually thought Dougie was going to go through with it. And then he'd felt like absolute shit for being so relieved when Dougie didn't. This was what he wanted, wasn't it? For Dougie to give in to Nikolai's desires? To not *suffer* anymore?

But it seemed that even not suffering was its own form of torture, a torture that maybe didn't hurt as much as punishments and *consequences*, but chipped away at you just the same. He couldn't sit by and let that happen to his brother. Nikolai's logic sounded okay in theory, but that was what Nikolai *did*, just kept talking and talking and talking until you believed what he said, until you accepted his worldview as your own. Guys like Roger weren't happy in their submission, they were *dead* inside. That wasn't happiness, that was numbness. And maybe if your only options were numbness or pain, you would choose numbness, but at what cost? And what if your only options *weren't* numbness or pain? What if freedom was still on the table?

Yes. They could get out. Mat would save them. Dougie still had some piece of himself left, but it was a light going out fast, flickering like a fluorescent bulb on its last legs. Mat had to get him out of here. God, if only he didn't have this fucking *gag*, he could talk to him, tell him everything. Tell him about his deal with Nikolai, tell him he was sorry, tell him he loved him more than anything, more than his own life, and he'd save him even if he had to die trying.

But he supposed that was why Nikolai had gagged and tied him in the first place. The fucking bastard. He'd promised to let them see each other; he hadn't promised to let them speak to or comfort one another. He hadn't promised not to turn their meeting into another torture—to the contrary, in fact; he'd warned Mat to be careful what he wished for.

I should've known. I should've seen this coming somehow.

Now if he could just get out of this fucking chair. He was pretty sure he understood why Dougie hadn't untied him, why Dougie probably *wouldn't* untie him. No mistaking the confusion, the torment in his brother's eyes. The self-recrimination. The helplessness. The desire to please Nikolai, the fear of failure. This whole setup might've made Dougie question, but it wasn't going to make him risk more than that. So Mat would be stuck in this fucking chair all night, wouldn't he. Probably end up pissing himself. He balled his hands into fists and twisted his wrists again, glad for a moment of the penis gag to bite down on when pain flared breathlessly sharp in his torn skin. Nikolai would punish him for doing that to himself, but he didn't fucking care, wasn't even afraid of the serum, not if it meant he could get his hands free, get this gag off, talk Dougie back to him, back to sanity, to resistance, to escape.

No dice, though. The rope was thick, the knots solid. Maybe if his skin got slippery enough and the ropes wet enough—enough sweat, enough blood—he could pull his way free. How much time did he have left to try? Dougie's room, unlike his own, had a clock for some reason. Six thirty. Dinnertime.

He went back to flexing and torquing his wrists. Ignored the pain, ignored the trembling in his overtaxed muscles, ignored everything but the goal. He thought maybe the left rope was starting to feel a little looser. Not enough to pull free as of yet, but progress was progress. *Keep at it. Don't think. Just do.*

It was after seven when next he looked up, breathless and bloody, unable to continue without at least a few minutes of rest. His body had had enough, arms and chest and back muscles so overtaxed he could barely move. The pain was starting to poke through his concentration with barbed hooks. And Jesus, was Dougie still in the fucking shower? What was he *doing* in there? Why was it taking so long?

Was he . . . was he okay?

Oh God, what if he *wasn't* okay? What if he wasn't okay and it was Mat's fucking fault for insisting he be allowed to see Dougie when Dougie clearly wasn't in a position to cope with it?

Mat had to get out of this fucking chair. Had to be sure for himself. Had to be the big brother. He rocked forward, the soles of his feet hitting the floor, then pushed himself back with every ounce of strength he could muster.

Let himself fall.

Dougie heard the crash even over the running water. He froze, listening. Held his breath. There it was again, accompanied by a muffled shout. Mat. What was he fucking *doing* out there?

Dougie should go check. Not because he was worried or anything. Just . . . in case.

He heard another crash as he shut the water off, another muffled yell. And something else this time, a sound like . . . cracking wood?

Oh no, tell me you didn't, you damn idiot, tell me you're not breaking the chair. Nikolai would kill him. Kill them both. He couldn't be a good boy and do what Nikolai wanted if Mat was wandering free.

He darted from the shower, snagged a towel along the way and swiped at himself with it as he ran into the bedroom. Found Mat lying dazed on the floor on top of a pile of splintered wood, arms and legs still bound to broken bits of chair, groaning in pain.

"You idiot!" Dougie shouted, and then he saw the blood on Mat's arms and wrists and hands. "Oh God, Mat, what have you done? You're bleeding!" He rushed to his brother's side and fell to his knees, quickly untangling the wood and rope from Mat's raw skin. Nikolai would probably consider that to be helping, but they were already in shit anyway, right? "God, what have you done?" He took his wet towel and dabbed gently at the wounds, his hands shaking so badly he could barely manage. Not that Mat seemed to care; he pulled his arms away, and for a second Dougie thought he was just that disgusted by Dougie's touch, but then he saw Mat's fingers curling around the straps of the gag—two on each side, strong and thick, one buckled tight at the base of his skull and the other higher up on the back of his head, connected to each other by smaller straps that prevented Mat from slipping the top one off. Mat yanked and twisted and clawed, but Dougie hadn't missed the two little padlocks holding the buckles shut, and not even his big strong brother could break out of those straps. He couldn't even fit one fingertip beneath them for leverage.

"Stop it, Mat. They're locked. You can't open them, Nikolai probably has the key. You're just going to hurt yourself and make Nikolai even angrier than he's already going to be. Please, just stop." He realized he was crying again, fresh tears, except this time they didn't feel desperate, they felt strangely cleansing. "Oh Mat, I'm so sorry, this is all my fault. This could have been over and done by now if I—if I—"

He couldn't even say it.

Mat grasped either side of Dougie's face and pulled him down so that their foreheads touched. He didn't speak, not that he could. Didn't even grunt around his gag. Just closed his eyes and breathed slowly, slowly, slowly, until Dougie felt himself breathing along. He wanted to pull away, wanted to say, *Too late. You threw me away. You can't have this anymore just because you're desperate. You're not my brother anymore*, and then pin Mat down and ride him, just like Nikolai wanted.

But he couldn't, because even though Mat couldn't speak, Dougie heard his words loud and clear: *I love you. I love you.* Breathing, in, out. *I'm sorry. Please.* In. Out. *I love you.*

And Mat was crying again. Those big, stupid, silent tears.

"You idiot," Dougie cried back, softly. "You stupid, fucking idiot. Why— I was finally— And then you—"

God, I love you too, Mat. I love you so much, even though I wish I didn't. Even though you don't deserve me. Even though you don't really want me, not forever like Nikolai does.

Despite his endless list of *even thoughs*, Mat must've seen something, some change in Dougie's eyes, because he took his hands from Dougie's face and threw them around Dougie's shoulders instead, pulled him down tight, chest to chest, and locked his arms behind him, crying into his shoulder and bleeding all over his back and he was so warm—God, feverish—so hungry and alive with need, desperation, joy, relief, a thousand conflicting emotions Dougie felt welling in his own chest, too.

And no matter how much Dougie didn't *want* to feel all those things, no matter how afraid he was that Nikolai would come in at any moment and find them together like this, hate him for it, cast him away for it, he just . . . *couldn't* make himself stop.

He didn't know how long he lay there like that, half on top of Mat, them clinging to each other and choking on tears like drowning men. He lost track of time, lost track of *everything* because it was all so fucking slippery right now, broken and sharp and dangerous, and he couldn't even begin to figure out how to navigate his way through it without doing irrevocable damage to one or the other or both of them.

All he knew was that he loved Mat. And he *hated* Mat. Hated him in ways he'd never even been able to conceive of in his "before" life, because Mat had broken everything, hadn't he, he'd ruined it, ruined it all, and now Dougie didn't know how to fix things with Mat or Nikolai or *anyone* and he was still fucking *stuck here* and had to live this fucking life and how was he supposed to when all he'd given and suffered and worked for had been shattered in a single fucking minute with his brother?

He should leave. He should go right now, walk out that door, find Nikolai, fall to his knees and beg and beg. *Correct me, punish me, take me back. Make me see the right path.*

But he didn't. He couldn't. He just eased out from beneath Mat's arms, rose shakily to his feet, and hauled Mat up beside him. "Come on," he said, and "God damn you," and led Mat to the bed so he could take care of him properly, like Mat needed, like Mat *always* needed because he was a fucking mess, a train wreck, a wild beast, the bull in Dougie's fucking china shop and fuck him, seriously, *fuck* him.

He should've. He should've just fucked him and been done with it. Said good-bye for good. Everything would've been so much simpler that way.

Instead he went into the bathroom, into the medicine cabinet, found a roll of gauze and some tape, wet a clean washcloth and brought the whole mess back to Mat. Cleaned and bandaged his wrists. Surely Nikolai wouldn't fault him for that, would he? The master's property had been damaged, he was fixing it. That's all. Just looking out for Nikolai's interests. Most definitely *not* looking at Mat's eyes, which had gone all round and soft and dewy. But Mat would have looked like that at *anyone* who showed him some fucking pity, that was all. Nothing personal. Nothing personal.

Dougie didn't know what to do with himself after that was done. Wait, he supposed. Just . . . sit here and wait for Nikolai to come back and make everything okay again. Even if Nikolai was the one who'd broken everything so badly.

No, you did. *You should've listened to him. Everything would've been fine then. You would've been free. For the first time in your life, totally, honest-to-god free.*

His "before" voice scoffed. *Just the opposite, idiot. He was trying to trap you forever.*

"No," Dougie moaned, and covered his ears with both hands even though it was stupid, pointless, the arguments were coming from within and he couldn't run away from that, now could he? "Stop it. *Stop it.*"

Mat looked at him like he was losing his fucking mind.

That's because you are.

No. Everything had been fine, better than fine, *great* even, until Mat had shown up. He wasn't crazy. He was fine. He'd get through this. Nikolai would help him get through this. He just needed to trust. Be patient. Wait. Just like always.

He stood, walked around to the side of the bed Mat wasn't sitting on, and climbed in. Put his back to Mat and pulled the blankets up over his head. He'd just . . . lie here until morning. Think of nothing. Trust. Be patient. Wait. Run piano exercises in his head because he couldn't ever focus on anything else when he was trying to remember all that complicated fingering.

Except he couldn't *not* focus on Mat, somehow. Couldn't avoid noticing when Mat stood up from the bed, started pacing around the room, looking for . . . fuck-all knew what. A weapon, maybe. Oh, God, he wouldn't *hurt* Nikolai, would he? Because then Dougie would have to try to stop him and that would be *ridiculous* because there was no fucking way in hell he actually could stop him and—

Stop. Stop thinking.

He lurched upright when he heard the door open, halfway to sliding to his knees before he realized it was just Mat, not Nikolai. Just Mat, hand frozen, looking stunned beyond comprehension that the knob had actually turned beneath his fingers.

Nikolai must have kept Mat's door locked all the time. No wonder, he supposed. Couldn't exactly have a wild animal wandering free in his own house, could he.

Dougie figured Mat would make a break for it now, abandon him like he had before, but he didn't. He just stood there another moment, blinking stupidly, then peeked out into the hallway, then pulled back inside, and very, very quietly shut the door again.

Dougie buried himself back under the covers after that, but he couldn't help but hear Mat, whose activities around the room had turned downright frantic. Opening and closing drawers, rummaging around, tearing through the closet, the bathroom, every cabinet and nook. What was he *looking* for? Why wouldn't he just sit down and wait for Nikolai to come back?

When Mat finally, *finally* stopped poking around, he sat himself down on the edge of the bed by Dougie's hip and rubbed his back and shoulder through the blanket. The gesture was so familiar, so very Nikolai, that Dougie let himself be soothed by it, let himself be coaxed from his cocoon to meet Mat's questing gaze. His heart both thrilled and sank at what he saw there: that old familiar calm competence, steady and loving, that had seen him through so many trials in his past. That openness—*Do you trust me?*—that had fooled him so often before into believing Mat had offered him real, selfless love.

He did. He does. He will again if you let him. Even if you don't let him.

Dougie covered his ears again.

A little furrow formed between Mat's brow, and God he looked so frustrated at his inability to speak, even as Dougie was grateful for it, so grateful he wasn't sure he'd be able to speak himself if the need arose. He couldn't hear what Mat had to say. He'd lost enough for one night already.

Mat just sighed through his nose and held up his index finger: *wait.* Stood, extended all five fingers flat, palm down, and gestured once, then a second time: *stay here.*

As much as Dougie hadn't wanted to look at him before—still didn't want to look at him now—he couldn't help following Mat with his eyes as his brother walked back to the other side of the bed and pointed at a pile of stuff he'd accumulated there. The first things

Dougie saw were two fairly long, jagged pieces of broken chair, and he understood, even before his eyes next landed on the clothes and shoes and jacket Nikolai had bought him for their winter-weather hikes, that Mat planned to escape.

Escape. Escape.

But I live *here. I can't run away from my* life.

Except he had left his life behind before, hadn't he? And that small part of him that'd gotten louder and bigger throughout this disastrous clusterfuck of an evening, the "before" part, was *screaming* at him to do it again. To go, now, before it was too late. Before that part of him was dead forever, before Nikolai drowned it in the tub like a fucking unwanted baby and all that was left was *here, this,* whatever this was.

Because whatever this was, it wasn't Mat. It wasn't the real world. And as much as he didn't want to leave Nikolai, as much as he knew Mat didn't *really* love him, as much as the "real" world terrified him, as full of wild animals as it was, that little part of him, "before" him, was still alive and kicking and strong enough to recognize this for the chance that it was. Maybe his only chance. His *last* chance. And if he'd really blown it with Nikolai for good, then what was left for him here anyway? Why stay at all?

His eyes went back to those two bits of broken chair. Mat had let him down before, let him down a *lot,* pushed him away and hated him and let people hurt him, but Dougie had seen him with *yantok* sticks in his hands before, fluid and elegant and *deadly,* and knew, *knew,* that Mat wouldn't let him down tonight if he chose to go with him.

He looked at the clothes again. Then at the door—the unlocked door because *Nikolai trusted him.* Then at the clock.

Ten p.m. already, really? Wow. The household would be in bed by now. Yesterday at this time, he'd been curled up in bed with Nikolai and Roger, listening to the two men breathing softly in sleep before nodding off himself.

Now he was downstairs with Mat, and Nikolai was angry with him, and every scrap of stability he'd found for himself was fucking *gone* and there was no right answer here, no way to fix this, any of this, he couldn't stay and he couldn't go and he was broken, *broken,* didn't know what to do, needed someone to tell him what to do.

Mat must've seen him staring at the clothes and weapons, seen the despair on his face, the confusion, the anger, the fear, because he picked up the jeans Nikolai had given him and held them out.

Those were a gift, Mat, please don't—

Mat shook the jeans—*Take them, damn it, put them on!*—but when Dougie stood frozen, doing nothing, Mat threw them down on the bed and picked up the sweater instead. Fumbled with it until he'd opened the neck hole. Held the sweater, neck hole first, out to Dougie, and when Dougie was still too stunned to move, physically pulled the sweater over Dougie's head. *Dressing him?* Dougie let it happen, raised his arms so Mat could pull them through the sleeves. Then the jeans again. Mat held them out for him, and this time, Dougie took them.

I'm actually going to do this, aren't I? I'm going to put on these clothes and follow Mat out of this house and leave behind the only person who truly loves me without so much as a by-your-leave. What will I do then? How will I survive on my own?

His hands had fastened his jeans for him while he'd been thinking.

You think too much, Douglas, always think *too much.*

Mat kept Dougie's socks for himself, thick warm wool, but it wasn't as if Dougie would need them with the leather sneakers Mat was handing him. He took them numbly. Put them on himself because he didn't think he could bear Mat doing it for him. His jacket next, warm but lightweight down. It didn't escape his notice that he was bundled up to his eyeballs and Mat was still naked. Well, except for Dougie's socks.

Protecting you, he's protecting you. Willing to freeze so you don't.

That thought warmed him better than the clothes ever could. Scared the fucking shit out of him, too. There had to be a reason Mat was doing that. Had to be something he wanted, something he needed. He'd kept Dougie around all these years as a post-fighting-days meal ticket, Dougie knew that. No other reason to put up with him. So why was he being so selfless now?

You think *too much, Douglas.*

Yeah. He knew that. He just didn't know how to shut it off; only Nikolai had ever managed to silence the storms that raged in his head.

He scrubbed his face with both hands and stood up from the bed, waited for Mat to show him what to do next. If he could just . . . *obey,* follow orders, trust and be patient and wait, then maybe everything would be okay. Somehow.

Mat nodded at him and handed him the two jagged sticks. Or tried to. Dougie wouldn't take them. There wasn't one person in this house he would be willing to use them on, not for himself, not for Mat, not for anything.

Finally, Mat sighed around the gag and laid them on the little round table. Then he stripped the blanket and top sheet from the bed, laid the top sheet aside, and folded the blanket into some insanely complicated toga-like thing that left his arms and legs free for fighting and running and wouldn't trip him up during either. The sheet he folded down small and handed to Dougie. In case they froze, he supposed. Dougie tucked it into his jacket and looked to Mat—*Is that right? Is that okay?* Mat nodded again. Pulled his lips back from the gag in what Dougie thought might be a smile. Clapped him once on a down-poofy shoulder, and retrieved his *yantok* sticks.

Then he crept back to the door, opened it, and peeked down the darkened hall.

CHAPTER FOUR

Mat nearly melted with relief when Dougie followed him into the hallway. To be honest, even after getting him dressed, Mat still hadn't been sure that he would.

He tightened his grip on the makeshift *yantok* sticks and squinted into the dark. Saw nothing, heard nothing, sensed no one but Dougie at his back, crying softly though God knew why. They were getting out of here. That was something to celebrate, not mourn.

Or had Nikolai already fucked with his head so badly that he thought he'd miss this place?

Mat couldn't afford to think about that possibility right now. Not how true it probably was, not how big a role he himself had no doubt played in it, not how he'd ever figure out how to make things right again. He needed to be sharp now. Alert. Keep them alive and get them the fuck off this mountain. He could deal with the fallout *after* they were both safe. Right after he found a knife or scissors or something to cut this fucking gag off his face. It wasn't just about how uncomfortable it was, or how it constantly left him feeling on the edge of choking, or how it made it hard to breathe every time he looked at Dougie broken and begging and he teared up too. No, it was how fucking close to *shattering* Dougie was, and how much Mat needed to be able to talk to him, talk him down, tell him everything he should've said that awful, awful night with Mr. Baseball Bat.

Fix things. He had to fucking fix things.

Somehow.

God, they'd work it out, they always had. Mat refused to believe that this was less fixable than the deaths of their parents or Dougie being taken into foster care. He just needed to be able to talk. To comfort Dougie in a way that touches couldn't.

He looked over his shoulder again. Dougie was still behind him, eyes wet and shining in the dim light that streaked out from under the door at the top of the stairs. Would that door be unlocked too? Were they that lucky? God, were they lucky at all, or was this some kind of fucking trick? Would there be attack dogs at the top of the stairs, waiting to tear them apart for their betrayal?

No. We're too expensive for that.

Still, he didn't trust it. Couldn't.

Maybe Nikolai would be waiting at the top of the stairs. Or the guards. Only one way to find out though, and at this point, they didn't have much more to lose and a whole hell of a lot to gain.

How much more could Nikolai punish them? Could that ever outweigh their chance at freedom? Mat cast one more look at Dougie over his shoulder, still fucking *crying* (although at least he was doing it quietly)—just at the thought of leaving this place?—and decided it was worth the risk. Because it was either risk it, or leave Dougie to lose himself entirely. Tonight, Dougie had refused to rape him. Would he do the same again tomorrow?

Mat crept up the stairs, shifted both sticks into one hand, and put out his other hand to signal for Dougie to wait below while Mat put his ear to the door. No sounds of stirring at all.

Okay. Here goes. Lady Luck, don't fail me now.

Mat took the knob in hand.

Turned it.

Raised his weapons.

The door swung open, revealing . . . nothing at all of note. An empty cupboard, and outside of that, an empty hall. He gestured to Dougie to climb the stairs, stared out at the hall again. Right or left? Mat barely remembered the house's layout, and turned to Dougie for help. He needed to get this fucking gag off. He pointed at the straps. Made a scissoring motion with his hand.

"The kitchen?" Dougie whispered back. "Left."

So Mat turned left, but froze when Dougie's hand caught his wrist. When Mat turned to see what was the matter, Dougie shook his head until fresh tears fell. "We can't," he whispered. "I forgot. Jeremy."

Jeremy must be the cook. The one who made Mat all those surprisingly not-bland meals of lean protein and complex carbs.

What, the fucking guy cooks in the middle of the night? He was really starting to wish Dougie could muster up the energy for some full fucking sentences. It wasn't fair to be angry at him, he knew that, but he needed more information and couldn't ask for it, and Dougie wasn't fucking volunteering it.

But then, suddenly, he did. "His bedroom's off the kitchen. I . . . I've spent some nights there. He never shuts his door."

Mat didn't want to know why. He just reached out with one hand to cup Dougie's cheek and hoped that would serve as comfort. The way Dougie closed his eyes and leaned into the touch, like some needy cat but *sexual,* somehow, made him want to pull his hand away again. But he resisted the urge. *He doesn't know what he's doing. He doesn't mean it. He just . . . needs you.*

And you need him, too. You can't live without him. Not his fault he's too fucked up to express that properly anymore.

Okay, so Mat would be stuck with the gag a little longer. Maybe there was a shed or something in the garden. Not that he wanted to put rusty gardening equipment anywhere near his face. Oh well, no point in worrying about tetanus when they hadn't even made it out of the house yet.

Shit. Which way was out? How to ask? He tucked one stick beneath his arm and made a walking man with two fingers, mimicking going down steps with them.

"Stairs?" Dougie asked, and then his eyes lit up. "You want to go back downstairs?"

No! Mat shook his head vehemently. Damn, well, it was hardly Dougie's fault for not thinking of the stairs that led down to the front drive. He tried again. Drew a rectangle in the air with one finger, then mimed turning a doorknob—*The front door, kiddo, where's the front door?*—and when Dougie just cocked his head at him like some confused dog, he tucked both sticks between his knees and wrapped his arms around his blanketed chest, shivering as if outside in the cold. Made a broad, expansive gesture for the sky.

Then took a hold of the sticks again because he felt fucking naked standing here without a weapon, never mind that he'd been trained as one himself.

And *still* Dougie didn't seem to get it. God, how messed up was Dougie that he didn't instinctively know where they needed to go? They were wasting fucking time here. If he didn't figure it out soon,

Mat would just have to pick a direction and hope. There had to be night guards or something prowling the halls, preventing slaves from escaping, preventing cops or even unwitting outsiders from getting in. They were running out of fucking *time*.

"Front door," he said, trying his best to whisper through the gag, but it came out as something a little closer to *hrnt oor*. Well, *oor* rhymed with door, at least. He tried again. *Oor. Oor.*

Click, and Dougie's addled fucking mind jumped into action. "You want to go out. A-are you sure that's a good idea?"

Good idea? Probably not, but it's our only option now. I have to get you out of here, good idea or not, suicide mission or not. Mat nodded.

"Follow me," Dougie sighed. Sniffled. Stepped forward.

Mat caught him by the arm and shook his head. *No.* Pointed. *You stay behind me.* He brandished his sticks. *If we come up against anybody, I want them tasing me first.*

"Please don't hurt anyone," Dougie whispered, and Mat's teeth dug so hard into the bit he hurt his fucking jaw, but Dougie slunk behind him and meekly pointed right. *Like an obedient little slave,* and that thought made Mat as sick with fury as Dougie's twisted fucking concern for the members of this twisted fucking household. No room for anger now, though, no room—just like in a match, and God, he'd never fought one so important, except for maybe the one he'd lost against the bruisers who'd first brought them to Madame's—so he forced it all down, buried it for later, and led Dougie right.

The hall was mostly dark, thin slivers of light spilling in from somewhere—moonlight through a window, perhaps, or maybe a guard's flashlight. His eyes had adjusted enough to see, but just barely, and every twitch and shadow sent his heart jumping, his hands jerking with the instinct to strike. He wouldn't have even half a second to spare if they stumbled across someone; he'd need to knock them out before they could alert anyone else, make any noise, scream for help.

But all the shadows were just shadows. No threat, no danger. Just an overactive limbic system in a house full of all-too-real horrors.

At last, the hall opened up onto the broad, fancy foyer he remembered from his first day here. He froze in the shadows of the archway, put an arm out to tuck Dougie behind him, then raised both sticks and peered ahead. The foyer was brighter, moonlight spilling in through oversized windows and reflecting off white marble tile. It was also empty. He poked his head around the edge of the wall, looked in one direction, then the other. Still no sign of anyone. Where were all the guards? Wasn't anyone on watch? Or was Nikolai so fucking *certain* of himself that he thought he didn't need them? Or maybe he just didn't want the unwashed masses polluting his house.

No. This is a trap. It has to be. You're missing something. Look again.

Except he didn't see anything out of the ordinary on second glance, either. Or on the third. And he couldn't cower in this fucking hallway forever. He was the one wasting time now.

He looked over his shoulder, locked eyes with Dougie, darted his gaze toward the front door and then back. Nodded once—*Are you ready?*

Dougie's chin wobbled, and the terror that bloomed in his eyes was so stark Mat was *sure* he'd rabbit. But he didn't. Just canted his head up and held his ground despite his fear. It broke Mat's fucking heart to think of how Nikolai had trained that discipline into him. He wished he knew what exactly Dougie was so afraid of right now. Was it the possibility of exposure, of being caught? Or was it the fear of leaving this place behind them for good?

Worry about it later, asshole. You have bigger problems right now.

Like getting the hell out of here. Speaking of which, it was time to bite the bullet. He turned back to Dougie one last time, gave him a brief, purposeful nod, and streaked across the foyer to the front door.

Unlocked. It was unlocked, too. After a long, lingering look through a decorative glass panel—*No guards, where are all the fucking guards?*—he threw it open.

And was hit face-on with cold air and starlight so fucking beautiful he could have cried.

Probably would've, if not for Dougie crowding up behind him, pressing right into his back, as stubborn as a barnacle.

This was it.

Freedom.

Gotta move. Appreciate it later. Preferably from the lobby of a police station.

Of course, the big fucking question was: where to *go*? They could follow the driveway, but if someone woke and noticed them missing, that'd be the first place they'd look. The forest was safer. Maybe they could parallel the driveway from thirty or forty feet deep in the tree line. Shit, he was freezing. His feet were already numb just standing out here on the porch. Maybe that was for the best, though; a single pair of wool socks wasn't exactly much protection from all the rocks and sticks and shit littering the forest floor, and at least this way he wouldn't feel the pain so much. Dougie was shivering too, but he was dressed pretty warm; Mat didn't think it was the cold making his little brother shake.

Damn it. Fuck shit damn! His fingers tightened around his sticks. He'd never wanted to hit something so badly in his entire life.

Behind him, Dougie made an awful little mewling sound. Like he'd sensed Mat's anger and was terrified by it. Mat forced himself to relax. Stay loose and easy. Stay sharp. Get moving. *Come on,* he tried to say, but it came out, "Kuh uh." Whatever, close enough. He darted down the stairs and onto the driveway, and Dougie followed. Still a lost puppy, hugging himself, body small and frightened as he darted behind Mat and followed him into the shadowy overgrowth.

Stay close, kiddo. Just like when we used to go running. Stay close to me.

Mat had never bought into the barefoot running fad, a fact that was becoming really apparent now. It felt like he was walking on broken glass, and they'd barely made it past the tree line. Oh well, at least out here in the wilderness there was no risk of stepping on somebody's used hypodermic like back in Vegas.

Dougie followed close behind, still hugging himself, breathing heavily so that plumes of white breath erupted from him like from a steam engine's stack. It was darker in the trees. Harder to see. Mat tripped over something, stumbled three or four feet down an incline, stubbed his toe before regaining his balance. He'd dropped one of his sticks in the process. Didn't really see a point in picking it back up. In tight quarters like these, poplar trunks growing skinny and close, he'd be better off bare-handed. He dropped the other stick. Squinted up through the canopy at the stars. Found the Big Dipper and then the North Star, off to his left. Which meant the mountain was sloping down to the east. Perfect. If they were anywhere near where the foliage seemed to suggest they were, the ranges in this area ran mostly north to south. Heading east meant they'd run into civilization sooner rather than later.

Except they didn't. The going was painfully slow in the dark and the muscle-cramping cold, especially with Dougie lagging behind, still sniffling like a child. Mat was freezing, and thirsty, and it was hard to breathe through this fucking gag, and God, he didn't even want to *think* about his feet. If he managed to survive this ordeal with all his toes intact, he'd be genuinely surprised. The cold had numbed nearly every inch of him, and what it didn't numb, it shot through with burning pins and needles. He lost sight of the driveway without even realizing it'd happened. Hiked down and hit a gulch. No way out but back up. Nearly fucking vertical. No easy feat wrapped in a fucking blanket. Dougie didn't seem to be faring much better. He was dressed more appropriately, but not for this, not for winter in the fucking mountains in the middle of the fucking night. The wind tore at their hair. Dougie looked . . . listless. Like he was going where Mat led him only because he couldn't bear to be alone. Like he hated every fucking step of it. Like a man walking to the gallows who didn't even have the balls to be indignant about it, just scared and small and sad.

They scrambled their way back up the other side of the gulch. Sat to rest, just for a moment. Too long was dangerous—they'd freeze if they stopped moving. Dougie pulled the folded bedsheet from his down jacket with trembling fingers and wrapped it around his head and shoulders. Turned to Mat, eyes wet and luminous in the moonlight, and spoke his first words in what must've been hours: "I want to go home."

I know, kiddo. I'm doing my best. We'll hit a town eventually, I promise. We'll talk to the cops. Maybe we'll get home, maybe they sold our home like Madame and Nikolai said, but it doesn't matter. We'll get a hotel, and then we'll get an apartment, and home will be wherever we're together. I'll take care of you. I'll never fail you again.

Dougie just blinked at him, shivered, shook his head like maybe he'd read Mat's thoughts right off his face. "Mat, I want to go *home*."

Fucking gag. Mat nodded back instead. Hauled himself to his throbbing feet. Reached out to take Dougie by the shoulders and pull him into a gentle hug. God, he could barely stand to touch the kid right now; it all felt so twisted and sexual. He wanted to hug his little brother like a normal person, hug him and pet his hair and even kiss him, and know one hundred percent that there was nothing ominous or inappropriate in it.

Damn Nikolai for taking that from them.

Dougie tore himself out of Mat's arms, hugged himself instead, tears streaking down a face twisted with grief and fury. "It's cold out and I'm tired and you're *lost*, Mat! It's not safe out here and you've . . . you've ruined *everything*, damn you! Why did you do this? Take me back. Take me back and we can still *fix this*. Nikolai can fix this!"

No stopping himself—Mat hauled back and slapped him.

Regretted it the instant the sound of impact rang out in the silent woods. Dougie crumpled, falling to his knees in the frost-covered duff. He cradled his cheek in both hands, sobbing bitterly.

God, what have I done?

"Take me home. Take me b-back. I hate you. I hate you." Dougie rocked himself, clutching his cheek. "Hate you. Hate you. Hate you."

Something in Mat's chest seized so hard he couldn't breathe for several long moments. He wanted to vomit. To scream. To rip Nikolai's face off and shove it up the fucker's ass.

"I *hate you*," Dougie spat again.

No, kiddo, no, you can't mean that. You can't mean that. I'm so sorry. I shouldn't have hit you, but damn it, what else am I supposed to fucking do?

Mat couldn't say any of it. He just crouched there, watching Dougie cry, repeating "Hate you" over and over until it stopped sounding like words. When Mat reached out to try to touch him, try to apologize by gesture at least, Dougie fell back, swinging wildly to knock Mat's hands away.

"Don't you fucking touch me, don't you fucking touch what's not yours! You don't get to touch me anymore. This is all your fucking fault! If you had protected me, if you hadn't gotten into those underground fights, started meeting all the wrong people! If you hadn't been so fucking stubborn, hadn't fought everyone at Madame's like a fucking animal and caught Nikolai's eye for it! If you—" He hiccupped a sob, swallowed it down, clutched at a handful of duff and hurled it at Mat's chest. "If you— If you hadn't let me go to fucking foster care in the f-first place . . ."

All true. All true. But none of that—*none* of that cut as deeply as what followed: "If you'd just *left* me back at Nikolai's where I f-fucking *belong*!"

Mat thumped to the ground, stunned senseless. It took him far too long to realize that awful keening noise wasn't coming from Dougie.

And fuck, but Dougie had shouted so loud they'd probably been heard for miles. How far had they gotten from the house? Would people be coming now? They needed to *move*. He stood back up, but when he tried to go, Dougie didn't follow.

Damn you. Get up. He grabbed Dougie by one wrist and *yanked*, not caring if he broke the kid's arm if it would just get him fucking *moving*. Not caring how much Dougie hated him. Let him—they could fix this later. They *would* fix this later.

As angry as Dougie was, that good slave-boy part of him responded to the harsh treatment; he let himself be pulled to his feet, and kept up when Mat took off at a stumbling run.

Over his harsh panting, he thought he heard that keening sound again, except this time he was certain it wasn't him. Wait . . . no. That wasn't keening, that was the sound of a car.

That was the sound of a fucking *car* driving on a fucking *highway*. No crunch of gravel, that sound Mat remembered so clearly from when he'd been taken here. Oh no, that was the sound of a good ol' public road. And public road meant friendly strangers, meant a sheriff's car, even. An ambulance. A fucking bus full of nuns, it didn't fucking matter. They'd flag down whoever it was, and hopefully Dougie would be together enough to ask to be taken to the police. But fucking hell, even if he didn't speak a word, what else was there to do but bring them to the cops or the ER? They were bleeding. Half-frozen. One of them naked but for a blanket and gag, the other crying inconsolably.

All they had to do was make it to that highway. Hope another car passed by soon.

Free. We're going to be free. We're going to go to the cops and I'm going to tell them everything and I'm going to bring this whole fucking operation down. The thought made him downright giddy.

Even if Dougie hates me for the rest of his life, at least he'll be free.

But maybe, just *maybe*, Dougie wouldn't hate him. Because when he took a second to think about it, he realized he wasn't dragging

Dougie anymore. Dougie was running *with* him, beside him, just like old times, and when Mat stole a glance at Dougie's face, he saw . . . God, was that *hope*? Excitement, even? Had he heard the car too and realized there was another answer, another way out of this mess?

Or was Mat just projecting his own wants and needs onto a half-second look in the near dark at his brother's moving face?

Whatever. Didn't matter. Road. Car. Freedom. *That* was what mattered.

They were both panting hard when they breached the tree line and emerged out onto the gravel shoulder of the two-lane highway, Mat struggling anew not to choke around the gag, to take in enough air through his running nose. It was quiet and dark, no sign of any vehicles, but that was okay. One would pass by soon. All they had to do was stay out of sight for now, pick a direction and keep walking until a car came from the east. If anyone was driving from Nikolai's house, they'd be coming *down* the mountain, from the west just like Dougie and Mat had. Mat wished he could communicate all that to Dougie, but the kid looked too shell-shocked and dazed to be signaling anyone of his own volition, anyway. He'd follow Mat's lead.

Because in his eyes, with Nikolai gone, you're *the master now.*

You even beat him like one.

No. Stop thinking about it.

He reached out and took Dougie's hand as they trudged along the shoulder. Held it tight. Dougie's fingers were as stiff and cold as his own, even half-stuffed in his jacket sleeves as they were. They'd ask whoever they flagged down to crank up the heat, and Mat would hold Dougie's hands to the vent. Prove he cared, that he wanted Dougie to be safe and well and comfortable. Prove he *loved* him, more than Nikolai ever had or would, because he didn't expect anything in return. Nothing at all.

I just want you to be safe. I just want to protect you.

He wished he could say it. Wished he could say anything at all, even if it was just *Holy shit, it's cold out here, hey kiddo?* Would they ever have a normal conversation like that again?

Don't think about the future. Keep your eyes on the road. Mat peered to the east, into the impenetrable darkness. Sometime during their little escapade, the moon had set, but there was no hint of the sunrise yet, either. And no streetlights on this windy mountain drive, so remote from civilization. No light pollution, either. *Too* remote. Nikolai had chosen well; he was like a civilized Leatherface, or something.

And wouldn't that suck, if they got this far only to freeze to death on the side of a highway, waiting for a savior who never came? *Keep walking, just keep walking. You won't freeze if you keep walking.* At least no snow had fallen yet.

He squeezed Dougie's hand. Dougie didn't squeeze back, but he kept pace beside him, and he didn't pull out of Mat's grip. Hard to make out his features, but the whole angle of his body, the set of his shoulders, told Mat that his hope was gone—if it'd ever been there in the first place, if Mat hadn't just been seeing what he'd wanted to see. Apparently mirages weren't just for deserts.

Dougie looked like he was on a fucking death march, just waiting for the end to come and swallow him up and take away his pain.

An end would come. Dougie's pain would be taken away, too. But not in the way he clearly thought.

And just like that, the brighter ending came: a car rattling up the highway from the east, an old rust bucket by the sound of it, its muddied headlights cutting a huge curve across the scenery as it rounded a bend, blinding Mat as they hit his eyes. Dougie, too, judging by how he shielded his face with his forearm.

Mat lurched forward, throwing himself onto the shoulder, waving his arms wildly.

"Help! Help!" he shouted through the gag, and then, halle-fucking-lujah, Dougie snapped from his fugue and joined in too, screaming in a high, hoarse, but clear voice: "Help! Please, help us!"

When it started to look like the car might pass them by, Mat realized just how insane he and Dougie might seem to some innocent driver. Like a pair of drunks or drug addicts, or worse, some psycho kinksters out cruising for unwilling victims. Fuck-all knew how long it'd be before another car came along. He couldn't take the chance of losing this one, not after all the screaming they'd just done, not after everything they'd been through, not after Dougie had finally snapped out of his fucking nightmare and realized it'd all just been some awful dream. He *couldn't*.

Without another thought, he freed his hand from Dougie's and ran full tilt into the middle of the road. If the car hit him, so be it. At least then it would have to stop. At least Dougie would make it home.

It didn't hit him.

The driver braked hard, swerved nearly sideways, but managed to pull the car to a stop just a few feet short of impact.

Dougie rushed up beside Mat and grabbed his hand like he thought he could stop him *now* from throwing himself into the road. The figure inside the car seemed to stare at them for a moment, unmoving, and he and Dougie stared back at the darkened shape of him—her?—behind the wheel, afraid to spook their would-be savior, afraid he'd start up again and run them over, afraid that if they stepped out of the way for even a second, he'd just take off into the night and—junker or not—leave them in his dust.

But then the driver waved to them, leaned across the front seat, and threw open the passenger door.

The time for hesitation and caution had passed. Do or die, quite literally.

Still clutching to each other, tears streaming down both their cheeks, Mat and Dougie rushed over and climbed inside.

THE FLESH

SEASON 3: TRANSFORMATION

CARTEL

EPISODE 10: FALSE GODS

CHAPTER ONE

Mat had quite deliberately steered Dougie into the backseat rather than the front, despite the open passenger door. He didn't know this person, this shadowed would-be rescuer with a knit cap pulled low over his forehead against the winter chill, and though he *hoped*, he couldn't bring himself to trust. So he clung to Dougie as long as he could—*safe, he's safe, he's finally safe, please let it be true*—as they settled in the back of the car. Had to force himself to let go, turn away just for a moment, so he could close the door.

"Slowly, now."

Mat froze, arm outstretched toward the open car door. Tried to swallow past his dry throat. Felt a fresh chill crawl up and down his clammy, frigid skin.

He knew that voice.

Of course he did.

Roger. Turned around in the driver's seat, arm extended, the muzzle of a handgun jabbed into Dougie's cheek. Dougie, trembling and tear-streaked, so wide-eyed Mat could see the blue of them even in the dark car.

"Close. The. Door."

Don't hurt him. You're supposed to be my friend. Please don't hurt him.

Very slowly, every inch of him fighting not to run like a fucking coward and leave Dougie behind, Mat reached for the door handle with one hand, the other hand palm up near his head. Pulled the door carefully shut—no sudden movements, no loud startling noises. He heard the click of the automatic locks, noticed immediately there was no way to open them again from the backseat—someone had broken off the manual lock lever—and by the time he'd turned back again, the gun was pointed squarely at the center of his chest.

Good. Better him than Dougie.

Roger squeezed the trigger, and the world went black.

"*No!*" Dougie threw himself at the gap between the front seats, knocking Roger's hand away, knocking the *gun* away, but he was too late, too late, heard a too-quiet pop-hiss and Mat grunted and jerked, hand flying to his chest and then slumping, limp as the rest of him, in the darkened chasm of the backseat. "No!" Dougie screamed again, even though it was too late, even as Roger shoved him against his seat with a hard hit to the sternum from the butt of the gun.

"It's just a tranq dart. Master doesn't want him rabbiting again. I don't have to shoot you too, do I?"

"No," Dougie said, for the third time, but this time it was a sad little whisper. It seemed to be enough for Roger, though, who lowered the gun and then lifted a cell phone to his ear. Distantly, Dougie heard ringing, heard the faint "Hello, Roger" from Nikolai on the other end. His chest hitched at the sound, one-quarter conditioned pleasure, three-quarters terror.

"I've got them, Master."

Speech from Nikolai then, something short that Dougie couldn't make out beyond the general tone of satisfaction.

"No, no trouble, Master." Pause. "Yes, Master, just like you said, about half a mile south of the forest service road. We'll be there soon."

He hung up, pointed a silent finger at Dougie—*You be good now, you hear?*—then turned and started the car.

Started back to Nikolai's.

Dougie eyed the dart sticking out of Mat's chest, fingers itching to remove it, but instead he clenched them in his lap. Pressed himself against his seat, exactly equidistant between the dangerous car door and his dangerous brother. Not touching anything. Especially not Mat.

Mat, who wasn't dead but wasn't alive either, wasn't okay, would never be okay again, not anymore, not now that Roger was dragging them back there. But Dougie? Dougie was fucking *relieved*, at least in part, to be going back to Nikolai, back to routine and responsibility, all the things that Mat didn't have, that Nikolai wouldn't give him.

Mat deserved to be free. *Needed* to be free.

Dougie wasn't sure what he needed. Didn't even know what he *wanted*. To be free out in the wilds by his brother's side, or to be a *good boy*, loved and safe and cherished?

He wished he'd never run. When he'd woken up this morning things had been so clear and simple, and now they were all fucked up. Roger was focused on the road, no answers coming from the back of his head, and Dougie was too afraid to ask the questions because what if he never stopped? Questioning, that's what had brought him here in the first place, questions and doubts cracking away at his safety and certainty and what had it gotten him?

Your brother back. Yourself *back. Clarity. Distance. Perspective.*

Yeah, and what had *that* gotten him? Nothing but fucking trouble. What the fuck was he supposed to *do* with perspective in a locked fucking car or a locked fucking room in a locked fucking house in the middle of nowhere with a master who wouldn't let him keep it? Oh God, he'd have to start all the fuck *over* again now, wouldn't he? Have to . . . have to *suffer* again, bleed again, *need* again before he could ever kneel again at Nikolai's feet and mean it, be happy there, survive and thrive, and *fuck* Mat for forcing that on him, for stripping him of weeks, months of labor, of scant inches torturously gained. He couldn't go back to that. He *couldn't*. He didn't want to *be* Nikolai's good boy again. Wouldn't survive another transformation.

Another breaking. He broke *you.*

But you were happy then.

No. He turned to Mat, slumped on the seat beside him, thought of all his brother had tried to do, how brave (*foolish!*) he'd always been, how strong (*stupid!*), how willing to risk it all for what mattered (*prideful and stubborn!*), thought, *I should be more like him. I should be brave. I should take control of my own life. I should stop this.*

He looked at the back of Roger's head again. Roger's hands on the wheel. Roger's car on some dark lonely two-lane highway in the middle of nowhere. He could grab Roger. Choke him. Snap his neck, even, like he'd seen in the movies. Except he wasn't that strong, was he? But he *could* grab his arms and make him swerve the car, and maybe they'd all die in some dark ditch but at least that would be the end of it. This sad fucking story.

Or maybe it wouldn't. Maybe Mat would die and Roger would die and you'd have killed them both and Nikolai would never take you back and you'd be alone, all alone, fucked-up and unlovable and lost.

Or he could go back. Go back and take his punishment and let Nikolai fix him no matter how much it hurt, how long it took, and then be happy again. Loved again. Never, ever alone again.

You scaredy-cat. Chickenshit. Coward.

No. Just . . . practical. He wanted to live. No matter what that took, no matter how ugly it might get, he wanted to *live*. And he wanted Mat to live, and Roger to live, and even if he did crash the car and even if they did all survive, what then? Nikolai would just send more men when they didn't return.

Nikolai's punishment would come. It was always going to come, and there was no stopping it, and wasn't that what Dougie wanted? A world that made sense, a world that followed rules, a world where what you saw was what you got and every promise was fulfilled.

I want to go home. *Back to school and back to Vegas and back to Serena Chang's tits half falling from her too-tight shirt. Home.*

Nikolai *is your home now.*

Oh God, maybe he should crash the car after all. Just crash it and kill himself and put an end to this fucking shouting match in his skull.

But too late again, too late. The tires were already crunching up the graveled driveway. For all the hours he'd stumbled blindly behind Mat, stupidly trusting, stupidly *hopeful*, the drive back to Nikolai's had only taken ten or fifteen minutes. God, they'd been fooling themselves even worse than he'd thought, hadn't they? There'd never been any hope at all. They hadn't gotten *anywhere*.

No wonder there hadn't been any guards. They'd never stood a fucking chance.

Roger pulled up in front of the house, put the car into park, and turned to face Dougie. Dougie didn't miss the tranq gun held firmly in one of Roger's hands. Steady hands. A man with no split loyalties. A man who, yesterday, he thought he might've died for, if the need had arisen. But now . . . God, what *now*? He felt . . . nothing. Not even hate.

Roger inclined his head toward the house. Toward where Nikolai was no doubt waiting to bring Dougie back to heel. "It's not too late to fix things," Roger said, and Dougie *hated* how sincere he sounded, how sympathetic, how *loving*. "I know it may seem like it is, but it's not. The master is a reasonable man, and he cares about you very much. I think you know that."

Dougie wasn't willing to reply to that last bit, not just now, because he *didn't* know that. Oh, he did, he *did*, but at the same time . . .

Instead he just lowered his eyes, stared at his hands fidgeting in his lap because it was so much easier than looking at Mat or Roger or the house, and said, "I'll go quietly." Because, really, what else was he supposed to do? What options did he have? The thought of walking back through that door twisted his insides so bad his heart felt choked by his lower intestines, but fighting would only make things worse. So, so much worse.

"I know you will, little guy." Roger killed the engine, and the locks popped. "Go on up. He's waiting for you. I'll deal with your brother."

"But—" Dougie looked to Roger, to Mat still slumped unconscious beside him, to Roger again. "I mean, aren't you—" *coming with me? I can't do this alone. I'm not strong enough. I'll run, I'll panic, I'll stand frozen in the yard until the cold takes me, I'll . . . I'll . . .* Please.

Roger smiled sadly and shook his head. "You need to make the choice, Douglas. You need to prove to the master—and to *yourself*—that you're strong enough. You are, I know it. I've seen it. You've made some terrible choices tonight, it's true, but your brother can't mislead you now; you'll make the right choice this time."

Dougie wished he had half as much faith in himself as everyone else seemed to. Roger, Mat, Nikolai. But he'd let everyone down, hadn't he. Every last one of them. Even though they each expected different and conflicting things, he'd somehow still fucked up in every conceivable direction. Why did they still believe in him? Why did they still keep him around?

It didn't matter why, only that they did.

Dougie took a deep breath, opened the car door, put one foot in front of the other.

His fate was waiting. The least he could do was walk to it like a man.

CHAPTER TWO

J ust like before, the front door was unlocked. Except this time, Dougie didn't have Mat to hide behind. And he *knew* what was waiting on the other side.

His captor. His torturer. His master.

His lover.

The stereo was on in the living room, soft classical music drifting into the front foyer, nearly too quiet to hear. It felt all at once like the soundtrack to a fated love story and to a slasher film, and Dougie swallowed down his dread and followed the notes. Didn't even have to force his feet to move; they went on their own, as trapped by the sheer inevitability of *Nikolai* as the rest of him was.

He found the man at ease on the huge antique armchair near the fireplace in the massive living room, a space where Dougie had spent many happy hours curled at Nikolai's feet or draped over his lap, reading to him or just keeping him company while he watched old movies. Now, Nikolai was sitting like a king in his throne, one side of his face cast into sharp shadows and angles by the light of the fire. In front of him now, Dougie didn't even feel like a man. He didn't realize he'd fallen to his knees, hadn't meant to, but here he was, looking up at Nikolai from the floor.

"Hello, boy. Back from your little excursion?" His face revealed nothing. Not anger, not happiness, not frustration . . . nothing. His eyes glittered dark in the firelight.

Dougie swallowed. Swallowed again. The fire had sapped every drop of moisture from the room, from his body. He didn't know what to say here. Didn't know how to react because he didn't know how *Nikolai* was reacting, and if there was one thing he knew for certain in all this clusterfuckery, it was that his fate was in Nikolai's hands.

Best not to keep him waiting, then. He opened his mouth, and "Yes, sir" came out. Not "Yes, Master" like he realized he should've

said. Like he would've said yesterday without hesitation or thought—
with pride, even. With love.

Fuck Mat. Fuck him and his fucking stupid gallant stupid plan.

"Is that all you have to say?"

"I . . ." No, he had more to say, *so much* more to say, but it was
dangerous, all of it, and Nikolai fucking *terrified* him now. "You want
me to say I'm sorry," he found himself saying, his damn mouth working
on its own again, and he clapped his hands over it, mortified. He was
in enough fucking trouble already, thank you very much.

Yet Nikolai's expression didn't so much as twitch. He lifted one
hand from its resting place on his thigh in a little I-can't-quite-even-
be-bothered-to-shrug sort of way, and said, "I want you to tell me the
truth."

"I wish I'd never left." There, that was easy. A truth Nikolai would
like. So why was he still fucking talking? "I wish we'd gotten away. I
wish you hadn't put us together in the first place." He sniffed, broke
position to swipe at his nose, and Jesus, when had he gotten into
position? "I *told* you I was fragile!" he shouted, and he hadn't meant
to do *that*, either. "I'm broken now! You broke me. Mat broke me. I
see now. I *remember*. I don't . . . I don't want to be what you made me
again." And yet he laid his hands palm-up on his thighs, squared his
shoulders. The good little pet. "I hate it. I hate you."

"Oh my sweet, stupid boy." Nikolai stood, and he was *towering*
over Dougie, elevated from king to god, and then he dropped to one
knee, just a man again somehow. He took Dougie's chin in his hand
and laid a soft kiss on his lips, and Dougie wanted to tear away, to
bite him, to spit into his mouth, but he was too afraid and what good
would it do him anyway? "I'm so happy you're home."

No. Be mad at me. Be furious. *I just told you to go fuck yourself, I
just told you I hated you and hated me and hated what you've done to me.
Don't love me, you fuck. Don't.* Don't.

"I know this wasn't your idea, Douglas. You were just doing what
I taught you to do, what you were *meant* to do: submitting to another
man. But your brother isn't a man, even though he styles himself as
one. He's a *slave*, Douglas."

Yes. And so am I. Thinking anything else was vapor and air. Foolish.
Dangerous. He was trapped here, could never go home, could never

escape his fate. Whatever glimmer of hope he might've been holding out for that, it was gone now. Mat had ruined that too. He couldn't go backward. And the only way forward now was through. Suck it up. Take his licks. Put himself in Nikolai's hands again, no matter how much they were sure to hurt him. At least, when it was over, there'd be no more pain. No more confusion. No more doubt. "Yes, sir."

"And I suppose I owe you an apology, too, for not recognizing how weak and impressionable you still are. That you wouldn't be able to understand the nuance between a man who merely seeks to dominate you, and one who truly *deserves* to."

Nikolai pressed Dougie against his chest, wrapped his arms around Dougie's back and rested his chin on the top of Dougie's head. Loving and possessive all at once, as if to demonstrate what a *deserving* man felt like.

Was returning to the fold really going to be this easy, after everything?

No. This won't be easy because you still hate it all. You'll always hate it all if he doesn't destroy you again. Break you. Remake you.

Maybe this time, if he was lucky, Nikolai wouldn't leave any stray bits of his old self lying around to trip him up again.

Apparently, hug time was over; Nikolai eased him back, held him by the shoulders and looked down into his eyes. "So I'm sorry, Douglas, I truly am, but I also can't let this behavior stand. You clearly have lessons yet to learn. Time to teach you the difference between a *master* and a common brute bully."

Yes. Please. I need it. I don't want to hate anymore.

"And, while we're at it, remind you of the value of a master who *loves* you. Who values and cherishes you. Who cares for your happiness."

God yes. Tell me. Whatever it is, I'll do it. Make me love you again. Make me love myself again. Please.

"Remember when I taught you the value of pleasure?"

The plugs. The cage. The milking. Days and days and *days* of horrible pain, ending in surrender and revelation and sweet release.

"Yes, sir."

"How did I teach you that lesson, Douglas?"

"Through denial, sir."

"Very good. And now is the time to deny you again."

Of love. Pleasure. Happiness. All the gifts Nikolai had given him over the past weeks and months. *God, please, no. No, no, no.*

"Starting with these." Dougie hadn't seen Nikolai draw a knife, but there it was, wicked sharp and long and curved and glittering with firelight like it had been forged in hell. With his other hand, Nikolai grasped the fabric of Dougie's coat. "These clothes were a gift, Douglas, and you sullied them. You used them against me."

"I'm sorry!" Dougie sobbed, because Jesus, he really was—sorry he'd ever followed Mat out that door, sorry he'd ever been reminded of *before*, sorry he'd angered Nikolai and *especially* sorry that he'd slid back so far, so far, would have to suffer so fucking *much* again to become something he didn't even fucking want to *be*. But it was too late again, too fucking late, like every fucking thing this whole fucking night. The glinting tip of the blade slid beneath the collar of Dougie's coat. One swift, decisive movement, and the fabric split, feathers and down flying everywhere, and all Dougie could think was *He's going to make me clean this up later and it's going to take me all fucking night.* Another slice. Another. Another. Surgically precise. The fabric slumped from Dougie's shoulders and then fell to the floor in ragged pieces.

Nikolai made quick work of his sweater, and then had Dougie stand so he could cut the button from the fly of his jeans before tugging the denim taut and slicing down from Dougie's waist all the way to right behind his balls. A twist of the blade from there and Nikolai had split the seam wide, opening the most vulnerable part of his body to the sharp tip of the blade.

He felt the flat of the knife scrape along that sensitive skin, and then it turned, following his inseam down until the whole pant leg hung open. The other leg next. The jeans fell, scraps of denim pooling at his feet. Dougie realized he was panting, his newly naked body slick with sweat.

Would Nikolai fuck him now? Complete this ritual, reassert his place as master? Dougie almost wished he would. It was easy to give his body, even if it was painful, even if Nikolai didn't prepare him at all. It would be easy to suffer the pain, take Nikolai's cock and Nikolai's teeth and Nikolai's cum. Do that enough times and he'd be new again, the broken toy repaired in Nikolai's image. No more pain, then. No more pain.

But that wasn't what happened.

"Throw it all in the fire, Douglas, and kneel there until it's burned away. I want you to watch my gifts to you crumble into nothing but ash and smoke. And as you watch, I want you to think of the life you worked so hard to build for yourself here, and how you almost made ash and smoke of that too, and of how saving what's left of it will mean reaching into the fire—willingly thrusting your hands into cleansing flame. You *can* save it, though. I'll help you to save it. I'll help you to rebuild, because I love you and I would never fail you, never disappoint you, never leave you dangling alone in the world. Because you are worth more to *me* than these clothes—my gifts, my love—were to *you*."

No! Dougie wanted to protest. *I do love you, I'm sorry, I'm so sorry, you're everything to me, oh God.*

But he didn't. He didn't because he didn't *feel* it anymore, not really, not like he used to in his heart and his gut and the rawest, most primal centers of his brain. He only knew that he should. That he once had. That he needed to—*desperately* needed to—again.

Wanted to, even. Felt the singed edges of it, the remnants of this ruined night. Burning hot to the touch, but he'd cling to it, drag it back, take it in. He *would*. He just needed . . . he needed . . .

"Punish me, Master." He gathered his tattered clothes in his arms, crawled over to the fire, threw them in. A strange erection throbbed between his legs, hungry for something he'd never wanted before. "*Please.*"

Nikolai shook his head. "Oh Douglas, I do intend to. But not in the way you want, because that wouldn't teach you anything at all."

The clothes caught slowly, as if the fire were just as reluctant to destroy the evidence of Nikolai's love as Dougie was. He shook his head. He didn't need to be taught, to learn, because that involved thinking. He needed to *stop* thinking.

Then do. Trust Nikolai. He'll fix this. He'll make it right.

Oh, how *easy* it was to think that, how naturally it came, how *right* it felt. For the first moment since he'd climbed into Roger's car, he was beginning to believe he could have that again, do that again, trust like that again. It wouldn't be easy. But maybe . . . maybe it'd be worth it.

A silhouette, framed by the doorway. Roger, ever the perfect slave, not entering the room without an invitation.

"I'm ready for him now, Master."

I'm ready too.

This room was new. Not that Dougie had seen many down here in Nikolai's basement, but so far he'd been spared the sort of harshness that lay beyond the door Roger led him to and then through. Like a dungeon, all raw cinderblock and concrete, irons dangling from the ceiling and bolted to the walls, rack upon rack of implements purpose-built to inflict pain. He'd experienced a few, but not many. Some he couldn't even identify.

And there, in the corner, strapped by his wrists, hips, and ankles to the iron frame of a twin bed without a mattress, lay Mat. Still gagged, glaring up at the ceiling as he struggled and pulled against the fat leather straps. Beside his bed stood another, empty, and Dougie assumed that was for him. After all, if he was meant to share Mat's bed—to rape his brother—Nikolai would be here to watch.

Except Nikolai wasn't here, and Dougie couldn't decide if that was for the better or the worse. Part of him wanted Nikolai, *craved* him—needed his master to give meaning to the suffering he knew would come, to care enough to oversee his punishment, to watch his penance and see the moment when he'd at last repent and mean it. Hold him after. Welcome him home.

But the rest of him—the part his stupid fucktard of a brother had shaken so forcibly awake tonight—was sickened by that thought. Terrified of its sheer inevitability. Maybe if Nikolai wasn't here, Dougie could keep his head, not give in, suffer without letting it change him.

No purpose to this pain.

No. Dougie didn't want that, either. He liked order and meaning and rules and cause and effect, and Nikolai gave him those things, and maybe the price was worth paying. Besides, he wasn't like Mat, wasn't strong enough to endure and endure for nothing, for ever. He'd held on to such stupid romantic notions once, but now he knew what *real* suffering was, and there wasn't anything romantic about it at all.

"Go lie down," Roger instructed, none of the usual warmth in his voice. Did he like this, being Nikolai's right-hand man, even for the ugliest jobs? Or was it just a burden he bore, the price *he* paid?

Roger sighed. It seemed he was no better at the tough-love facade than Dougie was at the tough-man facade. "I'm trying to help you," Roger said. "Don't make this worse than it already is."

Even if he hadn't added that bit, Dougie still would have gone willingly. He went to the bed beside his brother's and lay down. Didn't struggle or fight when Roger buckled him into the thick leather straps, even though the raw metal frame bit miserably into his skin. Mat was struggling enough for the both of them now, shouting around his gag, shaking his head. Like he couldn't *believe* Dougie would so easily submit to bondage. Or maybe Mat just knew what was coming and couldn't bear the thought of Dougie having to endure it; he might still hate Dougie, but old habits were hard to break, Dougie knew that better than most. Nikolai had said that Mat spent much more time being punished and facing consequences than Dougie ever had. *Bad* habits were hard to break, too.

Roger finished strapping him down, and Dougie braced himself for whatever might come next. Tried not to be afraid. He needed this, after all. Deserved it, even. Maybe when it was over, things could go back to the way they were before. Nikolai would take him back. He would want to *be* taken back.

Standing up straight above them, looking at neither of them, Roger spoke. "So. The master has instructed me to tell you that since you decided to tie your fates to one another instead of to him, you'll both be punished the same. Bound by pain."

A beating, then? Would Roger take one of the whips or canes or paddles off the wall and beat them both? Make him scream in front of Mat, who already found him weak and disgusting? And probably ten times more weak and disgusting after tonight's debacle. Was that the plan? Make it so that whatever thin thread of brotherly affection and responsibility still bound Mat to Dougie would snap?

And what of Dougie? Would Roger make even the great and mighty Mathias Carmichael beg and cry? Did Nikolai mean for

Dougie to see that even the man he'd once worshipped could be brought so low? Remind Dougie that no one—*no one*—could hold out forever so he'd best just let go now before he caused himself unnecessary pain?

Roger didn't move to fetch a whip, though. Or a paddle or a crop or anything else. Just reached into his pants pocket with one hand and pulled out . . . What the hell was that? Dougie strained to lift his head off the bed frame, get a closer look. Some kind of marker, maybe?

Whatever it was, it was apparently worse than any cane or strap, because once Roger had pulled his hand out of his pocket, Mat's howls intensified, became almost animalistic. No, not *almost* animalistic—he sounded like an injured stray at a shelter, backed into a corner by threatening strangers. Even through the gag, there was no mistaking the *No* and *Don't* and *Please* spilling on an endless loop from Mat's mouth.

Whatever was in Roger's hand, there was no way it could be as serious as Mat was making it out to be. And fuck him and his panic, anyway—wasn't he supposed to be the strong one for Dougie? He'd gotten them into this, after all, fucking dragged Dougie by the ear out of the house and into the woods and away from his master and any chance he'd had at a happy life, and now he was cowering and begging like Dougie at his absolute fucking worst and "Would you *shut the fuck up?*" Dougie shouted, because he was *sick* of this shit, the unfairness of it all, the pretending to be one thing and then behaving like another and he *needed* Mat to not fucking do this. "Just shut up! Shut up and take it like a fucking man, you ass!"

The noise cut off as suddenly as if Dougie had struck him, and when Dougie turned his head to look at Mat, see what bullshit excuse was printed on his face, Mat was blinking back at him, eyes huge and wounded, mouth slack around the gag and a single tear tracking its way down his cheek. His chest was still heaving, but he'd stopped struggling. He looked . . . sorry. And terrified. But mostly sorry.

Yeah, well, he should be. What kind of man was he, to get them into such deep shit and then balk at the consequences? Well, Dougie would show him how to bear it with dignity. Maybe he'd learn a thing or two. Learn to accept his place with grace and poise, like a slave was supposed to. *And lead me not into temptation anymore.*

Mat turned away from Dougie—probably couldn't bear the reprobation in Dougie's eyes, and wow, big bro was just revealing himself as one kind of chicken after another tonight, wasn't he? He looked to Roger instead, started trying to talk to him. Well, grunting around his gag, jerking his arms as far as the straps would let him, like he was trying to gesture.

Roger moved to stand by Mat's head, reached back into his pocket, and pulled out a second whatever-it-was. Placed them both in one palm and held them just over Mat's chest.

Mat stopped jerking and nodded. Frantically. Huffed what Dougie thought was a *Please* around his gag.

But then Roger straightened up and shook his head and said, "No, I'm sorry, it doesn't work that way. Not this time." Mat squeezed his eyes shut, and a few fresh tears leaked from the corners. He shook his head. Grunted another *Please*, more insistent than the last.

"I'm sorry," Roger said again, and Dougie's anger—quashed momentarily by curiosity—began to rise again. Whatever magical fucking psychic exchange they were having, it was fucking *rude* to be excluding him from it, he was *right here* for fuck's sake, and he was so. Fucking. Tired of all the bullshit. Just wanted this over and done with. Mat had already fallen off his pedestal and broken into a million pieces; nothing left for Dougie to do now but crawl away from the shards and hope he wouldn't cut himself as he went. Hope he'd still be fit for Nikolai's love when he came back.

Roger's back straightened, and in the blink of an eye his arm had moved, striking as fast as a snake. Oh, it was an auto-injector, like an EpiPen. Stuck in Mat's naked, trembling thigh now, and God, the *noise* Mat made at that, like some broken pup, like he was *dying*, half-swallowed like he didn't want Dougie to hear. Roger pulled the needle free. Rubbed at the site of the injection a second or two, then ran a hand over the top of Mat's head. Tears were squeezing out of Mat's eyes, and he was sniffling and hiccupping, teeth digging so hard into the gag Dougie half expected it to break.

Just stop looking at him.

A shadow fell over Dougie, and now Roger was standing over him, holding the second auto-injector in his fist. Dougie nodded at him, determined to show up Mat. He hoped that somewhere, Nikolai was watching. That somewhere, Nikolai would see how obedient Dougie was being, what a good brave boy. "Go ahead. I'm not afraid."

"I know you're not," Roger said, but he didn't seem proud or impressed. More upset than anything. Sad, maybe. Or angry. Dougie thought he knew Roger pretty well, but right now . . . right now he felt as if Roger were a stranger. Well, maybe he was. They'd been nearly brothers, there, at least for a while, but now some crucial understanding between them had been eroded away. Because Roger couldn't comprehend any reason to ever try to leave their master, while Dougie, even if only for a fleeting moment, *had*, and there was no bridging that.

Off to his right, Mat lurched and wailed, rattling the bed frame, and Roger winced.

"I'm not afraid," Dougie said again, even though he kind of was now. How could he not be, hearing the noises Mat was making? Mat, who'd take a beating in the ring that would bring most men to tears ten times over, and then brush himself off and go party half the night. Mat, his stupid, stubborn, strong-as-an-ox, fatally prideful brother.

Roger brushed thoughtful fingers over Dougie's bare thigh, like he was trying to re-map Dougie, find his way back to the man he knew Dougie could be. Should be. Had been, before Mat had ruined everything. Dougie wished he had a hand free, just so he could grasp Roger's, show him how serious he was when he said, "Help me come home, Roger."

Roger slammed the auto-injector into his thigh.

CHAPTER THREE

ougie had been sure he was going to die, couldn't foresee any other outcome to this unending agony, but suddenly he was surfacing into awareness, the pain still lapping at his body but most definitely receding. The tide going out. And when it did, what would be left of him—of his body, his sanity, his dignity—on the shore? He couldn't ponder it too closely, wade too deep; he'd drown again, drown except he wouldn't die, just lie there and suffocate and *suffer*, and the thought scared him so badly he choked on it.

He could hear himself crying now. Felt that he'd wet himself, too. That was new. For a while, the pain had wiped out all his other senses, sight, sound, taste, touch, smell, all of it subsumed by *pain*, which was the real sixth sense, fuck that bull about clairvoyance.

God, he stank like piss. Almost hurt too much to care. Heard a whimper he was pretty sure he hadn't made, turned his head toward the sound, and this time the whimper was *definitely* him, sand or iron filings or maybe broken glass grinding in the vertebrae of his neck.

When he could open his eyes again, Mat filled his vision. Sweaty and blotchy and tear-streaked, so still and pale with exhaustion and pain he looked dead.

Maybe I'd be better off that way.

He was too tired and wrung out to feel guilty about or disgusted by that thought, and anyway, the next moment Mat clenched his teeth on his gag, eyebrows tightening, and let out a low grunt. Definitely not dead. Dougie's own nervous system flared in symphony, or maybe sympathy, and he grunted too.

This is his fault. He brought this on us both.

Good. Use that. Grip it tight and never let it go. His fault. His fault. His fault. Hate him for it. Push him away. He's standing between you and Nikolai. Let him, and you'll just end up suffering like this again.

No. *God* no. He couldn't. He'd die. He'd make sure of it before he let this happen to him again.

He needed Nikolai. Needed Nikolai to come in and call him his good boy and his precious little pet and rationalize away all of Dougie's hurt and betrayal until he understood down to his bones why he had to be in so much pain and how much *better* that pain was going to make him. Nikolai would make sense, so much sense, too much sense, and then it would all be okay. He'd be happy again. Loved again. And he'd love back, and he wouldn't hurt anymore, and this whole horrible night would fade from his mind, just as surely as the pain would fade from his muscles and bones.

He'd be cleansed.

Yes.

The tide of pain washed back. Drew away. Dougie closed his eyes and slept.

Woke again almost free of pain, body heavy and exhausted and *desperately* thirsty but only hurting from overtaxed muscles and the uncomfortable bed he was strapped to and the bruises from the straps themselves. But none of that bone-deep grinding or sharp sparks of burning under the skin.

And *oh God thank you* Nikolai was here. A silhouette in the doorway, broad shoulders, stiff posture. Dougie wished his arms were free so he could hold them up, beg to be carried and held like a child. But instead he just lay back and waited, waited for Nikolai to come to his side.

Mat was gone, he realized. The bed beside him emptied and scrubbed meticulously clean while he'd slept. He started to wonder what was happening to Mat, whether this was the end of his punishment or just the beginning, but then reminded himself that he didn't give a fuck. Mat had brought this on himself and Nikolai was here, Nikolai was *here*, and he was all that mattered to Dougie. Had to be all that mattered if he didn't want to end up here again, strapped down in a dungeon and begging to die to stop the pain.

But then Nikolai stepped forward and the shadows fell from his face and he wasn't Nikolai at all. He was . . . someone else, a man Dougie had never seen before, middle-aged and handsome but wearing an expression crueler than even Jeremy's at his most bitter.

So this was how it was going to be, then? Of course he hadn't earned Nikolai's forgiveness. After all, he hadn't really *done* anything. Enduring pain was impressive, but passive. Of course Nikolai would expect Dougie to act, rather than simply be acted upon, in order to be forgiven. It was foolish of him to expect anything less.

But Dougie would earn that forgiveness. He *would*. He *had to*.

He lay still, trying not to let his fear or hurt show. Whoever this man was, Dougie would obey and serve him as if he were Nikolai himself. Yes, that had to be the best course of action now. Prove that even in his absence, Nikolai's training had truly made an impression on Dougie.

He just wished he could reclaim the feelings of *contentment* and *rightness* that had, until so recently, accompanied his obedience. But, if he were honest with himself, all he really felt now was fear. Panic. Desperation. Those old familiar friends he knew so well and couldn't fucking seem to escape.

"Hello, doggie." *No, it's Dougie*, he thought, but then realized his mistake. A heavy hand landed on top of his head and tangled itself in his hair. Gave an insistent tug.

For all his intentions, Dougie wasn't in enough control of his exhausted body to squash the pained whine that escaped his mouth.

"I'm Luke," the man said. *The one who killed the chicken*, Dougie's fevered mind filled in.

He's ruthless. He doesn't show mercy.

Dougie was a person, though, not a chicken.

Or maybe he wasn't a person after all, considering Luke had greeted him as "doggie."

Maybe Luke doesn't kill dogs. Maybe he just kicks and beats them instead.

"I—" Dougie started, but then realized he had no idea what he was supposed to say. But it seemed rude not to reply at all.

"What was that, doggie?" Luke asked. "You're thirsty? I bet. I hear you've been down here screaming your lungs out and crying and pissing yourself for hours. That's bound to make any pup a little dehydrated."

Or maybe he's kind after all. Maybe killing is its own mercy. Maybe he's kind.

Except Luke's voice didn't sound kind at all.

"Anyway, Master wants you to spend some time with me and my boys. Teach you some basic fuckin' appreciation for how good you got it here. But I'll get you a drink first."

"Please," Dougie rasped. Wow, his voice really was rough. Felt like he'd swallowed a big handful of broken glass. "Sir."

Luke nodded, and Dougie waited for him to get a cup, to unstrap Dougie's hands. But instead, he moved closer—climbed right onto the miserable bed frame and then straddled Dougie, sat on his chest and ground Dougie's back into the metal slats and Jesus, he *couldn't breathe* with this mountain on top of him, muscles already weakened and growing weaker by the second and then Luke was grabbing his jaw and pressing something to his lips and suddenly Dougie knew *exactly* how this would go.

No. God, please, no. Not that, not now.

But he'd been too well trained, and he was far, far too desperate to claw back into Nikolai's good graces, so he opened his mouth and sealed his lips around Luke's soft cock, and when Luke let loose a hot salty flood of bitter wretchedness against Dougie's tongue, Dougie swallowed like a *good boy*.

Choked and sputtered and *oh God* it was running out his mouth, up his nose, into his fucking *sinuses* and he'd be smelling and tasting this for fucking *ever* and it *wouldn't fucking stop* but he just kept on swallowing and swallowing.

"Ahhh," Luke sighed, and sat back again. Zipped his flaccid dick back into his mud-spattered jeans. "Good dog. Man, you must love the taste of piss to guzzle mine up like that. Guess I better remember that for later."

Dougie was too disgusted with Luke—with himself—and too busy trying to keep himself from puking to reply, so he just shut his eyes and nodded. *I'll be good. Whatever you want from me. Just, please, help me come home.*

"Yeah, that's right. You 'n' me are gonna have a good time then. Let me just grab your collar—dogs gotta be leashed on this nice property, you understand—and then we can be on our merry way. *Stay.*" He hopped off Dougie's body, surprisingly limber for his size, and strolled out of view.

The idea of wearing a collar somehow terrified and traumatized him even more than the thought of getting pissed in, but Dougie forced himself to breathe in and out, in and out, center himself, think of how worth it all this would be once he was at Nikolai's feet again. It would all be a bad dream. Just a bad dream.

Luke returned. The collar was heavy and thick, made of stiff new leather. Fragrant. So much bigger and more imposing than the delicate thing Madame had made him wear for the auction all those months ago. He had trouble lowering his chin in this one, and Luke was buckling it so tight he felt like he was choking, even though he could breathe just fine. The pressure against the front of his throat, that awful crush of his Adam's apple, was near unbearable already. How would he make it through the hour, the day, the God-knew-how-long he'd have to stay with Luke before he learned to *appreciate* Nikolai again, learned not just in his head but in his heart and gut and soul?

Luke hooked a leash onto the D-ring that hung front and center, and then and only then did he begin unbuckling the bindings at Dougie's wrists and ankles and hips.

"Up. Heel," Luke said, and Dougie forced his aching body to move. "And don't ever let me see you on your fucking feet, or I'll stick nails in your heels. Dogs crawl. Got me?"

"Yes, sir." Crawling was easier anyway; he wasn't actually convinced his legs could've held him. Besides, crawling reminded him of who he was—of *what* he was—and who he belonged to. He needed to remember that now. Needed it desperately. So he fell to his hands and knees. Winced at the scrape and press of the concrete floor, at the soreness in his muscles, at the fresh pain in his kneecaps.

He thought that Luke would lead him upstairs; after all, as far as Dougie knew, that was the only way in or out of this place. And maybe, on the way, they'd see Nikolai, and Nikolai would see Dougie, would see how good Dougie was being, even as a dog instead of a boy, and maybe he'd put a stop to this whole thing, or maybe not, but at least the sight of his pleasure or even just his approval would give Dougie strength to endure.

But they didn't go upstairs. Luke led him on his taut leash at an exhaustive pace down a narrow basement hall, up to a heavy steel door.

Three keys in three locks, all from a ring Luke kept in one battered denim pocket, and the door opened. Ice cold air hit Dougie head-on, knocking the breath out of him.

He realized for the first time that Luke was wearing a heavy workman's jacket. Steel-toed boots. A knit cap, even.

And Dougie, of course, was naked. *All my clothes—all Nikolai's gifts of trust to me—burnt away.*

His nudity didn't stop Luke from yanking him outside onto the frozen grass. It burned his knees and palms like fire, bumpy and gritty and so, *so* cold, but at least the path was free of snow and relatively clear of roots or twigs or sharp rocks. Luke led him down a trimmed path Dougie didn't recognize, down a steep slope, down into the trees. Through the woods, then, although still on beaten ground, thank God, and suddenly the path opened up into a clearing.

"This is the old cabin," Luke said. "Back before Master's mentor bought this property, the descendants of the original settlers lived here. Master fixed it up for me and the other guys working the property. Our own space, away from the pampered pets he keeps at the house."

Well, that didn't sound *too* awful, at least. Dougie could endure it.

"But before we let you in, we're gonna have to clean you off. You reek of piss, and I don't want any dog prints on my nice floor." Dougie realized they'd gone clear past the door of the cabin, which looked as old and rustic as Luke claimed it was but seemed at least in good repair, and were now right in front of a rusty old pump well, complete with bucket.

No. He wouldn't . . . would he? Not out here in the biting wind and the freezing cold. Dougie was shivering hard already, despite the exertion of keeping up with Luke on all fours. Dousing him with icy water would *kill* him.

"What, doggie afraid of a little cold? Well, there's a nice warm fire in the cabin you can stretch out in front of . . . once you're clean. Inside *and* out, dog. Master expects you to be well used while you're here, and I am more than happy to oblige."

"Yes, sir," Dougie mumbled, eyes locked on the pump. There was a layer of frost on the metal. Would Dougie's palms stick to it?

"Oh, one last thing. No need to waste all that energy with the *Yes, sirs* when you can just do what comes naturally to you and bark."

Dougie wanted to be out of the cold. He wanted to be clean. He wanted to be back with Nikolai, back in Nikolai's good graces. He'd done a million humiliating things since he'd been taken, a million things so very much worse than acting like the animal he clearly was, the animal Nikolai had tried so hard to break him free of.

So he barked. Didn't even mind. A dog was all he was now—he knew that, *understood* that in his heart as well as his mind. And a dog was all he'd be until Luke was through with him, until he'd relearned all the tricks Nikolai had taught him. Until Nikolai loved him again.

Luke didn't bother warning him not to run. Didn't need to. Just unclipped his leash, watched him crawl up to the old pump and bucket, watched him squat to clean his ass with frigid water, and then, satisfied that the job was being done, turned on his heel and left, the front door of the cabin slamming shut behind him.

When Dougie was finished, he crawled up to that door on limbs shaking so hard he could barely convince them to obey his mind's commands, knelt, and scratched at it to be let in. Whimpered once through chattering teeth. Sat on his haunches and waited.

Good dog.

The man who opened the door for him wasn't Luke, but he stooped to hook two fingers into the ring on Dougie's collar and drag him over the threshold with the same cruel authority. The sudden warmth of the cabin left Dougie breathless and sweating, and he barely had time to form an impression of a whole crowd of too-attractive middle-aged men, a large great room, a fire in a fieldstone hearth, a massive kitchen table, a row of bunk beds through the open door to a room on his left, before he was dragged to a hatch in the floor and shoved down a short, steep flight of stairs into . . . a root cellar? Raw earth walls and floor, damp and dank, lit by a single bulb. The space wasn't tiny by any means, but it *was* small and dark enough to remind him of—

No. Don't think about that don't think about that don't think about that. They're not going to forget about you down here. They're not.

And they didn't. Four men came down the stairs, cornering Dougie against the packed dirt wall. One pinched Dougie's face to open his mouth. Two others were unzipping their jeans. The fourth just stood there watching, smiling a nasty smile and rubbing his crotch. Just like the guards back at Madame's.

Don't struggle. Don't fight. Don't let this be rape. Don't. Just be good. Nikolai would want you to be good, serve these men like masters. Make them feel good, do everything they ask, anticipate their needs. Impress them.

Dougie licked his lips, though he doubted he looked terribly seductive with his cheeks still smashed between the man's hand. He looked up at the man through his lashes, tried to smile. Almost started to say something, but then remembered he was just a dog now, and dogs don't speak. Whined instead, nosing closer to the man's crotch. *Let me serve you. Let me show you what a good dog I can be.*

The man laughed, let go of his face, and backhanded him so hard his head bounced off the dirt wall. "Looks like our little bitch is in heat, boys."

Dougie wasn't stupid; he stayed down as the four men closed in. Hands, then, everywhere, pulling and pinching and slapping and grabbing. Teeth followed, and fingers and fists and tongues and cocks. They didn't want his cooperation, they didn't want his skill, they didn't want his service. No, they wanted his *pain*. And he'd have given that to them too, gladly, if they'd let him, because it was so much worse when they just *took* it instead.

"Did you really think you were going to escape?" Nikolai asked, and Mat couldn't help but laugh. He sounded like such a fucking evil supervillain sometimes.

"Kinda, yeah." He twisted his wrists in the leather straps that kept him secured to the chair he was sitting in. Metal. Nikolai was learning, apparently.

"I didn't expect you to be quite that stupid, Mathias. It wasn't like I made it very difficult for you to figure out you were walking into a trap. No locks? No guards? Really?" The guy obviously wanted to monologue, so Mat let him. Nikolai flicked Mat's left forearm. "And did you forget about the GPS tag, or were you just too arrogant to think it would matter?"

Huh. Mat had forgotten, actually. Must have been the distraction of having his own brother almost rape him. Or maybe just the fact that its implantation had been such a minor, long-ago horror compared to all that'd come after, symptomless and easily ignorable. But he wouldn't forget next time. Because if this little experience had taught him anything, it was that there *would* be a next time. That Nikolai wasn't perfect and no place was impervious to escape and if he'd just remembered to cut their damn chips out, they might've gotten into a car that hadn't belonged to Nikolai.

"All I had to do was let you go, let Douglas follow. I sent Roger out as soon as you cleared the property line. Had him wait in the closest town until your trackers showed you were returning to the highway. Now let's see your brother trust you enough to follow you ever again. You failed him, Mathias, to terrible consequence. He won't soon forget."

"Yeah, well, you mind-raped him, and I'm pretty sure he won't be forgetting that anytime, either. Not now that he knows freedom's on the table. Now that he knows you're the kind of monster who'd ask him to—" *To do such unspeakable things. To betray me, and himself, and everything between us.*

Nikolai leaned in close to Mat's ear and murmured, silky seductive, "Whatever you once were to him, Mathias, that's over now. You destroyed what remained of it last night. He's more mine now than he ever could've been without your help. I'm not a monster in his eyes. I'm his *savior*. The one you failed to be. And now it's time for you to see just how *badly* you failed him, and just how much he's willing to do to make me love him again." With that, Nikolai stepped back, turned to the table in front of Mat and opened the laptop computer resting atop it, right at Mat's eye level.

It turned on, and the sound of Dougie's screams filled the room.

"Douglas is learning what his world would be like without me. Without my protection and care. And since you've positioned yourself as the man who would tear him from me, that means the world he's learning about now is the one *you* would have him live in. He's just getting a small taste of it, but I expect the lesson will stick."

Nikolai stepped aside, and now Mat could see as well as hear what was being done to his brother. He was pressed to his back on a dirt floor, one man holding his legs apart, another fist-fucking him so hard it was like he was punching the poor kid over and over. A third man had his teeth on Dougie's nipple, and a fourth looked like he was trying to pull Dougie's hair out by the roots.

Mat squeezed his eyes shut and turned away, but it was way too fucking late for that. That image would be seared on his retinas until the day he died.

"You know by now that I have a habit of buying back some of my old charges." Nikolai nodded to someone standing behind Mat's shoulder, Roger maybe, or another tamed man, who stood watch at the door to this small room. "Well, not all of them come back as pleasant and even-tempered as Roger. Some come back to me . . . somewhat twisted by their experiences, and eager to take back their power by dominating those lesser than themselves when given the chance. Behind their well-trained facades lie feral beasts, but they're partly my creation, so I love them nonetheless. And let them indulge their true natures when it suits me." He paused. "Now you say whatever brilliant comeback you have for me."

Mat couldn't speak. He could feel hot tears on his face, could hear nothing but Dougie's sounds of pain. And God, not just that, he was . . . barking? Yes, that was definitely a tear-choked *woof*.

"I think that's Luke, who takes his pleasure from making men bark like dogs. I expect your poor brother will be getting his nutrition from kibble and table scraps instead of Jeremy's cooking over the next while. Crawling on all fours. Urinating outside."

"Stop this," Mat begged, his eyes squeezed shut. "Please, please just stop, go and get him, take him back, stop them hurting him. I'll do whatever you want, I promise."

"What I want is for you to *learn*. To learn your place, and learn the price of your disobedience. But most of all, to learn that you do not know what is best for your brother. You are not his master anymore, Mathias; you are not his idol or his god. You are nothing but a deceiver, and you lead him to pain."

Mat lurched against the chair, desperate to mute the fucking computer, make it all *stop*, scoop Dougie up and get him out of here for real this time. "Fine, fine! Just . . . please. God, please stop this."

"You had a chance to prevent this, Mathias, and now that time has passed. I hope you remember the consequences of your actions next time you consider doing something so spectacularly foolish."

Yeah. Next time he'd cut out the fucking GPS chips. Because there would be a next time. There *would*. Because if the only other option was abandoning Dougie to this life for good . . . well, that wasn't a choice he was willing to make, not anymore. Not when freedom had been so fucking close. Not when he knew now they could have it again.

And if Mat couldn't help him escape, Dougie would be better off dead. They both would.

CHAPTER FOUR

That night, Dougie slept on the foot of the one named Graham's bed. Graham liked having his feet licked, and his balls too, and decided halfway through the night that he was far too warm and cozy to venture out of his nest of blankets to use the toilet, so once again Dougie found himself standing in as a urinal. The man who slept in the bunk above Graham—Colin, Dougie thought his name was—must've woken to Dougie's retching swallows, because he patted his mattress and whispered, "Here, doggie doggie," and waited for Dougie to climb up and swallow his piss too. Then he fucked Dougie's mouth, came all over his eyes and nose, smeared it into his skin and then scolded him for it—*Filthy dog, you're disgusting, get out of my bed.* Didn't even let him climb down the ladder, just shoved him right off the edge, and Dougie hit the hardwood floor with a very doglike yelp and a jarring thud that woke the other four occupants in the bedroom. Which meant no more sleep for Dougie that night as they passed him from bed to bed, pissing in him and fucking him and complaining about how dirty and disgusting he was. Which meant, in turn, that he got tossed out the front door to wash himself at the ice-cold water pump under the light of the moon and stars.

He took the opportunity to vomit up every nasty fucking thing they'd shoved down his throat over the last couple hours.

To think Dougie had ever been happy to see the night sky.

When he was finished and shivering with cold again, he came up to the door—which stood ajar—and nosed it open wide enough to crawl through, then gently shut it behind him.

Just snores greeted him, thank God. He knew he should probably go back down to his sad little pallet in the root cellar now that nobody wanted to use him again tonight, but he just couldn't bear the thought of more cold dark silence, and unlike Nikolai, these men would beat him one way or the other, no matter what choices he made. So he went to the mat in front of the fireplace, curled up like the dog he was, and slept.

The first day he'd been here, Nikolai had presented him with bowls of food placed on the floor and the problem of how to eat them. Back then, he'd chosen to eat them like a dog, to debase himself for Nikolai's pleasure and entertainment, although by now he realized that Nikolai didn't want or need that from him. Just wanted loving submission, had only ever wanted such.

So it seemed like he was coming full circle now to be under the thumb of a man who *did* desire that debasement, and fed Dougie a metal bowl of dog food—*actual* dog food, reeking and lumpy, wet and dry mixed—to prove it.

He thought back to Nikolai, to the carefully prepared food on that very first tray, to all the goodness and happiness and love Nikolai wanted for him. Thought of what he'd lost because he'd been unable to let go of the past, because he'd made the terrible mistake of trusting Mat over his own *master*. Thought of the consequences of his choices—ice-water baths and brutal fistings and six men's piss in his gullet. Thought of the life he'd end up living if he couldn't be worthy of Nikolai's love again.

And ate the dog food.

Mat sniffed back horrified tears and closed his eyes, just for a moment, because he couldn't bear it anymore and surely his guard wouldn't notice—

Pain lanced through his shoulder, so acute he screamed, and he opened his eyes again because he knew damn well the guard's ability to shock him would far outlast his own ability to endure being shocked. It was a fine balancing act, walking the line of least agony. Sometimes that meant letting the fucker torture him. Sometimes it meant watching Dougie being tortured by some dozen other fuckers instead. And sometimes, if he was really, really lucky, it meant blacking out for a while. But he always came to strapped to the same fucking chair in front of the same fucking monitor with the same fucking command ringing in his ears: *Behold the consequences of your choices.*

Six days. Six days in this special brand of Hell, and Dougie knew because he'd been counting the sunsets, counting the trips outside to bathe in the icy water, counting the very fucking *seconds* until his master decided he'd suffered enough, learned his lesson, was ready to come home. And oh *God* was he ever ready. Or felt ready, anyway, felt it in his head and his heart and right down to his fucking *toenails*, which throbbed and ached just as surely as the rest of him from the unending abuse of Nikolai's buybacks. But he knew just as surely that he *wasn't* ready, not really, because Nikolai wasn't here to take him away from all this yet, and Nikolai knew best, *always* knew best, and forgetting that was what'd gotten Dougie into this mess in the first place so he'd never, ever, *ever* question Nikolai again. Which meant that if Nikolai didn't think he was ready yet, then he really wasn't ready yet.

Someone whistled. Dougie lurched to his hands and knees, barked once in acknowledgment, and trotted toward the source of the sound as quickly as his battered body would permit. Colin. He knew what Colin liked. Stuck his tongue out and craned his neck, trying to be a good dog, to anticipate the man's needs. Colin dropped his pants and settled himself over the edge of a bed. Dougie set to work with his tongue, ignoring the salty-sour taste of him, the fact that he'd clearly worked hard all day and hadn't washed before shoving his asshole in Dougie's face. Just licked like a good dog, licked and licked and then stiffened his tongue and fucked Colin with it when the man started pushing back against him. He was so focused on pleasing Colin that he didn't even realize someone had come up behind him until a lubed-up cock breached his hole, no warning, no prep, no pause for comfort, just shoved right in and off to the races. Dougie took it, trying not to think too hard of Nikolai's plugs, of his master taking him slow and easy, owning his ass but not hurting him, not unless the hurt was the point of the act. Even giving Dougie pleasure while taking his own. Nothing like that here. Dougie hadn't come once in six days. Not even close. Maybe he wasn't allowed, and the men here knew that. Or maybe they just didn't fucking care.

But that was okay. Bad dogs didn't get to come. Coming was a privilege, an honor, a sweet reward for best behavior. He knew that now, right down to his bones. Knew he might never deserve to come again, not the way he'd behaved, the way he'd spat on Nikolai's generosity and kindness and thrown it right back in his master's face. Nothing could ever make that right. He could never do enough, lick enough, suck enough, be fucked enough to be forgiven for that.

But he'd try. He'd *die* trying. And be grateful for the second chance.

The man behind him finished, came in his ass with a grunt. Someone else took his place. Not just a cock, either. Fingers, too. Spreading him wide, splitting him open. He whimpered into Colin's ass, eyes clenched tight against the pain. But he wasn't complaining, and didn't stop rimming. Wouldn't dare.

"So loose, doggie. Not sure if the master will even want you back, now."

No mistaking the distress in Dougie's whimper at that. The man was lying. Had to be lying. He'd be so good. He'd make himself tight again. The master would take him back. He *would*.

Mat jerked awake to the too-familiar bite of the stun gun. "Eyes on your brother, dog!" his guard barked. God, how long had he been sitting here subjected to this? His wrists and ankles were chafed raw and bloody. He was fairly certain he had pressure sores on his back and ass. They let him up three times a day to eat and piss and exercise, but then it was always back to the chair, even to sleep. But only when Dougie slept—which wasn't, as it turned out, very much—because God for-fucking-bid he missed a single moment of his brother's agony. Eleven men in that cabin and every single one of them took at least one turn a day. Didn't leave Dougie much in the way of free time.

But the worst of it—worse than the hard metal chair and the chafing bonds and the cattle prod and the sleep deprivation and

Dougie's endless suffering—was how obvious it was where this was heading. How eager Dougie had clearly become to endure—even to *enjoy*—the abuse. How deeply he was sinking into himself, into this world Nikolai had created. How far and fast he was slipping from Mat's fingers. What few remaining traces of the smart, passionate, ambitious young man Mat had once known were crumbling to dust beneath a steady stream of beatings and rapes and humiliations. It didn't take a genius to know that soon there'd be nothing left of that young man. Nothing left at all but what Nikolai would step in to put there.

And if Mat wept at that, well, there was no shame in mourning a brother's death.

No, not dead. Just buried. Just hang on. Hang on, and one day you'll have the chance to find him again.

Mat clung to that thought with every cell in his miserable body as he watched, watched, watched Dougie's feed.

They hadn't taken him outside in a day. Dougie *hurt* with the need to piss. He looked at the door, looked at the men sitting at the table playing cards, looked at the door again. Whined aloud.

"Shut up, dog," Luke snapped.

They always took him outside. Once in the morning, once before bed, maybe a couple times more in between. They took turns, and whoever's turn it was would walk him a ways from the cabin, tell him to get on with it, and Dougie would. No shame left in him; he'd squat like an animal while they watched, and then he'd be led to the pump to wash if they decided he needed a wash, and then it would be back into the house again.

But nobody was walking him today. Snowflakes swirled outside the window, and none of the men wanted to venture out into the cold. Dougie didn't want to, either, but he wasn't allowed to use their toilet, so he *needed* to. Badly.

He whined again.

"Shut up, dog, or so help me I will *shut* you up."

Dougie cowered. Nikolai had never denied him this way.

When he finally gave in and pissed himself, Colin rubbed his nose in it, repeating "Bad dog!" over and over again until the words were stamped on Dougie's brain, until it didn't seem unfair at all that he had to lick up his mess, that they beat him until he made a new one and had to lick that up too. Bad dog. He was a bad dog. And bad dogs didn't deserve their master's love.

CHAPTER FIVE

Luke was the one to say he thought it was kind of disgusting to piss in a dog's mouth and then fuck the same hole. Unhygienic.

Graham was the one who suggested they clean Dougie's mouth and throat with the scalding kettle water.

They had him on his knees, a man on either side restraining his arms, one behind him holding his face tipped up and his mouth open, and overhead was the kettle from the fire, the one Luke had to use an oven mitt to hold, steam pouring from its spout, and Dougie was fucking *howling* with fear, knowing that the moment it tipped, that would be it for his throat and tongue, he'd never speak again, but maybe that was what he deserved, to be a dog for the rest of his days, reduced to whines and yelps and grunts.

A quiet knock sounded from the front door.

"Shit!" Luke said. "Is it that time already? Shit, shit, shit!" He backed off, the kettle disappearing from Dougie's line of vision.

Dougie cried with relief, but there was no stopping the hyperventilation, his heart thrumming like a hummingbird's, his chest heaving as he gasped for air.

"Roger," Luke said.

Roger, Roger, oh thank God, thank you, thank you oh Master, Roger. If he'd had a tail, he'd be wagging it now too fast to see.

The men surrounding him all fell back, letting Dougie collapse into a heap on the floor. When he found the strength and coordination to raise his head, Roger was standing in front of him, looking down on him with an unreadable expression.

"C'mon guys, fun's over," someone said, but Dougie didn't care who.

He was too busy raising himself to his knees, lifting his chin, posing prettily. For the first time in ages, his cock swelled and rose between his legs, as happy as the rest of him. He nosed at Roger's crotch, whined plaintively in the back of his throat. *Please. Let me taste you, suck you, make you feel so good. I love you. I love you. Let me show you. Please.*

Roger looked . . . not like a man who wanted a blowjob, that was for sure, although his cock had gone erect too, tenting his soft, fine trousers. He looked sad, and happy too? And sad again. His smile wobbled, and his fingers carded through Dougie's hair, so, so gentle. "Oh Douglas, poor Douglas," he said, and cupped Dougie's cheek. "You don't have to do that. Not for me, my sweet little boy." Roger's hands slid down further still, to the collar, which he unbuckled. "Come on, time to bring you home."

Dougie swelled with such joy he could have died. He pressed his face into Roger's hands, rubbed and nuzzled and wished he could crawl right *inside* Roger he was so happy. *Home.* Yes. Where he could be a *good boy* again. Not a bad dog. Not a dog at all. Never again.

"Yes," Dougie said, because he wasn't a dog anymore, and then, "Please." Softly, so softly, because he hadn't used his voice in so long, and he smiled up at Roger through his falling tears. Roger smiled back, and Dougie nuzzled him again, cheek so close to Roger's cock and God, he *wanted* it, wanted that clean familiar taste on his tongue, that comforting scent in his nostrils, those breathy little moans of pleasure filling his ears. He mouthed at Roger, found himself whining again without meaning to but he didn't feel like a dog this time, he felt like a man, like a *good boy*, and Roger cupped his head in both hands and said, "Maybe later, if the master wants. But now we need to go, Douglas. Now your master's waiting, all right?"

Yes. *Yes.* Better than all right. Better than *anything.* Nikolai was waiting? For *him*? Tears flowed fresh and free at the thought, and he was unashamed, basking in the pleasure of it all, the sheer orgasmic ecstasy of Nikolai's forgiveness. Roger helped him to unsteady feet made even shakier by the thought of what glories might await him, what chances to prove himself, to please his master. He hurried as best he could. He'd never keep his master waiting again. Never.

Roger washed and waxed his body. Trimmed his hair and shaved his face. Gingerly helped him through a nice cleansing enema that Dougie was actually pretty happy to receive, considering how his ass had been used over the last week. Nothing to be done for all the bruises and scrapes, but Dougie liked to think they added color, that maybe Nikolai wouldn't mind them. Or, even better, that Nikolai would look upon them and see how much Dougie had suffered for his mistakes, how sorry he was, how much he was willing to endure for his master. No longer a pampered, naïve boy, Dougie was now a seasoned slave. Had proved his worth. And knew *exactly* how lucky he was to be Nikolai's sweet boy.

He'd eagerly take his place with Roger at Nikolai's feet, and be so, so grateful for it.

Once properly groomed, Roger led him back down to the basement. Dougie tried not to be disappointed by that—oh how he'd hoped and dreamed of being ushered into Nikolai's bedroom, of demonstrating his newfound devotion in his master's arms. But perhaps Nikolai wasn't done with his suffering yet. That was . . . well, not what he'd hoped for, obviously, but something he'd gladly endure for his master if need be. Whatever this new fate was, he wasn't going back to being a dog. He was clean now, clean and scrubbed and beautiful, *pristine*, the collar left far behind him.

Yet as Roger walked him to the door of the dungeon where this week's nightmare had begun, it seemed increasingly likely that Dougie's continued suffering was exactly what Nikolai needed.

His mind flashed back to those first endless hours of agony, then shied away, the memory of pain so strong he felt sick with it. But he'd do it. He'd lie down on that bed and let Roger strap him in and take the poison with his chin held high. For Nikolai. Anything for Nikolai.

"Easy," Roger said, smoothing a hand between Dougie's shoulder blades. "It'll be all right, Douglas, I promise."

"I know," he said, because he was done making stupid mistakes, and Nikolai was a good man, a forgiving man, a loving man.

And then Roger opened the door, and what Dougie saw there didn't surprise him at all.

Because of course it had to be Mat, naked and bound to a table that looked like it'd come right out of an obstetrics office, stirrups and all. He was seated half upright, a wide leather strap across his chest, another holding his hips and wrists down, ass hanging off the edge of the table, feet strapped into the stirrups. Meat on display. A body to be used, and Dougie had no illusions about who would be using it.

No reservations, either.

Oddly, Mat wasn't struggling this time, and he wasn't gagged. And since Dougie doubted Nikolai had resorted to cutting his tongue out, that meant he was being willingly silent right now. As Dougie walked into the room, Mat stared resolutely at the ceiling, and his breath came through his nostrils in harsh but controlled puffs.

To the left of the table, Nikolai stood against the wall, his arms folded across his chest. Not ready to welcome Dougie into them, not yet, not until Dougie did this one last thing, proved this one last point, passed this one final test.

He turned his eyes back to Mat. Saw an auto-injector lying ready on a side table, shining and immaculate atop a sterile blue sheet of paper. No question what was inside. And Dougie knew now *exactly* how torturous it was, how unspeakably, indescribably brutal, how utterly terrifying. He also knew it wasn't for him.

"Go on, Douglas," Roger said. Roger, not Nikolai, not the man whose voice Dougie most yearned to hear. Roger's hand at the small of his back, urging him forward. "Sever the final thread. Be free."

Yes, be free. Like Roger. Forever. Happy.

Dougie's treacherous hands trembled as he picked up the auto-injector, and his body betrayed him further when, just before jamming it into Mat's splayed thigh, his eyes moved of their own accord to look at Mat. Right into Mat's face as he whimpered and lurched in his bonds, then forced himself still and silent, gaze cast resolutely to the ceiling. He was panting like he'd just gone three hard rounds, fingers curled into fists, jaw clenched, blinking far too fast over watering eyes. Ever the tough one, the damned fool. Trying to pretend he wasn't terrified. Trying to hide his pain. Unable to let go of his stupid fucking pride.

Dougie raised his arm again, auto-injector clenched in his fist.

"Pl—" Mat clamped down on his begging so hard his teeth clicked, but he was *looking* at Dougie now with those big stupid blue eyes, wet and wounded, and fuck him anyway, he had *no fucking right* to look at Dougie like that, not after all he'd done to him.

Dougie glared back. Mat took Dougie's anger like he took everything else: silent and stoic, right on the chin. Swallowed hard and said, "I love you, Dougie. No matter what. Never forget that."

Then he closed his eyes and turned his head away and banged it twice against the back of the table like maybe he hadn't meant to say any of that out loud.

Or maybe he'd just realized he had no fucking *right* to. "Fuck you," Dougie—no, *Douglas*—growled. "My name's not Dougie anymore, it's *Douglas*, and I don't *belong* to you anymore, and you don't get to talk to me that way."

Mat—no, the slave, just a slave that meant nothing to Douglas at all—swallowed hard, jaw stiff like he knew if he opened it the words would keep pouring out of him and never stop. Good. Douglas was tired of hearing him, tired of words and meaningless platitudes, when the only thing that counted were actions.

And Douglas was ready to define himself by his. He slammed the auto-injector into the slave's thigh, then slammed his rigid cock balls deep into the slave's pre-slicked ass. He didn't remember getting hard, wasn't even sure how it'd happened, but there was no mistaking his master's approving hum, even over the slave's agonized screams and bitter weeping. Douglas ignored the slave's pleading, fucked the bound body harder, the slave's muscles spasming so tight around his cock it nearly hurt. He could feel his master's gaze upon him, feel his master's smile.

He'd never come so fast in his life.

He pulled out with a growl, caught the cum dripping out of the slave's hole and shoved it back inside with three fingers. Fucked him with them. He'd come too fast beneath the heady weight of his master's approval. He'd been supposed to *hurt* this slave. He meant to see it through. Maybe he could work his whole fist up there, beat the troublesome beast from the inside.

"That's enough, Douglas," his master said, his voice tremulous, full of weight and meaning. "Clean yourself and come here."

No towel, no tissues. Douglas swiped his hand over his cock to wipe away the traces of cum and lube, then forced his fingers into the slave's mouth and snapped, "Lick." But the slave was so far gone with the pain of the injection that Douglas was lucky he didn't lose his fingers to clenching teeth. He rolled them around the slave's tongue and lips until they seemed reasonably clean, then wiped his wet hand on the slave's trembling shoulder.

When it was done, he went to his master and fell to his knees. He was shaking. Hard. Vibrating with adrenaline. His master laid a hand on the top of his head, and it took every ounce of control Nikolai had ever taught him for Douglas not to lean into that touch without permission.

"Well done," his master said, and ecstasy washed through Douglas as fiercely as his orgasm had just moments before "Now let go of your anger, Douglas. Give me back my sweet boy. Come home to me."

Nikolai's sweet boy. Nikolai's alone. He owed nothing else to anyone, least of all the slave crying on the table.

He breathed out a sigh as the anger and hate drained from his body, replaced by the suppleness of submission, and then he laid his cheek against his master's hip.

Home. Yes. He was finally home.

CHAPTER SIX

One Month Later

Douglas had blossomed into perfection this past month, as evidenced by the absolutely spectacular foot massage he was currently giving Nikolai, strong hands and formidable attention focused on the sole of Nikolai's left foot. He'd found that magic spot that seemed to be linked directly to Nikolai's groin, honed right in, and rubbed and pressed—*yes, little pet, I know what you want*—but Nikolai just wasn't feeling it tonight. Was feeling rather maudlin, in fact.

Because he knew it was time.

And while he never much cared to part with his creations, this one in particular would feel like a surgical excision. He'd grown far too close to the boy, felt far too affectionate. He'd even seriously considered keeping him—after all, he was earmarked for no one—but the damn brother . . . Now there was a sticky wicket if ever he'd seen one. Just as he knew it was time to sell Douglas on, he knew it was also time to admit partial defeat with Mathias. The only way—the *only* way—to ensure his client's safety was to sell Douglas with Mathias. The beast was simply too unpredictable, otherwise. Only one person in the world could control him without breaking him, and that person was currently sliding oiled fingers between Nikolai's toes.

And kissing Nikolai's calf. Knee. Thigh.

"Douglas."

More kissing, and a soft little moan now, too.

"*Douglas*. I have to talk to you." He took the boy's face between his hands and tilted it up until he could see those beautiful blue eyes, half-glazed with arousal.

"Yes, Master," Douglas said, and fell back so he was sitting on his heels, in position and attentive.

"It's been a month now since you came back to me. Since you chose your loyalties."

Nervousness and a touch of fear fluttered over Douglas's carefully arranged features. The boy hated to be reminded of those dark days. Thought now, perhaps, that Nikolai was angry with him, that he'd done something wrong.

"And since then, your behavior has been exemplary. There's simply no other way to describe how far you've come, Douglas, and how very much you please me."

Beaming now, practically *glowing*, and yet he wrestled that under control as well because good boys weren't *giddy* in front of their masters, and said simply, "I learned from the very best, Master. I'm so glad I've pleased you."

Nikolai reached out to indulge a touch, and Douglas leaned forward into his palm, closed his eyes as Nikolai stroked his hair. He'd be purring if he were capable, but that soft, private smile was enough for Nikolai.

He leaned back again, waited until the boy's eyes were back upon him. This was too important to cloud with desire. "You've always known what we've been working toward here, Douglas." The boy said nothing, but when Nikolai didn't press on, Douglas nodded, once, the nervousness back. He knew where this was going. Had to. "And the hard truth is that you're ready to move on."

Too well trained now to protest, but Nikolai could see the tears springing up at the corners of his eyes until he blinked them back. "If . . ." His voice cracked, but he cleared it and pushed on, blinking back new tears. "If Master wishes. I'll, um . . . I'll do you proud, sir, I promise. I'll—" He blushed furiously and ducked his watering eyes, didn't finish his thought. But Nikolai could read it in his reddened cheeks, in the hunch of his shoulders: *I'll be so good you'll come back for me.*

Nikolai's fingers *ached* to touch the boy, stroke him, reassure him. But now was not the time for coddling. He laced his hands across his lap instead, and said, "You mustn't think I'm discarding you, Douglas. I would never. And you *will* come home to me someday, of this I have no doubt. But until then, I need you, Douglas. I need you to do something for me that only you can do."

Ah, he had the boy's attention now, wide eyes fixed on Nikolai's face, lips slightly parted. Trying to puzzle through what made him unique, how his master could possibly *need* him and whether he'd live up to the expectation.

No need to torture him by keeping him waiting. "It's Mathias, Douglas." The boy's nose wrinkled at the mention of his brother. It would've been adorable if not for how he also bared his teeth. "He goes to his new master soon, too, and I've come to realize that short of breaking him, the only way to guarantee my client's safety is to send you along to watch over him."

Douglas looked fit for bursting with the need to speak, so Nikolai inclined his head, gestured with an open palm. Douglas jumped on the invitation before Nikolai had even finished moving. "But Master, I don't—" His lips twisted into an ugly scowl. Nikolai couldn't decide if he was disgusted with the thought of babysitting his brother or with the fact that he'd nearly argued with his master. Both, probably. The boy's eyes closed for a long moment, and he took a deep breath through his nose, resettled into the perfect posture Nikolai had taught him. "I hate even looking at him," he finally said, so soft it was nearly a whisper. It wasn't fear that stole his voice; he simply didn't feel entitled to ask of this for himself. "He makes me so *angry*. He . . . he reminds me of all the awful things I used to do and say and be. He reminds me of *hurting you.*"

"Douglas. Douglas." Nikolai took hold of the boy's chin. "I'm not asking you to do this for him, I'm asking you to do it for *me*. Serve me in a way only you can. Mathias heels for no one else. No one but you. You're stronger than him now, stronger than he'll ever be. I need you to control him if he ever hints at going too far. I need you to protect my client, my investments, my very reputation. Do you understand how important this is? How much I'm trusting you with?"

Douglas's face fell, but when he raised his eyes again, they were full of resolute determination. Pride, too. *Good boy.* "Yes Master. Anything. Just tell me what to do."

Douglas crept down the hall, Nikolai's tea balanced on the tray in his hands. It was hard to believe that in a few days, maybe a few weeks, he'd be carrying tea for someone else. Or coffee, maybe. Or whatever his new master might like. Assuming his new master would like anything at all from him beyond leash duty for a dangerous slave.

No. Douglas wasn't going to think like that. Whatever the new master wanted, he'd offer with pride and be glad for it. For the chance to serve a man Nikolai deemed worthy. For the chance to show the world Nikolai's skill at training slaves, and for a chance to show Nikolai himself that Douglas was worth bringing back into the fold when the time came. Whenever that was. One year, five years, ten . . . No matter. He'd endure it. Even teach himself to enjoy it. For Nikolai.

He just wished he could keep serving Nikolai *here*. He could hardly be faulted for loving his master too much, could he?

Wait, hadn't that been Lucifer's "crime," too?

God, he'd even miss Jeremy. And Roger, of course. And that big antique piano in the parlor; he was getting pretty good, actually, and treasured his quiet time to practice. Would his new master have a piano too? Would he let him play?

He realized he'd been standing outside the door of Nikolai's study, tea tray growing heavy in his hands, for God knew how long while he'd moped and felt sorry for himself. *Shit.* He'd go in, and lay out Nikolai's tea, and then he'd fetch the cane from the umbrella stand in the corner, the fat one that left bruises for days, and beg Nikolai to correct him for forgetting himself.

Then everything would be okay again. Everything would be okay and maybe Nikolai would find someone else to keep his stupid awful brother in line and not make Douglas go.

But when Douglas nudged the door open with his foot and rushed inside, Nikolai was too distracted to disturb with a request for discipline, so Douglas just set the tea tray at his desk, prepared Nikolai a cup—one sugar cube, tiny splash of milk—and settled silently onto his knees at Nikolai's feet. Nikolai was on the phone, visibly bothered by whatever the person on the other end of the line was saying, but his tone was calm and even when he responded. "Yes, I understand," he said, the crease between his brows deepening, "but you know my work, Allen, and you know that when I tell you he'll make you happy, he'll make you happy. He's one of a kind, Allen."

Douglas closed his eyes, trying to let the words wash over him. Trying to ignore them outright; a good slave was invisible, after all, never spoke out of turn, never heard what he wasn't supposed to hear. By holding this conversation in front of him, Nikolai was trusting him to behave like he should. So he wouldn't let himself be upset, even knowing that right now, Nikolai was trying to sell him. To someone who, apparently, didn't even *want* him. But Nikolai thought he'd be a good fit for this man, and Nikolai knew best.

Master knows best. Master knows best. Master knows best.

Besides, Nikolai needed him. Needed *him.*

"I understand that you're bored with complacent pups, Allen. And I promise, the man I'm training for you now will fit your exact specifications in that regard. But this other boy is so much *more* than just complacent, Allen. He's exquisite." Nikolai took a quiet sip of his tea; the right corner of his mouth quirked up in brief satisfaction, and Douglas's whole center pulsed with pride, relief, though equally brief given the circumstances. "Yes. Yes. I understand."

No mistaking the disappointment in Nikolai's tone. Did this Allen man not want Douglas even after Nikolai's reassurances?

God, he shouldn't be feeling so thankful right now. What would happen if Mat went to Allen alone? Who would keep him under control then? Who would stop him from doing all the stupid shit he'd done here and worse? And what would happen to Nikolai, then? Would people still trust him to train their slaves? He was the best—the *best*. Douglas couldn't allow Mat to ruin that. He needed to convince Allen he was worth taking. Not just a *complacent pup.*

"Well, listen. Let me make it up to you. I'm having a debut party for this new boy, with all the usual clients. Show him off, find him some interested buyers, you know how it goes. Jeremy will pull out all the stops on the hors d'oeuvres, of course, and I'll pull your favorite Château Margaux out of my cellar. Best of all, your little investment will be there. Not quite ready to go home with you yet, but I think I could arrange a private preview for you. Supervised, of course, but that shouldn't affect your enjoyment, I don't think?" He laughed at whatever Allen said in reply, but when Douglas darted his eyes up to Nikolai's face, the little furrow was still marring his brow.

A couple more minutes of small talk, a few more sips of tea, and he hung up with a sigh.

Douglas shuffled forward on his knees until he could lay his head on Nikolai's thigh. Despite how the conversation had just gone, he couldn't help but think that this might be one of the last times for a very long time he'd be able to do this, and he didn't want to miss a single moment while it lasted. More than that, Nikolai was upset. And if Douglas could do anything at all to make him feel better, he damn well would. "Master? Would you like to get your frustration out? My mouth, maybe? My ass?" A pause—was he asking this for Nikolai or for himself?—and then, "Or should I fetch a cane for you?"

Nikolai shook his head. He didn't like hurting people, and he clearly wasn't in the mood for sex.

"Foot rub, Master? A massage? A drink? Should I find Roger and we can create some distraction for you? Master?"

Nikolai sighed, the sound no different than the one he'd made at the conclusion of that unpleasant phone call. Pinched the bridge of his nose between thumb and forefinger. Douglas shut his mouth, ducked his head. He'd pushed too hard. "I'm sorry, Master, I shouldn't have—"

Nikolai's hand came to rest on Douglas's head. For a moment he'd been certain Nikolai was going to strike him—God knew he deserved it for getting in his master's face like he just had, even if all he'd wanted was to help. It wasn't his place to help. Wasn't his place to push. And certainly wasn't his place to be so fucking *needy*. He was going away because Nikolai needed him to. He had to accept that.

Nikolai didn't strike him, though. He just carded his fingers through Douglas's hair, then guided Douglas's head back to his thigh. Douglas pressed his cheek against fine fabric and firm muscle and closed his eyes, all the better to remember this moment, this sensation, Nikolai's nails scratching lightly across his scalp.

"I love you, Master," he murmured. *No matter what.*

"I know, Douglas. Which is why I know I can count on you to change Allen's mind at your coming-out party."

Douglas's stomach clenched. "Of course, Master."

"Good boy. *Now* you can fetch my cane—but only once you tell me what you've done."

I wanted to stay. I needed you. "Thank you, Master."

CHAPTER SEVEN

Roger tugged a comb through Douglas's increasingly unruly hair while Douglas tried very, very hard not to fidget. He was sitting naked on the floor between Roger's bare legs, Roger perched behind him on a footstool, both of them freshly washed and waxed and manicured. Two men, two slaves, two lovers of the same master, separated only by time.

Two rooms over, in Nikolai's grand, cathedral-ceilinged great room, Douglas's coming-out party was winding up to full swing. He hadn't heard the front door open in a good ten minutes, which meant everyone was probably here by now, or nearly so. Clients, mostly, Nikolai had explained, but a handful of his fellow trainers as well—those who worked with different wares, no competition to him—unable to resist a good party and a rare opportunity to socialize with their fellows. Nikolai's parties were a popular affair, a chance to dress up and engage in luxurious debauchery and perhaps get a handful—or mouthful or cockful—of a freshly trained young slave. Douglas, to be specific.

"I feel underdressed," Douglas joked, and Roger chuckled even though there was no mistaking the nervous flutter in Douglas's voice. He'd caught glimpses of tuxedos and cocktail dresses through the open door to the hall. He, of course, was as stark naked as Roger was, both of them wearing nothing but decorative leather wrist and ankle cuffs. No collar for him, which was reassuring, but a short platinum chain hung from Roger's neck, the clasp stamped with a delicate "NP." Nikolai's chain, a gift to Roger, a sign of their permanent bond to one another.

Maybe Douglas *could* come around to liking a collar, not that anyone was offering him one now. He wasn't Nikolai's in anything but his heart, after all. He was a homeless boy, the ward of a trainer awaiting a real master. A master that maybe Douglas would meet tonight.

Strange, how much that reminded him of his early days in foster care. He was, he realized, just as scared now as he had been then. Desperately wanting the one thing he knew he couldn't have. Terrified of what he might end up getting. Or rather, who might end up getting him.

Roger put the comb down and used his fingers for the final touches. This long, Douglas's hair curled a little at the ends.

Douglas reached up and captured Roger's hand. "I'm scared," he said.

Roger kissed the crown of his head. "That's normal. It's all right to be afraid now."

"But . . ." Dougie turned around to face Roger, settled on his heels between Roger's legs, met his eyes. How much to say? If it were Nikolai here now, he wouldn't hesitate to speak the whole truth. Nikolai would know exactly what to say to make things better, to make him braver, stronger, the perfect slave.

Still, Roger was his friend. His occasional lover. And Nikolai's right hand in many ways. Maybe he'd know the right thing to say, too.

"The thing is . . . I don't want to go, and I'm afraid that maybe I'll do something or say something without meaning to, or that I won't be my best, that I'll disappoint the master, or worse, embarrass him in front of his guests. What if my subconscious tries to sabotage things? Tries to make it impossible for Nikolai to sell me?"

Roger shook his head, took both of Douglas's hands in his own. "That's not going to happen. We both know you're stronger than that. And you won't let the master down because *he* didn't let *you* down. All the time and care he's given you—you're perfect, Douglas. You're exactly as you should be. And when you go out there, you'll do exactly what you should do." He raised Douglas's right hand to his mouth, pressed his lips to it, then laid it back on Douglas's thigh with a gentle pat. "I know you'll make him proud."

"Did you? I mean, did you make him proud? Did you have a party like this?"

Roger nodded. "But that was back in the nineties, so the fashion wasn't as easy to take seriously."

Douglas laughed, bright and unexpected. "I guess there's something to be said for going naked," he replied, and there was no missing how much better he felt. Roger really did know just what to say, had even gone beyond Nikolai this time. Nikolai wouldn't have thought to make him laugh. He was a wonderful man, but humor wasn't exactly his style. He and Roger completed each other. Douglas liked to think that, in turn, he completed *them*. A perfect, comfortable triad.

And it was about to be shattered.

"Now, now," Roger chided, swiping a thumb beneath Douglas's eye, even though he wasn't crying—yet. "None of that. Think of how happy you're about to make the master, and smile."

Douglas did—closed his eyes and thought about the warmth in Nikolai's eyes when he pleased him, the calm wash of satisfaction and pride and *rightness* at being Nikolai's good boy. His heart settled. His breathing eased. The threat of tears receded.

Roger said nothing more, and neither did Douglas, just sat there in silence, in perfect position, eyes closed, holding on to that image of domestic bliss in his mind. He didn't know how long he sat there picturing forever with Nikolai. Only that he felt so very, very calm when at last Nikolai came to collect him.

He rose to his feet, leaned into Nikolai's touch when the man put a hand on each bare shoulder. Nikolai leaned down to murmur in his ear. "Remember, I'll walk you in, you'll fall into position, I'll announce you and then step away. I've eighteen guests. Three are trainers, you'll not need to perform for them, but the rest may sample as they will . . . though it's considered impolite to leave a mess. No matter their requests, you will of course offer them your very finest behavior."

Sample, Douglas thought, picturing them using his mouth, touching his body. He'd perform. He would. Because it would make his master happy, and that was all that mattered.

Nikolai's hands massaged his shoulders. "It's all right to be nervous, Douglas. Everyone is at their coming-out. But no one's ever let me down, and I know you won't either." One hand left Douglas's shoulder to stroke his cheek, and Nikolai offered him a private little smile. "You're one of my very finest, Douglas. You'll make me proud. Now, come."

All the usuals—Nikolai's best customers and a few favorite colleagues—had shown up for the occasion of Douglas's debut.

Most importantly, Allen was here, looking sour as ever sipping at his cocktail in one corner of the room. Nikolai had shown Douglas his picture earlier today, and he tilted Douglas toward him now with a firm squeeze to his shoulder, just to make sure Douglas knew who he was truly here to impress.

Douglas nodded almost imperceptibly, and then sank to his knees at Nikolai's feet, a picture of submissive perfection. So beautiful, and growing more so by the day. It strained Nikolai's heart to look at him now and know how very little time they had left together. But such was the way of things—always had been, always would be—and he took comfort in the idea that he'd likely be able to buy Douglas back sooner rather than later. Took significantly less comfort in the knowledge that Mathias's untimely—and likely brutal—death would be the precipitator of the opportunity. But after all Mathias had put him through, the thought didn't bother him quite so much as it might once have.

In any case, he had an introduction to make, and he needed to be on his best behavior just as much as Douglas did, so he pushed thoughts of *later* from his mind, took a glass of champagne and a silver knife from Luke's hand—my, he cleaned up nicely when he wasn't out mucking with Nikolai's edible livestock—and clinked his glass.

The room quieted, soft conversations fading into silence, and all eyes turned to him—and, of course, to Douglas. "Thank you all for coming, ladies and gentlemen—it is my honor to see each and every one of you here today. Allow me to introduce you to my newest creation, Douglas Petrovic." At the sound of his name, Douglas raised his head, and though Nikolai couldn't see his face, he knew the boy was smiling demurely, just as they'd rehearsed. "This one's quite special. For one, he's my first in nearly three years that isn't already promised, and I know many of you have been waiting some time for a new indulgence. More importantly, he's quite the unique creature. A sharp mind, a sweet body, a poet's heart, a burning desire to love and be loved . . ." A theatrical pause, a slightly naughty smile, "and an absolutely spectacular mouth. I invite you to try for yourself."

Now *that* energized his guests. They closed in, drinks in hand, to watch, or to try the boy for themselves. All except for Allen, off sulking in a corner with his wife (who looked quite eager to get closer to Douglas but resigned to stay by her husband's side), no doubt impatient to see what he'd really come for. He wasn't a popular man at these soirées—wasn't a popular man at all, really—but popularity took a backseat when one was as outrageously wealthy as he. Nikolai didn't sell to him often—he liked to pretend he was straight even though he owned *several* men according to rumor—but Douglas was pretty enough to tempt him once Nikolai had plied the man with enough fine food and drink. And the finale of the evening, of course. If nothing else would do it, that should.

He turned back from his contemplation of his difficult client to find Douglas eagerly sucking two cocks at once, fists jacking two more, ass out for a fifth man with three fingers—already?—up his hole. The sight left Nikolai instantly hard and wanting, but the boy wasn't for his pleasure tonight. If Nikolai were any less disciplined, he'd have slipped away to shove his cock down Roger's throat, let the man take the edge off. But he didn't. He stood and watched and smiled instead, trading small talk with his spectating guests, the proud proprietor of the finest merchandise, ready and waiting to fulfill his clients' needs.

Douglas brought the first man off in less than two minutes. The second perhaps thirty seconds later. Mouth now free, one of the men he'd been jacking claimed it instead. A different man filled the empty fist. Maria, the lovely wife of the equally lovely man with three fingers up Douglas's ass, knelt down beside her husband and inserted two fingers of her own. Douglas hitched a cry but didn't so much as skip a beat with mouth or hands, didn't even hint at squirming away from the painful stretching.

Gods, was he ever making Nikolai proud.

And jealous. He wanted to fill up that well-stretched ass, *really* give the boy something to cry about. No doubt someone would by the end of the party, but at this early stage of the evening, everyone was too polite to fist the merchandise. Even Maria and Roberto only stretched him so painfully for a moment. Likely they'd just wanted to see how he'd respond. Now Roberto had his tongue in Douglas's ass, and Maria's manicured fingers were toying with Douglas's cock and balls.

Douglas was rock hard. And no wonder—to be the center of so much attention, to be pleasing so many people at once, was a dream come true for his needy boy.

"What a little beauty," a woman at Nikolai's shoulder said. Ah, one of his fellow trainers, Leslie, a miracle worker with the fairer sex and a dear old friend of his mentor's. "And you don't have a buyer for him? Really?"

"I bought him on spec with his older brother, who is a custom job. Frankly, I've been enjoying him too much to put too much thought into his eventual sale before now." Well, only half a lie.

She smiled indulgently at him, like she found it quaint that he'd grow so attached. She probably did. "He almost makes me think about considering cock."

Nikolai chuckled into his drink. "You're more than welcome to try him." If Douglas could tempt a solid six on the Kinsey scale, perhaps he could tempt Allen as well.

But Leslie just shrugged and stood in amicable silence beside Nikolai, watching as two men lifted Douglas bodily and draped him on his back on a couch. Someone poured half a glass of champagne on his stomach and chest then bent to lick it away. Someone else had Douglas's big toe in his mouth.

The boy himself looked dazed, as if hypnotized, his eyes far away. Lost in all the physical sensations, perhaps. It didn't stop him from expertly sucking cock, though, head nearly upside down over the arm of the couch as a man took advantage of the angle to deep-throat him. At the same time, he was jacking himself slowly at someone's whispered direction, and his other hand had disappeared up Maria's skirt. Well, if worse came to worst and Allen wouldn't buy the boy, it seemed as if Nikolai could make a pretty penny from Maria and Roberto. Although gods knew what that would mean for Mathias. Well, Nikolai had done all he could on that front. Any future issues would be Allen's own fault.

At last, his boy came, and Nikolai couldn't fight down the pang of jealousy knowing it was by someone else's hand. He'd have to get over that soon, however, if he ever wanted to see the boy off to his rightful master.

The crowd golf-clapped at the sight of cum streaking up their new plaything's stomach, at the sound of him moaning and whining as his entire body arched with the force of his orgasm. Nikolai had trained him well—even in the throes of ecstasy, he kept working the cock in his mouth, the hand up Maria's dress. The man down his throat came just moments after he did—the vibrations of Douglas's moans had no doubt tipped him over. When the man pulled free, Douglas used his free hand to wipe the cum off his belly, then licked his fingers clean. To think, the boy had once retched and gagged at the sensation of cum—especially his own—in his mouth. Now he reveled in it. Completely debauched.

When nobody moved to claim his mouth or free hand anew, the boy grew daring and reached for Maria's hip, pulled her closer, closer, until she took the hint and straddled his face. Nikolai hadn't taught him how to please a woman, but it seemed he'd learned a trick or two on his own. Or perhaps the skills Nikolai *had* taught him simply more or less transferred. Certainly the oral fixation and the desire to please did.

Roberto, not wanting to be left out, took Douglas's soft cock in his mouth as Douglas moaned into his wife's pussy. Douglas went momentarily rigid at that, free hand curling into a fist, but then he sank back into his task, into the sensation, ignoring the oversensitivity. Good. It was important for his guests to see that he could. Some slaves whimpered and cried nonstop when touched so soon after orgasm, even if they'd learned to endure it. Douglas took it all in stride. An exemplary slave.

Still, his guests' interest began to wane after that—everyone who'd wanted a turn had already had one, and Nikolai's buybacks, pin-neat and beautiful in their tuxedos, were pacing the room with trays of Jeremy's finest hors d'oeuvres and Nikolai's finest liquors. The lull was to be expected; his guests had more appetites than just the one, after all. They'd be ready for round two once their bellies were full.

Once even Roberto and Maria had finished this first course, Nikolai signaled Luke to have Jeremy call them into the dining room for dinner. Then Nikolai went to Douglas, who was panting and glazed with cum, half-seated on the sofa, his hair a mess.

Nikolai spared him a kiss, grimacing at the taste of all the cock and pussy on his mouth, and pulled away. "You're doing so well, pet. I'll have Roger come clean and prepare you for the next stage. For now, rest and catch your breath, knowing you've made your master so, *so* happy."

I made him happy.

Douglas tried to hold on to that, tried to use it to beat back the fear that kept creeping into him. He didn't want to go with any of these people, least of all Allen, who hadn't even been *tempted* by the chance to use his body. He wasn't sure what he could do to fix that, either. He knew how much it meant to Nikolai, how important it was for Douglas to make Allen want him. But he didn't dare be forward with the man—he'd barely managed the nerve to be so forward with the woman, even when she'd so clearly wanted him—and he'd very much wanted her, the soft sweetness and beauty of something he hadn't seen, let alone touched, in God knew how long. He sat on the sofa awhile, head in his hands, trying to breathe, until finally Roger's hands closed around his shoulders.

Roger helped him stand, pulled him into a hug without a word. "Okay?" he asked into Douglas's hair.

Heart pounding. Throat dry and battered sore. Ass aching. Cock still tingling with torturous pleasure. "Yeah. Just tired." He let himself draw strength from Roger's embrace a while longer, and then it was back into the drawing room, where Roger wiped him down with warm washcloths, combed his hair again, gave him mouthwash to rinse with.

"Master wants us to fuck for them while they have dinner. They'll just be finishing the soup course now, so we have a few more minutes before I take you in. Do you want me to prepare you here, or do you want me to do it in front of them?"

Douglas wasn't sure how to answer that. "What do you think?"

Roger tilted his head back and forth, as if physically weighing his options on his ears. "I think they may want to see you in a little bit of pain. Or Allen, anyway, and he's the one to impress tonight. So maybe we lube you up here so there's no fumbling around with bottles, but I finger you in front of them and then take you a little prematurely? You can exaggerate the pain a little, too."

He what? "Really? I mean, isn't that . . . I don't know, like, lying?"

Roger shrugged. "I can hurt you for real, but I'd prefer not to, and I'm sure Master would understand. You're putting on a show, after all; I'm sure a little acting is fine. But if you're worried, we can tell Master tonight, together. It'll be a secret between the three of us."

The three of us. Master and Roger and me. Douglas felt love from his head to the soles of his feet. "Yeah." He nodded. "Okay." Impulsively, he stood up on his toes and kissed Roger, square on the lips. "Thank you."

Roger chuckled and ruffled his hair (and then promptly fixed it). "Lube up, now. Don't make us late."

The dinner fuck was hard and fast, Douglas on his hands and knees on a little raised platform by the long, formal dining room table, Roger behind him, gripping his hips for leverage and slamming in. Douglas turned his face toward Allen and telegraphed every drop of his discomfort. What pain he didn't feel, he faked. Truth was, he kind of liked it like this sometimes, rough and mindless. It was almost relaxing, in a way, not to have to do anything—to just crouch there and take it. Plus Roger had stretched him a little before they'd come out, and yes he had a very nice cock but it wasn't a porn star cock or anything, and he was awfully good at finding Douglas's prostate with it, so it wasn't long before Douglas got hard again beneath the barrage.

The guests ate and drank and watched and commented, and occasionally grabbed one of the outdoor slaves—doubling very nicely as waitstaff tonight, though their civility didn't fool Douglas, not one bit, and he really, really wished they'd leave—and shoved them to their knees to blow a load down their throats. So strange to see his tormentors *used* that way—strange and also satisfying, even if they did seem to be enjoying their tasks. Just slaves, no better than him. Their throats and asses just as good for fucking.

Speaking of fucking, Roger went on *forever*, fucking like a champion, possibly thanks to the thick leather cock ring he wore at the base of his dick. Mostly, though, he was just that insanely well disciplined, and Douglas knew that Nikolai was using Roger's prowess to reflect well on all his trainees. Trying to convince Allen, maybe, that Douglas could last that long too. Not that he actually could. But what he *could* do was enjoy it the whole time, especially when Roger indulged him with a reach-around and teased him to the edge of orgasm and back a dozen times over throughout the meal. By the time the main course had been cleared and Nikolai *finally* said, "All right, Roger, you can stop torturing the poor boy," Douglas was incoherent with need, *begging* for relief, and Roger gave it to him at last, riding Douglas's orgasm through to his own a moment after.

The applause this time was slightly more enthusiastic than the predinner offering, but one look at Allen confirmed to Douglas that they hadn't impressed the one man who really counted.

What the hell did Allen *want*, damn it?

Not a complacent pup. Well, maybe the finale over dessert would make it clear that Douglas was more than just a well-trained fuck doll, more than just a plaything to be tossed around from arm to arm, used until there was nothing left. No, this pup had teeth of his own.

CHAPTER EIGHT

S omething was going on upstairs. At first Mat had run for ages on his treadmill, trying to drown out the voices and the laughter, but now he was sitting on his bed, listening attentively for every scrap of sound, hoping for something that would help him puzzle out just what the hell was happening.

It was strange, actually, that he could hear anything at all. He'd been sure these rooms were soundproof; he'd certainly never heard a peep from outside his own walls in all the time he'd been here. And yet.

More mindfucks?

Well, consider him fucked. Many times over. If he hadn't resolved against suicide, decided *definitively* to save Dougie and get him out of this hell, well, he'd be dead now, especially after his and Dougie's last meeting.

Don't think about that. Don't. Just don't.

That'd been weeks ago already, had to be, yet at so much as the slightest thought of it, he still felt as raw as if it'd happened yesterday. Could even still feel the physical pain of it, though God knew that was the least of that particular constellation of suffering.

I said don't fucking think about it, you fucking asshole.

Saved by the bell, or rather, the door opening. He perked up just in time to see some bruiser in a tux—one of the animals who'd tortured Dougie in the cabin for a week straight—stride through the door and slam it shut behind him.

Mat wondered if he'd have time to knock all the fucker's teeth out before more of them came for him.

But it was an idle thought, strangled at birth. He knew how such a course of action would end. Besides, it was a bit late to be defending his brother's honor, wasn't it.

"Party time," the bruiser said. "And don't think about fucking this up for the master. Your buyer's here stinking up the place with a big sulk, and he needs some cheering before he brings the whole party down. Seeing you get smacked around should do the trick."

"Fuck you," Mat snarled. Seriously reconsidered the teeth thing.

The bruiser studied one cufflink, completely unfazed. "Be a shame if he had to smack around your little brother instead. Poor thing's already been entertaining the guests all night."

Oh, for fuck's sake. It was like he had a fucking sign on his forehead or something: "Dougie's Whipping Boy."

Not that he wasn't willing.

He just didn't understand why anyone needed to whip anyone at all. Nikolai hadn't seriously hurt him in at least a week or two; maybe he was just overdue. He hated how the thought of that was significantly less intimidating than the thought of being in the same room with Dougie again. He was fucking terrified of what he'd see—or not see—when he looked into his brother's eyes.

"You coming? Or do I tell the master you said to take it out of your brother's ass, instead?"

"Fine. Whatever." Mat stood, stripping his shorts and sneakers without being asked. He was expecting to be prepared or something then, the way he'd been at Madame's, but the bruiser just clipped him into a big collar on a pole, like the ones used for catching rabid dogs, then cuffed his hands behind his back. Pushed him out ahead. No way he could fight anyone like this. Which was probably smart of Nikolai. Or maybe all just part of the show for his buyer. Should he act rabid? Let his anger loose? What would make the guy happy? What would make the pain end the quickest? *Give the buyer what he wants and it's over faster.* Isn't that what Nikolai had told Mat oh-so-long ago, back when Dougie had still been . . . Dougie?

The bruiser marched him up the stairs, out the open door. The noise was louder up here, murmured voices and the clink of silverware and the occasional laugh or moan. Something smelled amazing. Several somethings, actually, much of which were either coming or going on trays carried by tuxedoed middle-aged models, who Mat only belatedly recognized as Dougie's other rapists all dressed up in their finery.

"Put on a show," the bruiser told him just as they approached the door to what must've been the dining room, shaking the pole to rattle him. Like the good dog Mat was, he struggled against the collar and let out a furious howl. The conversation in the room went silent. All his entrance needed was a record scratch.

What he got instead was Nikolai, casting an appraising gaze, then announcing to the room, "And to go with your dessert, I thought I'd show you my other little project. Mathias Carmichael, my fighting dog, never to know the true pleasure of submission. He'll struggle until he dies." And even with all his twisting and shouting, Mat didn't miss the way Nikolai's eyes strayed to a short, dark-eyed man seated at one end of the table, his dessert uneaten, a glass of some golden liquor on the rocks in one hand.

"Is that the fucker who wants my ass?" Mat shouted, twisting his shoulders, nearly bucking the bruiser off him. No show anymore—he was *furious*. "What do you think, you rich old pervert? Nikolai train me up nice for you?"

The man put down his drink and smiled. Turned to Nikolai and asked, "Does it bite?"

"Oh yes, if you let it. I suggest a bit gag or ring gag, depending on your pleasure. But I assure you he won't be biting anything tonight. And he *does* know how to heel; I've beaten that much into him, at least."

Nikolai strode around the table, to the corner of the room off toward Mat's left. Mat followed with his eyes and saw—oh God, *Dougie*. Kneeling there with Roger, glaring daggers at Mat. He couldn't . . . he just *couldn't*. He looked away. But not in time to miss Nikolai laying a possessive hand on Dougie's shoulder, or Dougie leaning into him like a spoiled cat.

"Like night and day, these two, wouldn't you say? Now here's the fun part. They're brothers. They came to Madame together by happy accident after that one"—the bruiser yanked hard on Mat's collar, and Mat, too distracted by Dougie to respond, fell choking and spluttering to his knees—"interfered with his brother's procurement. Noble fool. I'm sure he regrets it now. Look at me, Mathias."

Mat debated ignoring him. The client wanted a *tamed* beast, after all, and if Mat behaved badly tonight, maybe the client would reject him. But then where would that leave him? Nobody else wanted an animal, which meant Nikolai would either have to kill him or break him. Neither thought appealed; he couldn't escape if he was dead or . . . or like Dougie.

So he turned his glare on Nikolai and spat, "Yes, master?" with all the bitter resentment he could muster. Which was quite a fucking lot.

"My man is going to unclip you from the pole and free your hands. When he does, you will crawl to that chair"—he pointed to a straight-backed, armless metal chair at the end of the room, in full view of every seat at the table but closest, unsurprisingly, to the short old fuck who planned to buy Mat—"and sit yourself down in it. Do you understand?"

What to say? *Yes, sir,* or *Untie me and I'll kill you all*? He wished he knew the right answer here, how much fight was right for his master-to-be. The man had seemed downright gleeful at Mathias's wildcat routine on the way into the room, so maybe option two was the wiser choice. But then he'd have to follow through, or prove himself all bark and no bite. And follow-through meant pain: being tackled, tied down, punished. Probably a hell of a lot more pain than was necessary tonight if he behaved.

He'd pondered too long; the bruiser torqued the pole to one side and pulled, slamming Mat's back to the floor. The crowd murmured excitedly, vultures scenting blood. Nikolai took the opportunity to come over and step on his nuts.

Mat roared and made a halfhearted attempt to throw him off—a wholehearted attempt would've ended with Nikolai's own balls popping out his fucking throat, hands tied or no. Mat knew better than that, though. The threat still hung over Dougie's life.

"I said," Nikolai repeated, clipped and cold, but Mat could see the sparkle in his eyes that told him he was doing right, "do you understand?"

"Yes, master," he gasped through the choking collar.

"That's what I thought." Nikolai slowly lifted his toe, relieving the pressure on Mat's balls by inches. The collar came off after that, and then Mat sat up so that his wrists could be released as well.

From this vantage point, chest heaving with anger and pain, rubbing at his abused throat, Mat could see his buyer, drink emptied. Practically salivating. One day, he'd be sucking the guy's dick.

One day, he'd have his hands around the guy's throat, crushing every last drop of life out of him.

Just a matter of time.

"Crawl," Nikolai reminded him.

Fine. Whatever. Just keep your buggy eyes off my brother.

The crowd *ooh*ed and *aah*ed again when he obeyed. Like they'd thought he wouldn't. Like maybe they'd thought he'd turn on them all. But instead of frightening them, that little edge of danger just titillated them more. Fuck them. He wished he could launch himself onto the table and start busting heads, take out as many of them as he could before Nikolai's bruisers came at him with Tasers.

But instead he just crawled to the chair, then sat. He wasn't meek about it, though; he was glaring the fuck at everyone. Promising violence with his gaze. Even though he knew they had him by the throat as surely as if he were still strapped to that pole.

He lowered his chin. Took a deep breath, nostrils flaring. And waited. Someone had better tie him up. Because whatever they planned to do to him, the anger was way too fucking close to the surface right now for him to find enough control to sit through it otherwise.

The pervert party gasped as one as hands closed around Mat's wrists, yanking them back behind the chair. Mat grunted at the rough handling, but didn't struggle. Would he be hooked up to something electric next? A gag? His ass was protected by the seat of the chair, which meant his buyer wasn't planning on fucking him. Not that there weren't a million other ways to abuse and humiliate him. Starting with whoever was tying him up. Way too tight, rough rope, elbows and shoulders twisted miserably, knots pinching his skin.

"Remember"—Mat lurched at the sound of Nikolai's voice so close behind him—"he needs to be able to perform." Perform? Perform *how*? "Don't hurt him *too* much." Oh. Nausea flared low in Mat's gut. Perform like *that*. So Nikolai expected him to get it up in front of this sicko crowd? What for?

"Yes, Master," Dougie said, and nausea burst so violently through Mat's middle he almost hurled right then and there. So it was *Dougie* tying him up with so much force. With so much anger. And now he knew *exactly* what for.

He squeezed his eyes shut and turned his head away—*don't cry in front of the perverts don't cry don't let them see you cry*—but there was no escaping the oily crawl of their gazes across his skin.

And no escaping this chair, either. When Dougie circled around him to tie his ankles to the outsides of the front legs, he couldn't fight. He wouldn't kick his brother. Wouldn't hurt him, not even knowing how much Dougie was about to hurt them both.

"See how docile the beast becomes around the boy?" Nikolai announced to the gathered crowd. "How well he behaves for his brother? This was what attracted me to them in the first place. They put on a lovely show at Madame's, and that was before they'd had a moment of training."

Dougie's face barely twitched, even though he must have been remembering that night. Mat had assumed the guilt at what he'd done at the auction had torn Dougie apart, yet here he was, not even registering.

"Before they came to me, their only loyalty was to each other. Now Douglas answers to me alone. Isn't that right, Douglas?"

"Oh yes, Master." No mistaking the joy in Dougie's voice, the only emotion besides anger at Mat he'd shown tonight. Dougie wasn't checked out. He just didn't care anymore. Like Mat wasn't his brother anymore, but more than that. Worse than that.

Like Mat wasn't even a *person* anymore.

"Shall I give you all a demonstration?"

Enthusiastic murmurs from the crowd, leering eyes on the both of them. What kind of sick fuckery inspired people to cheer for forced incest? Mat started struggling in earnest, but the ropes were tight and the chair was bolted to the floor. All he was doing was hurting himself. Nobody seemed to care, except the man-who-would-be-his-master, who stared at Mat's straining, sweating body as if devouring Mat with his eyes, licking his lips and breathing way too fast. He was *getting off* on this. On Mat's pain. Mat's panic. Mat's struggle.

Nikolai let it continue for a minute or two, then clamped a hand down on the jointure of Mat's neck and shoulder, fingers digging hard enough into a pressure point that Mat's whole arm went tingly. He was too disgusted, too enraged, to be meek about it, and shouted, "Ow, you *fucker*, get off me!" Tried to shake free. Nikolai only pressed harder. Mat's next cry was wordless, whimpering. Nikolai didn't let go. If he was waiting for Mat to beg in front of all these people, he'd be waiting a long fucking time. Even if he got out the serum injector.

Not that he would, Mat didn't think. Nikolai needed Mat to get hard sometime this year.

Mat squeezed his eyes shut. When he pried them open again, he saw the extra-special sick fuck right there in the first chair, cock out of his unzipped pants and shoved down one of the waiter's throats. He was fisting the guy's hair so hard that Mat half expected it to come out by the roots. He wasn't letting the guy breathe at all.

Maybe letting Nikolai break you would be better.

No. *No.* Who would save Dougie then?

Didn't matter anyway. It was too late for him change the outcome of the evening. He was already tied down, helpless not to obey.

Finally, Nikolai unclenched his hand from Mat's shoulder. "Get him hard," Nikolai said, softly, but the eyes of the crowd let Mat know they'd heard.

"Of course, Master." Dougie's reply was faux-sweet, edged with something that wasn't disgust, wasn't fear, wasn't shame, most fucking certainly wasn't apology. "With pleasure."

Mat shuddered and squeezed his eyes shut, tilting his head until his skull smacked the back of the chair.

"Watch your brother work," Nikolai warned.

"Fuck you, you sick fuck," Mat snarled back, but lifted his head all the same. Opened his eyes. Tonight would be bad enough without making Nikolai punish him.

Dougie was kneeling in front of him now, all perfect poise and professional disinterest. It should have made Mat feel better to know that this wasn't harming Dougie, wasn't hurting him at all, but that somehow made it worse. Because it meant that Dougie, his brother—who'd hurt him before but then cried with shame, apologized and kissed him and *cried*—was gone. And Mat couldn't help but wonder how much of that was his fault. He'd had his chance to save Dougie, and he'd blown it, and so what if it'd been a trap—he'd still walked right into it, should've known better, should've overcome it somehow. They'd be free now if he had, but instead he'd killed whatever last vestige of hope Dougie had harbored, had caused Dougie a week of such abject brutality that Dougie had shattered completely.

And of course Nikolai had picked up the pieces, glued them back together just the way he wanted. Glued them back into a slave who was not just willing to rape his brother, but *eager*. Downright *mean* about it. Because of course Dougie hated him now. Between Nikolai's lies and Mat's own incompetence, was it any wonder?

But maybe . . . just *maybe* it wasn't too late. Maybe there was still some tiny seed of the old Dougie buried down deep in there somewhere. And maybe Mat could reach it. After all, Nikolai hadn't gagged him this time. He could *speak* this time.

"Dougie," he tried.

Between his knees, Dougie's eyes flicked up, stared hard at him a second, and then swept down again as he let out a theatrical moan, wrapping a hand around Mat's flaccid dick. Mat shuddered bodily at the touch, felt his nuts try to crawl right up into his belly.

"What a big uncut cock your brother has," Nikolai said, his voice taunting.

"Mmm," Dougie replied, fisting Mat slowly. In his tight grip, Mat's dick flopped around like a piece of meat. They had to be crazy to think he'd get off on this sick show.

"Much bigger than yours. Are you jealous?"

"No, Master. Mine pleases you; that's all I need. This is an animal's dick. Only useful for donkey-shows like this."

Had they rehearsed this? Mat couldn't bear to think that Dougie was speaking honestly right now.

"Dougie," Mat tried again, then gagged horribly when Dougie sucked his entire cock into his mouth, worked a nut in there as well, swirled the whole package with his tongue, hummed to send vibrations shooting through his flesh. Despite everything—the pain in his arms, the fucking *chasm* in his heart—Mat felt the first stirrings of arousal. No, not arousal. Physical stimulation, that was all. "Dougie, listen to me, *please*—"

Dougie wedged his hand between Mat and the chair, pressed his palm into Mat's taint and wiggled a finger up his ass to find his prostate.

"Dougie, stop it!" Mat jerked so hard the chair rattled. But Dougie was persistent, followed along, even used the opportunity to work his hand further back, drive his finger in deeper.

"You can hardly expect him to answer to someone who doesn't even know his name," Nikolai said.

"Fuck you, asshole." Mat grunted and twisted in his bonds, trying to ignore the sensation of Dougie's finger—no, fingers now—stuffed in his ass and Dougie's ruthlessly efficient mouth on his cock and balls (*don't think about how he learned this don't think about it don't think about it*), even as his erection started to swell. "I'll fucking kill you for this. I'll kill you for what you've done to him."

I'll bleed you dry. I'll strangle you. I'll disembowel you. I'll beat your face to a pulp, feel all the bones in your body break in my hands. I'll rip your cock off and stuff it down your fucking throat.

"Be a dear and silence him, would you, Douglas? I'd hate for him to upset our guests."

Dougie mumbled "Yes, Master" around Mat's half-hard cock. He didn't pull off, didn't pull his fingers from Mat's ass. Just lifted his own ass off his heels, leaned against Mat's lap, and thrust the fingers of his free hand into his own hole. *What the fuck?* How was *that* supposed to silence him? Shock value, maybe?

Well, Mat wasn't going silent without a fight. "Stop this! Somebody fucking stop this. God fucking damn you, all of you! He's sick! Can't you see he's fucking sick? He doesn't know what he's doing!"

Silence from the peanut gallery—unless you counted all that heavy breathing and the occasional moan and the sounds of slurping and sucking from all the waiters who'd been commandeered for, well, *other* purposes.

He himself was fully hard now, goddamn it, Dougie's fingers rubbing mercilessly on his prostate, Dougie's mouth doing abso-fucking-lutely *obscene* things to his cock and balls. Not even staring right at his brother—*my brother, this is* my *brother*—could seem to short-circuit his body's response. He just kept on screaming: "Please" and "Stop it" and "Damn you" and "God please" and "Just fucking kill me" and "Leave him alone."

Then Dougie looked right up at him through the fringe of his too-long hair, took his fingers from his ass—covered now in cum and lube from God knew how many previous fucks—and forced all four fingers into Mat's mouth.

Mat gagged. Squeezed his eyes shut against tears and swallowed hard against the urge to vomit. Tried to jerk his head away, but Dougie hooked his fingers behind Mat's teeth and held on. Sucking and licking and finger-fucking him all the while, perfectly unconcerned—he knew damn well Mat wouldn't bite him.

"I think that's enough, pet," Nikolai said, and Mat had one single glorious moment to think *Oh thank God it's over* before Nikolai added, "Can't let him come too soon."

"No, no more," Mat moaned around Dougie's vile little fingers.

Nikolai clapped him on the shoulder, fingers threateningly close to where they'd caused such pain before, but not squeezing. Not yet. "But we can't end the show without the finale, Mathias," he chirped, like some fucking schlock ringmaster. "Up you go, Douglas. Give my guests a night they won't forget."

No stopping it. No stopping their audience leering, no stopping Nikolai's pronouncements, no stopping Dougie's sick assault on his body, no stopping the tears that had started to run down his face. And the whole time, his buyer watched with hungry lizard-like eyes, taking in every inch and every second, cock thrusting almost absentmindedly in and out of that slave's throat. It was perfectly clear that wasn't the throat he *really* wanted. Mat supposed he'd be on his knees before the fucker soon enough. Would happily do it now, in fact, if it meant an end to this cruel performance.

But that option wasn't on the menu. No, only he was. Dougie ripped his fingers from Mat's ass, pulled his lips off Mat's cock and his hand from Mat's mouth, rose to his feet with all the grace of a well-trained fighter, spun around to face the audience, and straddled Mat's lap. He bent forward at the waist, spread his ass cheeks in both hands, swayed his hips as he lowered himself closer and closer to Mat's erection. He was clearly conscious of putting on a good show, and though Mat couldn't see his face (*thank God thank God*), he had no doubt that Dougie's eyes were half-lidded, eyelashes fluttering, tongue running over parted lips. Jesus, he didn't want to be picturing that—*why* was he picturing that?

Because it's easier than watching your own brother spearing himself on your cock.

"Please," he cried again, even though he was long past the point of hoping for mercy. Of saving either of them from this. Dougie had already raped him once, injected him with poison and then taken him rough and furious after their failed escape. But this was worse, so much worse even than that first shock of pain and betrayal and disbelief. Because this wasn't heat-of-the-moment fury and fear. This was cold and calculated. This was using Mat's own body against him. Making him rape himself. Making him rape his brother—because Dougie's consent was an illusion here, no doubt about it—even as his brother raped him. Why should he hope for anything? "Dougie, you're *killing* me, please!"

"Hear that?" Dougie purred, rolling his ass back, guiding Mat's dick up and down his cleft. A drizzle of old semen ran out of his twitching hole to slick the way. Mat tried to will himself soft. Couldn't, not with the stimulation Dougie was forcing on him. "He's begging me. Begging for my ass, Master."

"Any man would, my beautiful boy." Nikolai sounded like a proud father. This sick fucking family affair. "Best not keep him waiting, then."

"Yes, Master," Dougie breathed, and plunged down on Mat's cock.

Mat gasped as he sank balls deep, twisting and shouting as Dougie's ass came to rest against his thighs. He hadn't fucked anyone in forever, and God but it felt *good*—amazing, even, as Dougie expertly worked him with his muscles—and that more than anything drew out Mat's scream, his struggles, he couldn't let this happen, couldn't let his body like it, he'd *die* if he came in his brother's ass, he had to stop it, had to be stronger than this, better, fight harder, break free, stop it—

Dougie planted his hands on Mat's thighs and began to rock, moaning like a cat in heat. Mat's whole body shuddered with revulsion, and he cried openly as pleasure streaked up his groin and pooled low in his belly.

It's not him, it's not him, he's not my brother anymore, he's not my Dougie, he's not the kid brother who followed me on my runs, he's not the brother I bought beer for, he's not the brother whose knees I put Band-Aids on, he's not, he's sick, he's sick, he's sick, he's trapped somewhere inside his body and this isn't his fault and I'm going to find the real him in there and save him but not yet, not tonight, tonight he's gone, he's sleeping, he's gone and he's not my brother and the faster I come, the faster this ends; he can't rape us on a soft cock.

Dougie shifted position, throwing his head back against Mat's shoulder and locking his arms around Mat's neck, and now Mat could see over him, down his body, to his cock bouncing hard and eager against his stomach in time with his ass bouncing on Mat's lap. The tears flowed fresh then, so hard they obscured his vision—thank God for small mercies—and he closed his eyes and tried to forget absolutely fucking everything—where they were, who was on his lap, who was watching—tried to strip it down to mechanics, to make all the parts work as efficiently as possible. But he wasn't a machine, and he couldn't shut it out, it was too fucking big for that, and the bitter irony of it all didn't escape him: the more he wanted to hurry things along, the more upset ("upset," hah) he got, and the more upset he got, the more distant any hope of orgasm became. He was trapped in some hellish limbo of just enough arousal to stay hard, not nearly enough to end the torture.

And Dougie showed no signs of tiring, no signs of stopping. No signs of guilt or even conflict. God help him, they'd be at this all night.

"Who wants to touch him?" Nikolai asked, and for one sick, twisted moment, Mat thought—hoped—that Nikolai meant *him*. That maybe a second rapist might help to end this nightmare sooner. But no, he was pointing to Dougie, to his flushed, leaking cock, and a smarmily handsome Hispanic man and what he assumed was his smarmily pretty wife raised their hands like they were in fucking school or something, but then another voice rang out.

Mat's buyer. "No. Nobody touches him. Let him come from his brother's cock. Let big brother know that his cock can bring his slutty little brother off." *No. Stop talking, please stop talking.* "Let him live with that. Let him picture that every time he orgasms for the rest of his miserable life."

You sick fucker. Why are you doing *this? Isn't this cruel enough for you already?*

Meanwhile, Dougie bounced and moaned, even turned his face until his tongue was running sloppy lines of saliva over Mat's cheek and the corner of his mouth, some disgusting porn-like approximation of kissing, and Mat wasn't sure whether that was better or worse than a real kiss.

Better. At least this way, when we've escaped this place and put it all behind us, I just might have a chance in hell of not thinking of this moment every time I kiss someone for the rest of my life.

"Can he do it?" Mat's buyer asked, looking up over Mat's shoulder, to Nikolai. His hand was fisted tight around that slave's hair again. How had he not come yet? Or suffocated the guy between his legs? "Can your slutty little pup come just like that?"

"Of course he can," Nikolai said, all proud father again. "Show him, Douglas. Come for him now."

It wasn't an instantaneous thing, but it was as close to coming on command as Mat had ever seen. Dougie moaned, utterly wanton, fingers tangling in Mat's hair as his hips sped up. The sound of flesh slapping flesh filled Mat's ears, the feeling of Dougie's muscles milking him drowning out everything else.

A hole. Not your brother. Just a tight hole. A tight hole. A tight hole. A tight hole. Nothing else.

Mat squeezed his eyes shut, ignoring the tears streaking down his cheeks, the whine of pain and misery and pleasure that escaped through his clenched teeth. He should have killed himself. He should be dead right now, not here, not enduring this thing so far beyond endurance it made even the serum look like a day in a fucking amusement park. Dougie's hands clenched on his neck, his moans quick and high and raspy. His hips stuttered and he bore down hard, and every one of those internal muscles clenched and spasmed around Mat's cock as he cried out and shot all over his stomach and chest.

And Mat, weeping over their wasted lives, was quick to follow, his orgasm ripped right out of him by spasming muscles, vise-tight. Flooding his brother's ass with cum as he screamed and howled and cried.

He wished he were dead.

But he wasn't. He was alive, and this was his life, and he fucking deserved it for the part he'd played in what Dougie had become. Penance, that's what this was. And staying alive, suffering through this, was the price he'd have to pay for the chance to make things right again. Somehow. Some way.

Nikolai walked around the chair, tugged gently on Dougie's shoulder. Dougie slid off Mat's lap without hesitation—and no, Mat felt no shame at all about his sob of relief at that, didn't even begin to try to hide it—and tucked himself happily into Nikolai's embrace, his back to Nikolai's chest, Nikolai's arm slung around his shoulders. "That was perfect," Nikolai murmured near Dougie's ear, and Dougie *beamed*, so young and innocent-looking with that sweet, toothy smile on his face, and Mat found himself sobbing afresh at how much it reminded him of sneaking Dougie to the ice-cream parlor on their Saturday morning runs, watching him attack his contraband with such perfect glee. "Let's get you washed up, and then you can say your good-byes to my guests."

"Yes, Mast—" Dougie began, but then Cruel, Short, and Ugly darted a hand out, grabbed Dougie's wrist and said, "No."

Nikolai peered down at his guest, one eyebrow arched in an all-too-familiar expression that made Mat's skin crawl with sick anticipation, and the man added, "Let him keep his brother's cum inside him." Before Nikolai could remind the little shit who was the master of ceremonies here, the buyer turned to Dougie, and there was no mistaking how tight his grip was getting, even though Dougie didn't let the pain or fear show—or at least, didn't let it show to someone who didn't know him as intimately as Mat did. Or used to, anyway. Because this? This Dougie was a stranger. "I'll have him, Nikolai. I'll have *both* of them."

Like the deal was already done.

"Doesn't that sound wonderful, my little lovely?" the buyer said. "You can have your brother's dick like this every day, as much as you want. Again and again and again."

Again and again and again? I can't. I can't. We're better off dead.

"Yes, sir," Dougie said, seemingly unfazed, and not only that—was Mat going crazy, or was that a hint of *pleasure* in Dougie's voice? No, not crazy; a little smile was curling Dougie's lips now, too, but it looked . . . strained, somehow, like maybe Dougie was just putting on a show, doing what was expected.

Funny, but Nikolai's smile right then looked just the same.

Short, Cruel, and Ugly smiled back. All three smiles didn't reach their eyes. All three of them with their secrets, all three of them entangled in this mysterious power play, this twisted fucking bond of blood and cum and pain, with Mat the unwilling victim at its center, bearing the brunt of it all.

Alone.

Despite Dougie's presence—or maybe even because of it—for the first time in his life, Mat was completely, terrifyingly alone.

TO BE CONTINUED IN

THE
FLESH

SEASON 4: LIBERATION

CARTEL

riptidepublishing.com/titles/collections/flesh-cartel-season-4-liberation

ABOUT THE
AUTHORS

Heidi Belleau was born and raised in small town New Brunswick, Canada. She now lives in the rugged oil-patch frontier of Northern BC with her husband, an Irish ex-pat whose long work hours in the trades leave her plenty of quiet time to write. She has a degree in history from Simon Fraser University with a concentration in British and Irish studies; much of her work centred on popular culture, oral folklore, and sexuality, but she was known to perplex her professors with unironic papers on the historical roots of modern romance novel tropes. (Ask her about Highlanders!) When not writing, you might catch her trying to explain British television to her newborn daughter or standing in line at the local coffee shop, waiting on her caramel macchiato.

You can find her tweeting as @HeidiBelleau, email her at heidi.below.zero@gmail.com, or visit her blog: www.heidibelleau.com.

Rachel is an M/M erotic romance author, a freelance writer and editor, and the Publisher of Riptide Publishing. She's also a sadist with a pesky conscience, shamelessly silly, and quite proudly pervish. Fortunately, all those things make writing a lot more fun for her . . . if not so much for her characters.

When she's not writing about hot guys getting it on (or just plain getting it; her characters rarely escape a story unscathed), she loves to read, hike, camp, sing, perform in community theater, and glue captions to cats. She also has a particular fondness for her very needy dog, her even needier cat, and shouting at kids to get off her lawn.

You can find Rachel at her website, rachelhaimowitz.com, tweeting as @RachelHaimowitz, and on Tumblr at rachelhaimowitz.tumblr.com.

She loves to hear from folks, so feel free to drop her a line anytime at metarachel@gmail.com.

Enjoy this book?
Find more unconventional kink at
RiptidePublishing.com!

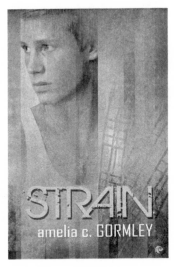

CPSIA information can be obtained at www.ICGtesting.com
Printed in the USA
BVOW08s0619070314

346947BV00001B/30/P